THE AMBITIOUS CARD

AN ELI MARKS MYSTERY

JOHN GASPARD

D1500433

HENERY PRESS

THE AMBITIOUS CARD
An Eli Marks Mystery
Part of the Henery Press Mystery Collection

First Edition
Trade paperback edition | August 2013

Henery Press
www.henerypress.com

ISBN-13: 978-1-938383-48-9

Printed in the United States of America

*For the magicians who have touched my life
in amazing and wonderful ways:
Ardan James, Tina Lennert and Suzanne.*

*But mostly dedicated to the brilliant Bill Arnold,
despite the fact that this dedication will annoy him.
Or maybe because of it.*

ACKNOWLEDGMENTS

Thanks to the folks who helped me get this idea down on paper: Jim Cunningham, Amy Oriani, Larry Kahlow, David Fogel, Amy Shomshak, Joe Gaspard, Steve Carlson, Dodd Vickers, and Richard Kaufman.

"My object is to mystify and entertain;
I wouldn't deceive you for the world."
Howard Thurston

Prologue

Ask anyone and they'll tell you I'm generally a positive person. But even I had to admit, this was a bad situation.

After the heavy wooden door closed behind us with an unforgiving finality, I'd come to a sudden insight—when it comes to being in the dark, there's *dark-dark* and then there's *inside-a-cave dark.*

We were definitely in the latter.

I'd never been in a place so dark, where the blackness of the space jostled up against us like an aggressive, surly crowd on a subway during rush hour.

My head was spinning from the lack of oxygen and even though I couldn't see my hand in front of my face, I was starting to see spots in front of my eyes. My lungs ached with each breath I took, the carbon monoxide that filled the cave a poor substitute for the oxygen I'd foolishly taken for granted until this late point in life.

We shuffled and slogged through the inky darkness. My foot slipped on a loose rock, hurdling me forward, where a stalagmite—or is it a stalactite?—connected with my forehead, breaking my fall. My head was now covered with small scrapes and contusions, and in the darkness I couldn't tell whether it was blood or sweat running down my face. I imagine it was a pretty even mixture of both.

Oh, and did I mention the bats? Well, I don't know how I could have forgotten them.

The flurry of winged pests had been just as surprised to encounter us as we had been to encounter them, leaving us the warm and sticky recipients of a rich shower of bat guano. It covered our hair and shoulders, a warm stream that slithered down my spine, making me wish I could actually remove my skin and send it out for cleaning. And as luck would have it, moments after the first battalion departed to points unknown, we were hit with yet a second wave of bat pee, the furry winged bastards slicing across the tops of our heads while their piercing screeches whizzed past our ears.

Even though I had more pressing concerns at the moment, I once again rebuked myself for getting us into this situation. It could have been avoided, I really think it could have.

Things would have turned out quite differently, I'm convinced, if I'd closed my act with something other than The Ambitious Card.

Had it been the cups and balls or the linking rings or a cut and restored rope or any of a hundred other tricks, I might be sitting home in front of the television right now happily munching popcorn, instead of asphyxiating in a cave while marinating in bat pee. But, as they say, hindsight is twenty/twenty, a lesson I appear to be learning and re-learning every day—even in the deadly pitch blackness of this stupid cave.

Chapter 1

"I find it puzzling, don't you? The rabbit, I mean. Very puzzling."

As a magician, I'm accustomed to people asking me about rabbits. However, in this particular instance, I wasn't being queried about your standard pink-nosed adorable bunny, suitable for producing out of a hat. My uncle was instead gesturing toward a large statue of a rabbit reclining on the grass. Perhaps five-feet tall, the dull bronze artwork gazed out at the cars as they passed by on the Minnehaha Parkway, a look of Mona Lisa-style contentment on its large, metallic face.

"Explain this to me, if you can," Uncle Harry continued without waiting for any response from me. "Is the statue meant to represent an oversized version of a normal-sized rabbit? Or, was the artist instead attempting to create a normal-sized depiction of a freakishly-large rabbit?"

I sorted through his questions in my head. "I guess I've never thought about it," I finally answered.

Harry clucked his tongue. "If we understood the context within which he—or she—was working, then I imagine we'd have a handle on it. It's never about what they're doing. It's always about *why*."

He gave the rabbit one more penetrating look as we drove past. "As a professional magician, these are the questions you should be thinking about," he added in his professorial tone.

Perhaps it's my imagination, but as he's gotten older, Harry's list of the questions I should be thinking about has grown exponentially. And to be honest, given recent events, I must admit that I haven't really made any attempt to keep up with his list. At this point, I am probably hopelessly behind.

I made a left turn on Chicago Avenue and we headed away from Minnehaha Parkway, driving the final two blocks home in reflective silence. I pulled into an open parking space across the street from the small shop that serves as both our abode and our business. Chicago Magic is the store and, surprisingly, it's a good 350 miles from the Windy City, nestled instead in a cozy neighborhood in South Minneapolis. The shop has been a fixture near the corner of 48th and Chicago for nearly fifty years. I've called the apartments above it my home—on and off—for just over twenty years, or since I was about ten. For those of you unwilling or unable to do the math, that would put me in my early thirties.

Uncle Harry gathered up the plastic shopping bag that slumped at his feet. The bag was filled to near-overflowing with candy bars of all varieties. And not the dreaded Fun-Size candy bars, which Harry loathes. ("Where's the fun in a candy bar the size of your thumb? That's about as much fun as a poke in the eye, if you ask me.") No, these were genuine, full-sized bars and they would join the other, equally-large bag we purchased two days earlier in anticipation of the supposed hordes of trick-or-treaters Harry was convinced would be visiting us that evening.

Harry is a man who does not like to be caught unprepared and Halloween fuels his already competitive nature. For years he has ranted about our business neighbors—the movie theater on one side of the store and the bar on the other—and their alleged stinginess in the matter of dispensing Halloween candy to the neighborhood children.

"Any business that charges an arm and two legs for a bag of popcorn," he would often say of the movie theater, "and then turns around and hands out miniscule candy bars at Halloween...that to me is a business with a heart the size of a gumdrop. And don't get me started with that bar," he would gesture toward what is actually a favorite hangout of his. "I swear to God, those cheap so-and-so's are handing out ice cubes instead of candy. I've seen them do it. They hold a bowl of something high enough over the kids' heads so they can't see inside of it, and then—plop, plop, plop—they toss ice cubes into the poor youngsters' bags, saying, 'Enjoy your Snickers bar and happy Halloween kids.' That, if you ask me, is lower than low."

Halloween had been a favorite holiday for Aunt Alice, and because this was the first occurrence of the holiday since her passing, I think Harry was over-compensating. I got the sense he was using the delivery of treats to random, roaming costume-clad kids as a sort of living memorial to her and their fifty-plus years together. But I sympathized with the feeling. So when he had insisted on making yet another run to the store that afternoon for more candy, I quickly agreed and even offered to drive.

As soon as the car came to a stop across from our shop, he opened the door and got out, turning back to reach in and pick up the bulging bag of candy bars. "Aren't you coming in?" he asked when he recognized that I hadn't turned off the engine.

I shook my head. "I've got that show in St. Paul to get to," I said, picking up a Snickers bar that had escaped from the bag. I handed it to Harry and he skillfully slipped it back into the bag, making it vanish from his hand. It was a good trick, but he did it without even realizing he had done it. Force of habit, I guess.

"Oh, that's right," he said, giving the side of his head a slight tap with his index finger. "Thanks for covering for me on that show. I'm just not up to it."

"I understand, no problem," I said, not wanting to make a big deal out of it.

He started to close the car door, then ducked his head back down for one last comment. "Give 'em hell, Buster." And then he closed the door.

I watched him as he waited for a couple of cars to pass and then tentatively made his way across the street to our shop. He glanced up at the sky as he slipped the key into the front door lock, looking to see if the snow that had been threatening for the last couple of days was any closer to becoming a reality. A few moments later the door was unlocked and he disappeared inside. And two seconds after that, a hand turned the sign that hangs in the window around so that it now read Open.

Chicago Magic was open for business and ready for trick-or-treaters. And I had to get to a psychic showdown—a mental cage match, as it was being advertised—in St. Paul.

But before I go, I thought, where's the harm in a quick interlude?

I pulled the car forward about thirty feet, which put me directly across from the shop on the corner—a mere four doors down from Chicago Magic. I pretended to be very interested in something on the car's dashboard, adjusting an invisible knob. And then slowly, oh so slowly, I turned my head to the left and looked across the street.

Bingo. I spotted her immediately, standing by the cash register and talking to a customer. Her face was slightly obscured by her curly brown hair—then she laughed and tossed her hair back, revealing that sweet, lovely face. She was gorgeous. It was evident even from this distance, clear across the street and through a fog of incense that hung around inside the store like, well, a fog.

I watched her for several long moments, with what I'm sure was a look of puppy dog infatuation on my face, until I reached a point where I was even starting to creep myself out. I said her name softly, like a sigh, "Megan," then put the car in gear and headed over to St. Paul.

The bluffs that border the riverfront, across the waterway from downtown St. Paul, are famous for their caves—miles of caverns and circuitous tunnels that cut deep into the tall, rocky hills. The best-known of these caves, and the only ones open to the public, are

The Wabasha Street Caves, which began their career as a mining site for valuable sandstone before becoming a private Prohibition-era nightclub. The Caves have gone through several permutations since that time, finally evolving into a rental space for parties and events. I'd only been there once previously, years before at a spooky magic show presented by a student of my uncle's. Although the event taught me nothing new about magic, I did learn one thing about The Caves that night that has stuck with me ever since—when the lights go out in a cave, it's dark. I mean dark-dark. Stygian darkness. Darker, as my uncle was fond of saying, than the inside of a nun.

It was immediately apparent that darkness wasn't going to be an issue inside The Caves that evening as I stepped into the steady flow of people making their way through the large wooden doors that framed the front entrance. The inside of the place was lit up like a crystal chandelier, with extra lighting courtesy of a TV crew that had moved in and completely taken over the main room.

Inside, t-shirted crewmembers with headsets and clipboards scurried around, as staff in charge of crowd control moved the people from the foyer into the rows of folding chairs that had been set up in the main room. I was instantly reminded that this was a Halloween event when I recognized that many in the crowd had come in costume, ranging from something as simple as a funny hat to one fellow who was dressed like the Gorn Captain, that shabby, shambling lizard from the old *Star Trek* series.

As the crowd slowly shuffled forward around me, I spotted a young woman wearing a black PBS t-shirt, blacker lipstick, a headset, and a determined expression.

"Excuse me," I said as I lightly tapped her on the shoulder, making the assumption that she wasn't in costume but was, in fact, in uniform.

She turned and looked at me, holding up one finger on her right hand while she pressed her headset closer to her head with her left, trying to hear above all the conversations in the cramped, echoing space. "Uh huh," she said into the mouthpiece. "Roger that." She lowered her right finger, giving me the go-ahead to speak. "Yes?"

"Hi. I'm Eli Marks. I'm in the show tonight."

She quickly paged through the stack of multi-colored sheets on her clipboard, then spoke into the mouthpiece again. "I've got the Debunker with me. Where should I put him?"

"Actually, the term Debunker is not one—"

She held up that one finger again as she listened intently to her headset. She nodded and then turned and pushed her way through the crowd, glancing back over her shoulder as she did.

"Follow me," she yelled, and then she dove further into the throng. I excused and pardoned my way through the packed foyer, as I did my best to keep the crewmember in sight. As we neared the entrance to the main room, she veered to the right, past the restrooms, and then made a left, bringing us into a new room that was, literally, cavernous.

A long bar ran against one wall, and the far end of the room revealed an archway entrance to another, similar room. If I was remembering correctly from my one visit to The Caves, that cavern connected to another cavern, which in turn connected back to the main cavern, which connected to the foyer we had just left, creating a circle of interconnected caverns.

This particular space was currently unoccupied, with the exception of a tall, rail-thin woman with spiky red hair standing by the bar. She was digging through what looked like a large fishing tackle box. Next to her were two lights on stands, which were directed at a high, canvas-backed chair. Ricky Martin screamed *Living La Vida Loca* from a portable iPod speaker system on the bar.

"I've got one who's ready for make-up," the crewmember barked over the music. "He's on last, so no rush."

"Great," the spiky-haired woman said. "What's the time?"

The crewmember looked at her watch, which hung on a braided lanyard around her neck. "We go live in twenty-five minutes," she said as she spun around and headed back the way she had come. As she left the cavern, her hand went up to the headset on her ear and I could hear her say, "Debunker's in makeup." And then she was gone.

"I'm Lauren," the spiky-haired woman said, taking a makeup bib off the chair and gesturing for me to have a seat. Her voice was husky and rich, the distinctive sound of a former or current smoker.

"I'm Eli," I said as I settled into the chair. She fastened the bib around my neck, yanking and tugging it until it was positioned to her satisfaction.

"So, Eli, what's a Debunker and why do you hate that term so much?" She ran a warm hand quickly through my hair, and then turned and began rummaging through the tackle box. From my new vantage point I could see that instead of hooks, worms, and bobbers, the box was full of makeup supplies. Powders, eyeliners, lipsticks, brushes, tubes, and small bottles I couldn't identify were neatly arranged in the box's tiers.

"How do you know I hate that term?"

She gave a little laugh. "Body language. They say that ninety-five percent of human communication is done via body language."

"Really?"

"Well," she shrugged, "I made up the number, but I stand by the concept." She turned back from the makeup case, having found a shade of powder that pleased her. She placed one hand over my eyes while the soft, feathery brush in her other hand gave my face a quick dusting. The song on the iPod speaker switched from Ricky Martin to an aria from an opera that I almost recognized. This was either an eclectic playlist or the machine was set on shuffle. "So, what's a Debunker?" she asked again.

"Well," I said, settling into my well-practiced description, "in the world of psychics, mystics, and the supernatural, a Debunker is someone who vehemently believes that all other-worldly occurrences are bogus and that they can always be explained by a simple, scientific explanation."

"And that's not what you do?" She pushed lightly on my forehead to get me to tip my head back as she deftly applied some powder to my neck.

"I'd like to think so. Debunkers are often as fanatical as the people they oppose. I've always preferred the term Skeptic."

"And that means what?" She replaced the makeup brush in the tackle box and produced a comb and what appeared to be a can of hairspray.

"That means that I approach each situation with an open mind. I don't immediately assume that every supernatural occurrence isn't simply a natural occurrence that has been misunderstood or faked in some way."

"Ever come across one that wasn't?"

"Not yet. But I'm keeping an open mind."

"Well, keep that mind open but do me a favor and shut those baby-blue eyes for just a second."

I closed my eyes and heard the hiss of the hairspray and felt the sharp tug of her comb as she attempted to give my unruly mop of hair a bit of well-needed discipline. When I opened my eyes I was surprised to see a deck of playing cards fanned out in front of my face.

"Pick a card, any card."

The fanned cards dipped for a moment and I recognized Pete's face behind the cards.

Before I go any further, I want to go on the record here and say that I like Pete. I really do. He's a swell guy. But there are two things that have me deeply, perhaps fatally, conflicted in my feelings toward him.

The first is that Pete is trying to learn magic. That's an unsightly thing to observe for anyone, but it's particularly gruesome for a professional magician.

The other somewhat larger reason I'm conflicted about Pete is that I'm in love with his wife, Megan. Which really isn't his fault, but there you go. And although I can fall back on the excuse that they're getting a divorce and all's fair in love and war, the truth is I had no idea they were getting a divorce when I first started to fall for her.

If it makes any difference, she hardly knows I exist.

"Come on, pick a card. Free choice." Pete held the fanned deck closer, swaying his clasped hands from side to side, in his sad attempt at what I suspected was intended to be an enticing manner.

"What are you doing here?" I asked, completely mystified. I was having one of those out-of-context experiences.

Pete and his soon-to-be ex-wife Megan own the row of shops on the corner of 48th and Chicago that includes Chicago Magic. I'm very used to seeing him around the neighborhood and I see far too much of him in the shop, but I was completely taken aback to encounter him and his ubiquitous deck of cards here in The Caves.

"I've got a client who owns this place. They're trying to unload it. Interested?" He switched effortlessly into realtor mode. "I mean, think about it. This place would make a killer magic emporium."

"Sure, but what would we do with the other ninety-five percent of the space?"

"You're probably right, there's way too much square footage here." He pushed the fanned cards at me once again. "I think I've got this sucker nailed, finally. Go ahead, pick a card."

I acquiesced reluctantly and pulled a card from the center of the fanned deck, showing it to Lauren.

"Now look at the card," Pete said as he fumbled to square the deck. He glanced up at us. "Oh, you already did. Good for you. Well done. Okay, now, remember that card. I want you to put your randomly-chosen card back into the deck. Anywhere in the deck, this is a free choice that I'm not influencing in any manner whatsoever..."

He lost track of his sentence as he began to drop the cards in a slow shower from his right hand, which hovered about eight inches above his left. "Say stop wherever you like."

"Stop," I said, trying my best to put a modicum of interest into my voice.

He stopped dropping cards from one hand to the other and indicated that I should put the card on top of the messy stack in his left hand. I did and he then continued to drop the cards in a painfully slow and awkward manner until all of the cards were in his left hand. He struggled to square the cards again as he said, in an overly practiced manner, "Now to keep things fair, I'll cut the cards."

Pete executed a sloppy cut, followed by a second, even sloppier one. I looked up at Lauren, who was watching with a look of sick fascination on her face. I looked back at Pete, who was attempting to roll the top card off the deck with an awkward thumb and finger flip combination. It was obscene.

"And here's your card, right?" he asked hopefully, offering the top card for our inspection.

Both Lauren and I shook our heads silently. "Really?" We nodded sadly as Lauren unsnapped the clasp on the make-up bib and pulled it off of me.

Pete began to sort through the cards, trying to trace his fatal misstep. "I think I screwed up the cut," he said.

"I think you did," I said as I stood up. I turned to Lauren. "Are you done with me?"

She smiled. "Have a good show."

"Thanks."

"And keep an open mind." She gave me a quick smile and turned back to her makeup kit, repacking materials and getting ready for her next victim.

I clapped Pete on the shoulder and turned him toward the archway that led to the foyer. "Come on, Houdini. You can watch the show with me."

"I must have screwed up the cut," he repeated as we headed out of one cavern and into another.

"Excuse me. They said up front that Mr. Marks could be found back there? Did you happen to see him?" The question was tossed at us by a costumed character who looked a whole lot like the Mad Hatter without the hat. The eccentric character tossed his question over his shoulder as he marched purposefully past us.

Pete and I were headed back through the foyer toward the main room, where the last of the crowd was taking their seats.

The fellow with the question wore a rich purple tailcoat and colorful plaid pants cut in a style popular back in the late 1970s. This ensemble was accessorized with a paisley silk scarf tied snugly around his neck. He was tall, thin, and long-legged, with an angular face and wild hair that must have been tinted at some point in the past, as I could detect a trace of blue in it as he moved past us.

"If you're looking for Mr. Marks, that's me," I said.

He stopped in his tracks about ten feet from us and turned, tilting his head to one side curiously. "Interesting," he said in what was either a British accent or a deep-seated affectation. "I don't know why, but for some reason, I expected you to be much older."

"I was," I said. "I mean, my uncle Harry was going to do this show when they booked it last summer. But I'm filling in for him." I stepped forward and put out my hand. "I'm Eli Marks."

He returned the handshake like a man new to the concept but certainly enthusiastic about it.

"Clive Albans," he said, almost bowing. "I was hoping I would have a chance to speak with you, either this evening or at some later point, for an article I'm doing for the London *Times*."

"Sure," I said. "What's the article about?"

"I'm doing an exposé on charlatan psychics and mentalists. Frauds, fakers, freaks, that sort of thing. My understanding was that you, actually, your uncle, is a bit legendary in the field of debunking. I'd love to include the perspective of the professional debunker, if I could."

I bit my tongue, deciding I would correct him on the use of that term during the actual interview. "Sure," I said. "No problem."

"Brilliant," he said, turning to follow us as we continued toward the main room. The three of us stood in the archway for a moment, marveling at all the costumed attendees; a truly exotic turnout. I heard Clive cluck his tongue loudly as he looked around the room.

"These people," he said, shaking his head slowly from side to side as he jotted illegibly in a small notebook. "They look ridiculous."

Pete and I exchanged a glance but kept our mouths shut.

"Okay, folks, we're going live in five minutes," the smiling television host told the assembled audience from his position near the front of the stage. The host wore his usual get-up—a tweed sport coat with a plaid scarf—but for once the scarf made sense in the crisp, cool constant fifty-five degrees of The Caves.

The floor manager gestured at him and he looked down at small stack of index cards in his hand as if he'd forgotten he was holding them.

"Oh yes," he said, "I've been asked to remind you of a couple of housekeeping notes. So, how many people here have ever been to The Vatican? You know, the one in Rome?"

This apparent *non sequitur* produced some puzzled looks in the crowd. A few audience members raised their hands tentatively.

"Okay, good, a few of you," the host continued. "Well, for the rest of you, when you go to The Vatican and visit the Sistine Chapel—which my wife and I did about five years ago, just stunning, don't miss it, get in line early, that sucker fills up quickly...they tell you the moment you enter the Chapel that you're not allowed to touch the walls. Da Vinci or Michelangelo or whoever it was who did all the painting in there, he did the whole thing, walls and ceiling. Just stunning. And they don't want you to touch the walls, because apparently they don't want the oils from your skin to get on the painting."

"Well," he said , unaware that the audience didn't have a clue what he was talking about, "the same is true here in The Caves, but for a slightly different reason. I've been asked to request that you don't touch the walls in here because they're made of sandstone and are very soft. They say that it doesn't take much to damage them. So, hands off the walls."

He added a laugh to emphasize this point and then flipped through his index cards for his next housekeeping note. "Also, be sure to get your questions into the crystal bowl...where is the bowl?"

The floor manager gestured toward the bowl, which was at the host's feet.

He grinned broadly and pointed at the bowl. "Yes, there's the bowl. You need to get your questions for Grey into this bowl before the start of the show. They tell me there's paper, pens, and envelopes up here and also on a table in the back of the room. Is that right?"

He looked to the floor manager for confirmation, received a quick nod, and continued with his pre-show warm-up.

An audio engineer had found me and was in the process of clipping a wireless lavaliere microphone to my sport coat. I ran the cord under my shirt and slid the small transmitter he handed me into my back pocket.

"So what's going on here tonight?" Pete whispered as the TV host cracked some more jokes and gave the audience a few more final instructions. Pete still held the deck of cards in his hands, which he fingered badly in what looked to be his sad attempt at a double lift.

"The local PBS station is doing a live remote, as part of their weekly local news magazine show. This week's special is a Halloween show," I explained. "They've got a psychic medium who is going to perform, and then, in the name of fairness or something, they want to bring me on."

"The voice of the opposition?" Clive suggested.

"Something like that," I agreed.

"So who's the psychic?" Pete asked.

"A performer named Grey," Clive answered before I could. He double-checked his notes. "Yes, that's it. Grey."

Pete looked at Clive quizzically. "Grey what?"

Clive shrugged. "Just Grey," he said as he paged through his notes. "Apparently he goes by only the one name. You know, like Cher. Liberace. Bono. Do you know him?" he asked me.

"Vaguely," I said, and then turned to Pete. "You may know him better by his former name...Walter Graboski."

A dim look of recognition crossed over Pete's face. "Now that you mention it, that does sound familiar. Wasn't he a realtor?"

"For years." Clive tapped me on the shoulder and I answered his question before he could ask it. "In Britain, you call them estate agents."

He gave me a nod of thanks and continued making notes in his small notepad.

"And now he's a psychic?" Pete asked.

"If you listen to his version of the truth, he'll tell you that he's always had *the gift*. But in reality, he was your garden-variety realtor for years. And then he started to get the reputation of being, shall we say, friendly to a fringe audience."

"Friendly to fringe audiences? Interesting." Clive asked, "Define please?"

"Well, if you were a witch or warlock who wanted to *mark* a property before you bought it...by urinating around the circumference of the house, for example...Grey was the type of realtor who would happily look the other way," I explained quietly. "Or if you felt the need to perform a nude cleansing of a space before you put in an offer, Grey was your guy.

"In some instances," I added, "I understand he was more than willing to strip down and join in. Then, after a while he discovered that he could make more money doing readings instead of doing real estate. So he made the switch to the psychic dodge full time."

"You can make more money as a psychic than a realtor?" Pete asked, his voice cracking as he attempted to whisper.

A crewmember turned toward us and signaled that less talking would be preferred. I smiled at her, then turned and gave Pete a knowing smile as well.

I considered adding a few more words to the topic, but at that moment the lights began to dim in the cavern as other lights grew brighter on the stage. The host looked directly into one of the large video cameras positioned in front of the stage and announced, "Yes, folks, we're coming to you live from The Wabasha Caves. It's Halloween and we've got a spooky treat for our audience here and for all of you at home. Please put your hands together for the one, the only...Grey!"

And then without warning, the lights went out, plunging the room into darkness.

Chapter 2

There was a yelp from the audience as the cavern suddenly went black. And then, just as the echo of that exclamation had died down, the room began to vibrate with the deep, eerie tones of a pipe organ. A moment later a spotlight snapped on, revealing an imposing figure, all in black, standing like a statue in the center of the stage. His sudden appearance produced the intended gasp from several audience members. He stood silently for a few moments and then the organ music dipped in volume and he began to speak in a rich, sonorous baritone.

"Good evening," he said. "Tonight we shall travel together, across the ether. We will summon souls from the other side and explore the terrain of the afterlife, step-by-step and hand-in-hand. We will touch the past and we will in turn be touched by the future. My name is Grey and this is my promise to you."

Grey spoke with an accent that could have been European, could have been South African, but was definitely not Minnesotan. I looked at him on the stage across the room, and then turned to get a better view on one of the wide-screen TV monitors that had been placed throughout the cavern. He was tall and wiry. His thick, jet-black hair was slicked back, exposing diamond studs in each earlobe, which sparkled in the spotlight. Other reflections were produced by the oversized diamond rings he sported on each hand. He was dressed elegantly in a tailored black suit coat, black turtleneck, and black slacks. His green eyes scanned the room methodically.

"To begin our journey, I require the assistance of a volunteer," he said as he launched into his act. He quickly found his first volunteer, a heavyset woman, about forty-five, who looked a little too well dressed for someone planning to spend Halloween on a folding chair in a damp cave. The woman appeared both thrilled and terrified as she jumped up and made her way toward the stage while a cameraman with a handheld video camera walked backwards in front of her.

As this matronly volunteer headed down the aisle, I noticed for the first time that Grey had an assistant, a figure who was standing silently at the base of the steps. She was a slim young woman. Like Grey, she was dressed all in black, with long dark hair that appeared to flow down to her waist and perhaps even beyond. If it weren't for her pale, almost translucent skin she might have disappeared completely into the black draping that spanned the back of the stage. Even from my vantage point across the room I could see that she was both exotic and stunning. While others in the room had decked themselves out for Halloween—from Jedi Knights to way-too old Harry Potters to your standard issue ghosts, witches and political figures—her wardrobe appeared to be something she had simply taken from her closet. Not goth, really, but just this side of Morticia Addams.

"Thank you, Nova," Grey said to her as she handed the woman off to him. Grey smoothly guided the volunteer up the steps and across the stage to where a heavy wooden table and three chairs had been set.

"What is your name, my dear?" he asked.

"Sharon," she said, her voice cracking a bit from nervousness and excitement.

"Excellent. Sharon, with your help I am going to begin the process of moving from this, the corporeal world, to the other side. I need to ask...Do you have any medical training?"

"I took a CPR class," she said almost apologetically. "But it was years ago."

"Then perhaps you know how to find my pulse? Do you think you could do that?"

With his guidance she proceeded to find his pulse. She held his wrist awkwardly, nodding that she had in fact found a pulse.

Grey nodded and then tilted his head back, with a sudden and sharp intake of breath. His body tensed and his head twisted oddly from side to side. Sharon continued to hold his wrist, her eyes widening at his near convulsions. And then she visibly paled. She moved her hand around his wrist, first slowly and then with growing concern.

"It's, it's stopped," she finally said, a tremor of fear in her voice. "You don't have a pulse."

"Excellent. Then I have crossed," Grey said, exhaling deeply. "I now stand on the precipice, on the border between the living and the deceased. For the next few minutes I will be neither alive nor dead, but instead will act as a conduit between these two disparate worlds."

He stood, and as he did Sharon lost her grip on his wrist.

"Thank you for helping me to cross." He put a hand on her shoulder and guided the clearly shaken woman to the steps at the front of the stage, where his assistant helped navigate her way back to her seat.

"How the hell did he do that?" Pete hissed in my ear. He's a couple inches shorter than I am, so this move had required him to stand on his toes.

"There's lots of ways to accomplish it, but my guess is that he's got a tennis ball strapped into his arm pit," I whispered back. "A little pressure and you cut off blood flow to the wrist, which gives the effect of no pulse. My uncle calls the trick the Armpit Tourniquet."

Clive clucked his tongue, in apparent agreement with my assessment.

Our brief conversation elicited another sharp look from one of the crewmembers, so I didn't continue my explanation. Regardless of his method, Grey had grabbed the audience's attention and they were listening raptly as he stepped back to his chair and withdrew a long strip of black fabric from his suit coat pocket.

"As I said, I have crossed and stand on the precipice between the living and the dead. However, in order to truly hone in on that connection, I need to do some fine-tuning." He looked up and smiled, his oily charm emanating from every pore. "For those of you who have taken long car trips, it's not unlike tuning a car radio in the middle of a remote desert, trying to find the point of greatest connection. To that end, I will attempt a couple of experiments— warm-up exercises, as it were. Experience has taught me that these are best accomplished without the burden of visual stimulation."

With that he sat down in the chair and placed the black strip of fabric over his eyes. Nova had silently joined him on-stage and she stepped forward to tie the blindfold for him, making a final adjustment to ensure that his eyes were completely covered. She then picked up a handheld microphone from the table and silently left the stage.

For the next twenty minutes, Grey skillfully performed some basic, almost rudimentary mentalism routines. With the help of the dark-haired Nova, he did a second sight bit, where she selected objects from audience members and he—still blindfolded—divined the nature, color, and size of the objects, much to the audience's amazement. After several short exchanges with various audience members—in which he divined the amount of money in a wallet, the age of an older gentleman, and the color of a pair of socks—Nova selected a nervous woman on the aisle. After a short, whispered exchange with the woman, Nova spoke into the handheld microphone. Her voice was soft and almost childlike.

"Grey."

"Yes, Nova," he said in a deep whisper. It sounded as if an audio engineer had added some reverberation to his microphone.

"See if you would tell me this woman's name," Nova said.

The audience looked from Nova to Grey, who sat stiff-backed and motionless on the stage.

"Her name is Joy," he finally said. The woman tried to suppress her surprised reaction by putting her hand over her mouth as the audience applauded. Nova had another brief, whispered conversation with the woman and then, as the applause died down, she continued.

"Now then, in what month was she born?"

Again the audience turned, almost in unison, from Nova to Grey.

"She was born in...in September," he said in a flat monotone.

"Would you tell me the date of her birth?"

"The fifth of September."

The woman nodded vigorously to the crowd, to demonstrate that every answer so far had been spot on. The audience burst into applause again.

"Someone's read his Corinda," Clive whispered to me out of the corner of his mouth.

"Classic presentation," I agreed. "Nothing new here."

Nova stepped back and looked the woman over head to toe. "Grey, can you tell me what color shoes Joy is wearing?"

Grey tilted his head to one side. "Her shoes are brown."

The woman looked down at her feet and then shook her head, first toward Grey and then toward Nova.

Nova seemed flustered for a moment. "I meant, will you tell me? *Will* you tell me what color they are?"

Even with a blindfold covering much of his face, Grey looked annoyed. But he quickly masked that emotion and continued. "Her shoes are black."

The woman nodded to Nova and to the crowd, and again they applauded, but this time with what felt to me to be a little less enthusiasm. Nova held out her open palm to the woman, who at first wasn't sure what was wanted of her. Then she pulled a ring off her finger. She handed it over to Nova, who clasped it tightly in her hand before continuing.

"Joy has given me a personal object. I want you to tell me what this is, now."

Grey looked momentarily puzzled. "A stamp?" he said, posing more of a question than making a statement.

"No," Nova stammered. "I want you to tell me what this is, *now then*."

Grey did his best to cover a sigh. "It's a ring."

Nova quickly rattled off her next request. "I'd like you to tell me what it is made of."

"Gold."

The woman smiled and nodded to the crowd, to let them know that Grey had been correct. The crowd applauded, some of their lost enthusiasm returning. Nova handed the ring to the woman and moved away, searching for another candidate.

"Grey, next we have a man—"

He cut her off brusquely. "For our next exercise, we will continue to strengthen my connection with the other side. For this demonstration, my assistant will pass out several recent magazines and books."

Nova looked surprised at the sudden shift in plan, but obeyed and headed back toward the stage. As she moved around the back row of seats, she passed an audio speaker resting on a stand. As soon as she moved in front of the speaker, there was a tremendous shriek of feedback. Nova held her free hand up to cover her ear. She clicked the *off* switch on the microphone, silencing the feedback and then she scampered toward the stage. There she picked up a silver tray that held a stack of magazines and books.

As new age music played through the sound system, Nova moved smoothly through the crowd, distributing the periodicals and books. By the time she reached me, the tray was empty. She shrugged impishly and turned back toward the stage, putting the tray under her arm while she flipped her microphone back on.

"Grey."

"Yes, Nova," he answered, still seated stiffly on the stage, his eyes covered by the black fabric.

"Distribution is complete," she said.

Grey then instructed those audience members who had received a book or magazine to page through it and find a single page, and then to concentrate with all their energy on that page. As I looked around the cavern I could see that people, God love 'em, were attacking the assignment with relish. Those who hadn't been lucky enough to receive one of the books or periodicals appeared to be wasting no time in assisting their neighbor in finding just the right page.

The first person selected from the audience was a heavy-set man in a blue denim work shirt and suspenders. He was holding a magazine. He held the cover up to Nova and then turned the magazine toward her to reveal his chosen page number.

"What is your name?" she asked.

"Scott," he said, leaning awkwardly toward her microphone.

"Grey," she said, turning back toward the stage, "your first reading is with Scott. Scott has this week's *Time* magazine and he is looking at page thirty-one."

"*Time* magazine," Grey repeated. "Page thirty-one. Look at that page and concentrate, Scott. Think of nothing else."

He held a hand up to his forehead dramatically, and then lowered it. "Scott, I'm having trouble seeing page thirty-one, because I'm seeing an advertisement for a ladies' razor, which consists primarily of a photo of a woman in a bathtub, shaving her legs. She appears to be completely naked, although I hasten to point out that the advertisement is in fine taste. However, there is no number on that page. Is that the page directly across from thirty-one?"

Nova held the microphone up to Scott, who shrugged his shoulders sheepishly. "Yes, it is. That's an ad."

Grey chuckled. "That was your first choice, wasn't it, Scott? But you didn't want to admit that to us, did you?"

"That's right," Scott mumbled into the microphone as the audience laughed.

"Thank you, Scott. You may sit down."

He sat amidst the good-natured teasing of several pals around him. Nova moved across the aisle to an elderly woman who was holding a paperback book. "What is your name, ma'am?" Nova asked.

"Bernice," the white-haired woman said softly. Nova looked at the book the woman was holding and the page she had the book opened to.

"Grey, Bernice is looking at page seventy-four of Shakespeare's *Macbeth*."

Grey again put his hand to his forehead for a moment, and then he spoke. "Bernice, through either choice or chance, you have picked one of my favorite passages from that great play. At the top of that page, Macduff speaks, does he not? Say the words with me, Bernice."

They began to read together, he onstage and she in the audience. *"O, horror, horror, horror. Confusion now hath made his masterpiece! Most sacrilegious murder hath broke open the Lord's anointed temple, and stole thence the life o' the building."*

Bernice closed the book and looked up at Grey with open-mouthed awe, her eyes tearing up slightly as Grey continued to speak the verse. *"Approach the chamber, and destroy your sight with a new Gorgon: do not bid me speak; See, and then speak yourselves. Shake off this downy sleep, death's counterfeit, and look on death itself!"*

His final words echoed through the chamber. Bernice slowly sat back in her chair as the audience applauded enthusiastically. Even Pete and Clive, on either side of me, broke into spontaneous applause. I didn't join in, but I had to admit, even though Grey was as dishonest as the day is long, he was a hell of a performer.

Chapter 3

The act continued in this manner for several minutes. Nova picked audience members and Grey read their minds as they concentrated on the books and magazines in front of them. The routine went smoothly—more smoothly than the previous exercise, that's for sure—with only one noticeable hiccup.

Nova had approached an audience member who had received a copy of *Business Week* magazine. She spoke with him briefly.

"Grey," she said as she turned back toward the stage, "I'm standing here with Chad. He's looking at page sixteen of *Business Week* magazine."

"Page sixteen of *Business Week* magazine," Grey repeated. "Let me see." He put a hand to his forehead and leaned forward in concentration. "I'm seeing an article about employee compensation, am I right?"

Chad nodded to Grey and then, realizing that the man was blindfolded, he leaned over to the microphone Nova was holding.

"Yes," he said. "Employee compensation."

"And the headline, the headline reads, 'More Employees Willing to Walk to Get Higher Wages,' is that correct?"

"Yes it is," Chad confirmed, shaking his head in amazement.

"I also see," Grey started to say and then stopped. He put a hand up to his forehead and then shook his head.

"I also see," he repeated, this sentence getting no further than the earlier attempt. "In addition to the headline..."

His voice trailed off as he pushed his hand harder into his forehead.

I turned from the stage back to the TV monitor, which was on a tight close-up of Grey. It looked as if he was beginning to sweat.

There was a long, awkward pause, as Grey shook his head from side to side. "No," he said in a raspy whisper. "No, absolutely not. No. No. I said no!" With a ferocious almost violent move, Grey stood up suddenly and ripped his blindfold off, throwing it down onto the stage. He looked out at the audience, his eyes squinting in reaction to the sudden exposure to light after having been covered for so long.

"I'm sorry, ladies and gentlemen," he said, quickly regaining his composure. "On rare occasions, while in the midst of the spiritual flow such as I was just immersed within, an unwelcome spirit will intrude upon the proceedings. A most unwelcome spirit. At times like that, it is best to simply break the connection with that particular entity. Permanently."

He ran a hand through his hair to ensure that each strand was still properly in place, and then stepped to the edge of the stage. "I think it's time to begin the portion of the program that most of you have come here tonight to experience. I will connect to the other side, connect with your loved ones, and answer questions that are near and dear to your hearts. Nova, are the questions prepared?"

By the sudden buzz of excitement that broke out in the room, it was clear that this was, in fact, the portion of the evening that the audience had come to experience. As effects go, it was simplicity itself. Nova presented Grey with a large punch bowl, filled with small tan envelopes. Before the show, each audience member had written a question on a slip of paper, folded it and sealed it in one of the small envelopes.

For the performance, Grey would then remove an envelope from the bowl, hold it to his forehead for a moment, then announce the question, the name of the questioner, and then provide an answer from the beyond for the hopeful participant.

"One important note before we begin," Grey said, pulling a match from his pocket and striking it on the table. "I should warn you that when the stream to the Other Side is opened, it is not entirely uncommon for an impatient spirit to jump his or her place in line," he said as he lit a candle on the table. He moved it to the center of the table, adjusting the position of a large silver ashtray next to it.

"When that happens," he continued, "I will have no clue that a new spirit has stepped in and taken the place of the spirit I was communicating with. Consequently, the information I'm receiving may no longer be relevant to the person I'm talking to. I will need your help...all of you," he said, spreading his hands wide to encompass the whole room.

"If the information I'm providing to you is correct, please acknowledge it by saying 'yes,' loudly and clearly. And if you're seated across the room and suddenly you feel that what I'm saying is applying to you, please let me know right away. Is that clear?" Like obedient students, the audience nodded at Grey as one.

"Good. Let us begin," he said as he pulled out the chair next to the table and sat. Lighting in the room shifted to increase the already moody ambiance and eerie organ music again began to echo throughout the cavern. He closed his eyes and reached into the bowl, taking out a single envelope and holding it up near his temple for a long moment.

"Rene T.," Grey said finally. "Rene, are you here?" A blonde woman in her late twenties stood in the crowd and meekly held her hand up. Grey turned his head in her direction as Nova moved through the crowd to her with the handheld microphone.

"You are curious about a relationship, are you not?"

Rene nodded, wringing her hands together nervously. Remembering Grey's earlier instruction, she quickly added, "Yes. Yes."

Grey closed his eyes. "This is a relationship of long duration, am I right?"

"Yes. A year and a half," she said.

"Rene, a year and a half is merely a blink in the eye of the universe. I'm seeing that this relationship has existed in this life and many previous incarnations. And that the two of you are working out issues now that have existed between you for millennia. You are arguing more now than usual, am I right?"

Rene nodded again. "Yes, it feels like it."

"One of the reasons you've been brought together in this life is to continue to work on these differences. But make no mistake...this person is your soul mate and you will indeed make progress that will help not only in this life, but in future lives as well."

"Thank you," Rene said as she sighed in relief and began to sit down again.

Grey raised his right hand and closed his eyes for a moment. "Rene, I'm also getting that you have a work relationship that is beginning to come to a boiling point, does that make sense?"

Rene cocked her head to one side, considering this. "I believe so, yes," she said, beginning to nod in agreement.

"Watch that closely for the next three weeks. Some changes are in order," he instructed as he picked up his letter opener and ripped open the envelope he had been holding the entire time. He pulled out the slip of paper and read it aloud: "Can you tell me if I should stay with my boyfriend, signed Rene T." He smiled at her as the audience applauded. He held the slip of paper over the candle and it began to smoke and then burned down to an ash. He held on to it for a long time, the flames flickering at his fingertips, before dropping it onto a large ashtray on the table.

He reached into the bowl and withdrew another envelope, as the audience appeared to lean forward as one in anticipation.

And so it went for over thirty minutes. Grey took envelope after envelope out of the bowl, identifying the owner and their question—and offering a detailed answer as well as other facts about the person and their life—before opening the envelope and reading their actual question aloud. Then he'd burn the question and move onto the next envelope.

"How the devil is he doing this?" Clive asked in a raspy whisper. "It's extraordinary."

I shrugged. "He's good, but it's all pretty simple stuff, really. He's one ahead, that's for sure. The rest is just a mix of cold reading, deductive reasoning and a solid understanding of human nature."

"One ahead? One ahead of what?" Pete asked, not taking his eyes off Grey, who was in the midst of giving a fellow a message from the man's recently deceased father. The guy was nearly in tears, his head bobbing up and down along with everything Grey was saying.

"Somehow he got a hold of the first question ahead of time," I explained quietly. "Probably a switch of some kind—the Al Baker or the Moldavian—and so every time he appears to be opening an envelope to read the question he just answered, he's actually reading the next question."

"One ahead," Pete repeated.

"Yeah, it's used all the time in magic. In cards, coins. Hell, even Cups and Balls is a one-ahead. It's all about having a piece of information the audience doesn't know you have...You can work tons of variations on it and the audience is none the wiser." I was going to explain further, but something Grey was saying snuck into my consciousness and grabbed my attention. In fact, for a brief moment, it sounded like he was talking about me.

Here's a little secret about how mentalism works—the audience plays the primary role in its success, much more than the performer. That's because the human brain, in all its evolutionary glory, insists on filling in any gaps. If you give the brain A and then follow it up with C, it's going to do its darnedest to connect the two with some form of B.

Consequently, all the mentalist really has to do is toss out random words that your brain can grab onto and try to make sense of.

If he says, "I'm getting a very powerful feeling about apples," then the average brain immediately searches for any connection it can make to apples, and pretty soon you're thinking, "Hey, I just had an apple last Thursday. This guy is pretty good."

The trouble is, even when you understand the principle, it's difficult to keep your brain from getting caught up in it. Which is exactly what happened to my brain when it heard Grey say, "Who here had something taken from them by someone named Ed? Or someone that sounds like Ed, maybe Ted?"

That immediately struck a nerve in my brain, because I did in fact have something taken from me by a guy named Fred, which my advanced brain immediately recognized as rhyming with Ed. Fred took my wife and he was the reason I was now living in a third-floor apartment above my uncle's magic shop.

Of course, on a purely intellectual level, I knew that wasn't the case. Fred hadn't actually taken anything from me. My now ex-wife, Deirdre, had left our marriage and married someone else. I might be angry about the manner in which she had done it, allowing the two relationships to overlap inconveniently, but nothing had been stolen. One husband had simply been exchanged for another. Not unlike taking one automobile and trading it for a new one. The only irregularity, of course, was that Deirdre had still been driving the first car while she test-drove the second.

But who could blame them, really? They had worked closely for a number of years, she as a fast-rising Assistant District Attorney, he as a hotshot cop on his way to becoming a hotshot homicide detective. Deirdre really had far more in common with Fred than she did with me, a guy whose greatest skill, it appeared, was the ability to make a gallon of milk disappear into a rolled-up newspaper.

All this flashed through my brain in a nanosecond and I mentally returned to the performance in time to hear Grey talking to a woman who had lost her virginity to a guy named Ned. Like I said, the brain will find the connection, regardless of how tenuous.

Grey finished his short reading of the woman and the audience applauded, as they had done each time, regardless of his level of accuracy. He held up one hand to quiet them.

"Ladies and gentlemen, I can feel my connection to the spirit world growing weaker, the braided strands to the other side unraveling by the moment. Could I impose upon my first helper to return to the stage to assist my journey back across that bridge?"

Sharon, the over-dressed, matronly woman quickly made her way back to the stage, moving toward Grey, who was still seated stiffly in the high-backed chair. She placed two fingers on his wrist, moving them once and then again and then once more. She shook her head. "There's no pulse," she said, a note of dread in her voice.

"No, not just yet," Grey agreed. "I'm still on the precipice." He closed his eyes and went through his deep breathing routine again.

As he did, Sharon adjusted her grip on his wrist. After several moments, she started nodding, a little at first and then more confidently. "There it is," she said. "I can feel the pulse. I can feel it."

Grey opened his eyes. "Yes. Yes," he said, smiling like a Cheshire Cat. "I have returned. Thank you, Sharon."

He stood and ushered her off the stage, and then turned to the applauding crowd. "And thanks to all of you. I will leave you tonight with the words of a great man, The Amazing Dunninger, who so wisely said, 'For those who believe, no explanation is necessary. For those who do not believe, no explanation will suffice.' Good night."

He bowed deeply, took a step back, and then bowed again. The pipe organ music began blasting through the room as the audience stood, en masse, applauding wildly. Some had tears running down their faces, some were hugging each other, and the rest were clapping their hands vigorously as Grey took yet another overly-dramatic bow.

"You're up next," a voice next to me yelled over the applause. The floor manager had appeared by my side, looking from me to the crowd. "Boy, that's going to be one hell of a tough act to follow."

"Thanks," I said. "That's just what I needed to hear."

Chapter 4

"Okay, we're back," the TV host said as the red light popped on above the main camera.

I was onstage, seated at the large wooden table, trying to look casual and relaxed and feeling neither. My unease was heightened by the placement of Grey, who was seated at the other end of the table. This was an unexpected development and the only solace I could take in the situation was that it seemed to be just as unanticipated for Grey as well.

During the break, as the host chatted casually with me while I settled into my place on stage, he suddenly turned to the floor manager and said, "Hey, why don't we get Grey back out here as well? Might be fun to have the two of them on camera together. Is he still here? Can we do that?"

This was followed by several energetic and hushed conversations by crew members speaking frantically into their headsets. A few moments later, Grey stepped back into the room, just pulling on a black wool coat. The host saw him from the stage and pointed him out to the crowd. "Hey folks," he boomed to the audience, "how many of you would like Grey to stick around for this next segment?"

Even if Grey had tried to decline, he would have been drowned out by the thunderous ovation the audience gave to this seemingly spontaneous suggestion. Moments later, he was re-wired with a microphone and seated at the other end of the table from me, where he still sat stiffly, refusing to look me in the eye.

"We just had a great paranormal experience with psychic, mentalist, and spiritualist Grey," the host continued, speaking directly into the camera. Without any prompting from the floor manager, the audience began applauding wildly. Grey smiled wanly and tilted his head a fraction of an inch, acknowledging their adoration.

"And joining us now," he continued, glancing down at his ubiquitous index cards, "is debunker and magician, Eli Marks."

He waited a beat too long, anticipating an interruption by applause, which clearly wasn't coming. The floor manager, standing just off-camera, frantically gave the audience the applause signal. Their response was at best lackluster, clapping with the same enthusiasm that a group of kids might display when being forced to welcome the man who was about to kill Santa Claus.

The host glanced at the index card again and then looked up at me. "So, Eli, you saw all of Grey's performance tonight, right?"

"Yes, I did," I said.

"As a debunker of paranormal events, did it set off all of your internal alarms? All the bells and whistles?" He chuckled good-naturedly.

"Well, to begin with, I prefer the term skeptic rather than debunker," I began, but he quickly cut me off.

"Debunker, skeptic, either way you don't believe that what Grey did here tonight was supernatural in any way, do you?"

I looked from the host, to the crowd, to Grey, who was ignoring my very existence.

"Here's the deal," I said suddenly, turning back to the host as I decided to just jump in and do it. "Grey is very good at what he does. Really. He has excellent crowd control, solid routines, and is obviously skillful. I have no issue with that. What gets me...what sticks in my craw, as my uncle would say...is that he presents the tricks that he's performing as if they were real."

"You're saying they're not real?" the host asked provocatively.

"Not one second of it. Look," I said, leaning forward and gesturing toward Grey across the table from me. "Grey has a great mentalism act. Really. He could make a handsome living in a Las Vegas showroom for years to come with that act. Not at one of the bigger hotels on The Strip," I added, "but he could still aspire to a job downtown." My joke, such as it was, got nothing from the audience.

"So then, if it's all bogus, can you tell us how he does it?" the Host asked provocatively. "Let us in on all the little secrets?"

I sat back in my chair with a sigh. "Well, you see, that's going to be a problem. Essentially what Grey did tonight was a magic show, and we magicians are not known for our willingness to let our secrets out."

"A professional magician never reveals his methods?" the host offered.

"Something like that," I agreed.

"Well, don't take this the wrong way, Eli," the host said, getting ready to go in for the kill. "But you appear to want it both ways. You say it's all fake and not real, but at the same time you won't explain how it's done. That's doesn't seem quite fair, does it?" He winked at the audience and got a smattering of applause in response. They still hated me, but now for a new reason. That was progress of a sort, I guess.

"Maybe I can meet you halfway," I said. "What parts do you want to know about?"

He glanced down at his notes. "Let's start at the top. How did he stop his heartbeat?"

I shook my head. "Sorry, folks, that's a magic trick. I can duplicate it for you, if you like, but I won't tell you how it's done."

"Okay, then," he continued, scanning through his notes. "How did he identify people in the audience...he knew their names, what they were wearing, objects they were holding...and he did it all while blindfolded. Can you explain how he did that?"

"Well, for starters, just because you have a blindfold on doesn't necessarily mean that you're blind. But, as for his method, I suspect he and his lovely assistant—"

"Nova," the host added, gesturing to the woman in question, who was seated just off-stage.

"Yes, the lovely Nova. I suspect that the two of them used a fairly simple verbal code to communicate the information. In fact, if you were paying close attention...or even if you weren't, for that matter...I think you might have recognized they were having a wee bit of trouble with it tonight." I looked over at Grey, who was glaring at Nova. She looked away and Grey huffed quietly and folded his arms in disgust.

"All right, fair enough," the host said, looking down and flipping to a new card in his stack. "What about his second-sight ability...reading the words from books and magazines held by audience members? There clearly wasn't any code going on there."

I nodded in agreement. "No, I think a more sophisticated technology was used for that." I picked up the wireless handheld microphone that Nova had left on the table. "Remember earlier when Nova got too close to one of the speakers in the audience with this microphone? How there was that loud, annoying feedback?"

I was saying this to the host, but I could see audience members nodding along with me as I spoke. "Well, that's because you don't want to get a live microphone too near a speaker—whether it's a great big speaker on a stand in front of the stage," I said, waving the microphone toward one of the distant speakers, "or a little tiny speaker hidden somewhere else."

With that, I waved the microphone past the left side of Grey's head, which produced a loud, shrill electronic shriek from somewhere near his left ear. He leapt up, holding his ear and moving quickly away from the table.

"Damn it," he said, rubbing his ear furiously. Then he must have realized that not only was he still in front of a live audience, he was also on live television. Ever the professional, he regained his composure just as quickly as he had exploded. He bowed slightly to the audience, ran a hand through his hair and glared quietly at the host as he returned to his chair.

"I didn't come on this program to be insulted," he said, sitting heavily in his seat. "I have a gift that I have proven again and again, countless times. I don't need the blessing of this, this...performing monkey." Grey spit out the last words like a curse. He flinched slightly as I moved the microphone toward him again, and then I set it midway between us on the table as a gesture of truce. The host was still flipping through the cards.

"Perhaps, Mr. Marks, you could explain how he predicted each of the questions in the sealed envelopes? And, even more impressive than that, there were all the facts he seemed to know about the audience members. People he'd never met before, according to him."

"Impressive? Perhaps," I began. "But not really all that difficult."

"What about when he revealed that someone in this room had a relative who died on the toilet? You don't just pull that out of thin air, do you? And he even knew how the fellow died...a heart attack, if I remember correctly." He nodded in agreement with several nearby audience members.

"To begin with, dying while on the toilet may be a unique event, but it's not as rare as you might think. How many people do we have in this room?" I asked, doing a quick scan of the crowd. "About 200 people?"

"Give or take," the host agreed.

"Well, in a group of 200 people, I would guess you have maybe a one-in-three chance of finding at least one person who knows of someone who died while on the toilet. For an act like Grey's...for any mentalist...that's a chance worth taking, because it's a big pay-off for very little risk.

"And, as for cause of death, there weren't really all that many options," I continued. "When death comes on a toilet, it's traditionally in the form of a heart attack or stroke, not a fall from a great height or a gunshot wound. Unless you're John Travolta in *Pulp Fiction*." This actually produced a ripple of laughter from the crowd. It didn't turn the tide, but finally I was feeling a little less hate coming from the group.

"Okay," the host acknowledged. "But what about divining the questions on the cards in sealed envelopes? I think of myself as a pretty smart guy, and to me that seems to defy explanation."

"Let me see here," I said. "How can I explain the technique without giving too much away?" I sat quietly for a moment, not trying to build drama—although that was the unintended effect—but to actually figure out a way to explain what Grey had done without screwing up about a hundred other magic tricks that use the same method.

"There's a technique in magic called One Ahead," I finally said, talking first to the host and then turning and addressing the crowd. "And it's as simple as it sounds...The magician is one ahead. That one might be a piece of information, a name, a question, or even a physical object, like a coin or a ball. The magician has it and the audience doesn't know it, so he's One Ahead."

I gestured toward Grey, who was still steadfastly refusing to look in my direction. "In the case of Grey's envelope trick, somehow he got the first question ahead of time...lots of different ways to do that, although I think I know the method he used tonight...and by being in possession of the first question, all he had to do was to pretend to read that question when he was actually opening the second question."

I was getting an equal amount of head nodding and blank stares from the audience. The host was going to say something, but even he seemed a bit baffled. I reached into my coat pocket and took out the deck of cards I always carry.

"Let me demonstrate the same thing, but with a deck of playing cards," I said as I spread the cards, face down, in a mess all over the table. "I'll need some help with this," I added, gesturing toward the host and then, in a burst of inspiration, toward Nova as well. As the audience applauded, the host bounded back up to the stage, while Nova moved at a much less enthusiastic pace.

"Let me see if I can remember the pattern for this routine," I said as much to myself as to the crowd. It took a few seconds for me to mentally sort through my card trick files, and then I remembered the routine. "Okay, I think I've got it."

I spread the cards around on the tabletop some more, to mix them even further. The host was standing over me and Nova had just crossed the stage. Grey, seated across the table from me, looked like an unhappy statue.

"Every time I try to write the word psychic," I said, rolling into the routine. "I somehow always end up writing the word physics. Now, except for sharing most of the same letters in common, the two words may seem unrelated. But they're actually a lot closer than you might think. You see, in quantum physics, it's understood that the very act of observing an action invariably changes the outcome. And, it turns out, the same is true in some psychic situations."

I moved the pile of cards around on the table, flattening it out, exposing nearly all the card backs. "Now, all of us are, to one degree or another, psychic. However, just like in physics, sometimes the very act of observing our psychic work will change the outcome. So for this effect, each one of you is going to use your psychic powers, but we're not going to look at the results until the end. Because looking at them might actually change that outcome."

I looked up at the host, who was anxiously scanning the cards spread across the table. "You can start," I said. "Using your psychic powers, I want you to point out the Queen of Hearts. Don't pick it up, just point to the card that your psychic powers tell you is the Queen of Hearts."

The host studied the cards for a long moment, finally pointing to a card in the center of the pile. I picked it up and glanced at the face of the card without letting any of them see it. "Good job, good job."

I looked up at Nova, who was standing nervously beside Grey. I caught her eye and gave her a smile, which she returned shyly.

"Nova, I'd like you to use your psychic abilities to find, let's see…why don't you try to find the ten of Clubs?"

Nova appeared to be taking her task very seriously. She considered the mass of cards and then, suddenly, pointed to one card on the far edge of the group. "Are you sure that's the ten of Clubs?" I asked. She thought about it for a moment and then nodded decisively. I picked up the card and glanced at the front. "Well done."

I looked at the cards spread out across the table, and then looked up at Grey, who was still stubbornly refusing to look in my direction. I glanced from him to the audience as I said, "How many of you would like to see Grey pick one of the cards?"

Without any prompting, the audience burst into an energetic round of applause. Grey smiled grimly at this outburst and then slowly turned his head and acknowledged me. His eyes were boiling over with hatred. He was seething and I think would have killed me with his bare hands if we hadn't been on live television.

"Great," I said, trying to keep my voice from cracking. "Grey, why don't you point out…point out where the two of Diamonds is."

Without taking his eyes off me, he pointed at a random card on the table. I reached for the card and inspected the front of it. "Perfect," I said, trying to keep things light. "And now, I'm feeling a little psychic myself, so I'm going to see if I can find a card as well. Let's see, I'll find…I'll find the Four of Hearts."

I picked up a card off the table, added it to the three others in my hand, and then placed each one down, face up, on the table with a flourish as I called it out. "There they are…the four of Hearts, the two of Diamonds, the ten of Clubs, and the Queen of Hearts."

The host gathered up the four cards and held them up for the audience, but it was an unnecessary step. The audience was already applauding wildly. The host clapped me on the back and Nova gave me a shy grin. Grey was the only one not smiling.

"That, without giving anything away," I explained as the applause began to subside, "uses the same technique that Grey used with the questions in the envelopes. I was One Ahead."

"We've still a couple minutes of the show left," the host said, treating me now like I was his best friend in the world. "Is there anything else you can show us tonight?"

"Well, let's see," I said as I gathered up the cards and straightened them back into a pack. I looked over at Grey, who was still fuming, and the part of my personality that often gets me into trouble suddenly spoke up. "How about a quick card trick with just Grey here?"

The audience showed their enthusiasm for the idea by bursting into applause again. "That sounds like fun," the host said over the ovation, and then he turned to Grey. "Are you up for it?" he asked, pretending that Grey had a choice in the matter.

Grey could see there was no way out, so he pretended, badly as it turned out, to be a good sport. "Sure thing," he said with all the sincerity of a used-car salesman.

I quickly shuffled the cards and then shuffled them again. "After seeing him perform tonight, I sense that Grey is an ambitious guy. So this will be the perfect card trick for him. It's called The Ambitious Card. Why, you ask?" I stated rhetorically, without stopping for anyone to answer. "Because, just like our friend Grey here, one particular card always finds its way to the top."

I fanned the cards and held them out to Grey. "Pick a card," I said, adding a carnival barker inflection to my voice. "Pick a card, any card." This produced more laughter from the crowd than it really warranted.

Practically dripping with contempt, Grey reached out his hand and pulled a card out of the cluster of the deck without even bothering to look at it. I gathered the cards together and pivoted in my chair, turning my back on him. "Now go ahead and sign your name on the face of the card, just to ensure that I don't try to switch cards later on."

I could hear him sigh deeply, then I heard the rustle of clothing as he pulled a pen out of his suit coat pocket. Moments later I heard the scratching of the pen on the card, then the click of the pen and the sound of rustling again. "All set?" I asked with a bit too much cheer.

"Yes, all set," he replied with no inflection in his voice.

I turned back to the table and once again held the cards out to him, slowly riffling through them. "Say stop whenever you like," I instructed.

"Stop," he growled.

I stopped riffling and told him to place the card at that spot in the deck, which he did with little enthusiasm. I cut the cards and then gave the deck two quick shuffles.

"So I've mixed the cards twice and cut them once. Your card is buried somewhere in the deck. But, like I said, it's an ambitious card, and so with a little coaxing from me," I said as I gave the bottom of the deck a hard flick of my index finger, "your card magically moves to the top of the deck." With that, I peeled back the top card, revealing a signed card—The King of Diamonds.

Grey stared at me with disdain, but the crowd applauded wildly. I looked at the card and then looked from the card to the diamond rings on Grey's fingers. "King of Diamonds," I said. "How fitting."

With that I launched into the trick with fervor. I shuffled the deck—the King of Diamonds returned to the top. The host shuffled the deck. The King of Diamonds returned to the top. I shuffled the deck and let Nova cut it three times in a row. The card returned to the top of the deck.

"It's a persistent little bugger, isn't it?" I said to Grey, who seemed to have only one facial expression—utter revulsion. Perhaps he was one of those rare people who didn't like card tricks.

"There may be only one solution," I continued, putting the card back with the others and shuffling them vigorously. "We may have to take lethal steps." I shuffled the cards one last time, and then spread all the cards face down across the table in front of me. "Grey, could I bother you to lend me your blindfold? And your letter opener—that wickedly sharp one you used earlier?"

I thought for a second that I had finally pushed him too far and that he was going to explode and come across the table at me. But, to his credit, he kept his cool.

Slowly, oh so slowly, he reached into his coat and withdrew the long strip of black fabric and the letter opener, setting both on the table just outside of my reach. Before I could lean forward to take the objects, Nova moved in and picked up both of them.

She moved into assistant mode, stepping behind me and placing the letter opener on the table, near my right hand. And then she took the blindfold and covered my eyes, skillfully tying a snug knot against the back of my head. I could feel her breath on my neck and her perfume wafted past my nose. Her hands danced lightly on my shoulders, straightening my shirt and adjusting my collar. And then I could feel her stepping back to her original position to watch the finale of the trick.

"The conclusion of this illusion," I said poetically, "comes courtesy of the great magician, Max Malini, who invented and perfected this move over his long and illustrious career." I felt across the top of the table, sliding the cards around with both hands to mix them up even more. I moved my right hand until I could feel the sharp point of the letter opener, carefully sliding my hand down the blade until I was able to grasp the handle.

"I would ask that if any of you have your hands, or any other body part, on the table, please remove them immediately, as I'm flying blind on this one." I could sense the host and Nova take a step back, but felt no movement from Grey's side of the table. I gave a few of the cards one final push with my left hand, as I raised the blade in my right.

"Let's just see if we can trap that ambitious card," I said, and then with a sudden movement, buried the tip of the blade into the tabletop. There was a surprised gasp from the crowd, which grew in volume and intensity as I pulled off the blindfold with my left hand, keeping my right firmly on the handle of the letter opener. I rocked the blade back and forth, carefully removing it from where it had jabbed the table. Several cards fell away as I lifted the letter opener, revealing that only one card had been actually stabbed. I tilted the letter opener forward, holding the face of the card up to the crowd— and, I'll admit—to the television camera.

It was the King of Diamonds, with the point of the blade cutting cleanly through his one eye. I removed the card from the tip of the blade and, reaching across the table, I slid it into the front breast pocket on Grey's suit, giving it a final pat as I did.

The host was wrapping up the show, the audience was applauding, somewhere the show's theme music was playing as the credits rolled. All that was lost on me, though, as my attention was directed completely at Grey. He was staring at me from across the table, seething with fury, anger, and even more hatred than before.

I was sorry to be the cause of all that and part of me considered, just for a moment, that I may have pushed him too far. And for a split second I felt bad about it, but only for a second. To be fair, though, I don't think it would have improved his mood any if he had known that, in less than four hours, he would no longer be angry. He would instead be dead.

Chapter 5

The beauty of living in Minnesota is that, upon awakening on the first day of November, you are just as likely to spend the rest of the day shoveling eight inches of snow as you are discovering that it's too hot and sunny to rake leaves. In other words, November in Minnesota is like one of those brown-paper grab bags they sell at charity auctions, where you never know what you're going to get, but odds are that it will at least be interesting.

Although the weatherman had been predicting snow for days, that particular November first dawned like a quintessential Indian Summer day, with a bright blue sky and a breeze that felt warmer than it had any right to feel.

I left my apartment on the third floor and made my way down the way-too-steep staircase to Harry's apartment. My divorce had come at around the same time as Aunt Alice's death and that had seemed like the perfect opportunity to come back to the apartment on Chicago Avenue and once again make it my home. Since returning, I'd made it a habit to share breakfast with Harry as often as I could. Although he never once commented on this new tradition, I suspected that he really appreciated it.

I really can't fathom the level of loss he experienced at her death. In addition to being his wife for over fifty years, Alice had also been his on-stage assistant for nearly as long. As many of his contemporaries had confided in me, Harry and Alice's act wasn't just a magic show—it was an on-stage love affair. Whether he was sawing her in half or she was helping him produce a cascade of doves, audiences sensed the chemistry they had together, which made their performance all the more special.

"Morning, Buster," Harry said without looking up from his in-depth perusal of the daily paper. I get all my news, and the comics to boot, online, but Harry is a diehard in many ways. One of those included the addictive need to feel newsprint between his fingertips at least once a day. I poured myself a cup of coffee and picked up the sports page to be convivial.

"How was the show last night?" he asked casually, although I knew he was deeply interested in any opportunity to expose mediums, psychics, and other frauds.

"About what you'd expect," I said. "Some mind reading. Some One-Ahead stuff. The Armpit Tourniquet."

"Ah, that old chestnut," Harry said. "And who was the alleged spiritualist?"

"Grey," I answered, as I added some cream to buffer the bitter coffee that Harry favored.

Harry shuddered. "That one gives me the creeps. Always has." He turned the page and scanned the fresh columns of print. "Did you give him a run for his money?"

"Well," I shrugged, "so much of his act is traditional magic that I really wasn't in a position to expose his methods. Not without ex-posing the methods of just about every working magician."

Harry grunted in understanding without looking up from his reading.

"So I just did some comparable stuff," I continued, absently paging through the paper. "Which, at the very least, took some of the shimmer off of his act."

"You pulled the rug out from under him?" he asked.

"I think I honored the family tradition," I said.

"And the audience hated you for it?"

"For a while," I said. "Although I think they warmed to me as things progressed. Then, just for fun, for my finale I did an ambitious card routine, which I ended with a nicely-executed Malini card stab, if I do say so myself."

This got his attention. His eyes peered at me over the top of the newspaper. One eyebrow slowly rose, like it was being pulled upward on a wire.

"Did you now?" he said, giving a low whistle. He set the newspaper down. "The Malini card stab was always one of my favorites. Did I ever tell you about the time I did that as the wrap-up of my act on the Sullivan show?"

He had told me that story on a number of occasions, but I shook my head and he launched into a blow-by-blow account of how Ed Sullivan himself had watched the act during rehearsal and made the decision—right there, on the spot—to move Harry's position in the show, in order to feature him more prominently. "It was a glorious evening," he said, stroking his thick white beard and smiling warmly.

"We should break out the video of that some night and look at it again," I suggested.

"Yes," he agreed. "Yes, we should do that. Some night."

I knew that he had been avoiding watching any of the old videos, as Alice would appear alongside him in every one of them, and he wasn't really ready for that. Not yet.

Of course, it wasn't as if she had entirely disappeared from his surroundings. Her smiling face, like a silent screen star, peered out at us from all the photos, posters and playbills on the walls up here—they lined the walls down in the store as well. Her clothes still hung in their closet. Her toothbrush and comb lay on the counter in the bathroom. Her needlepoint sat unfinished on the small table next to her chair in the living room, as if she had just stepped out to the kitchen for some tea and would return in a few moments to pick up where she left off. She was simultaneously everywhere and nowhere.

I could tell that he was sinking into a similar reverie, so I got up and brought my cup to the counter. "It's November first," I said with a little too much forced cheer. "If you want, I can walk the rent down to the landlord."

"What?" he asked, as he snapped back to the present. I noticed that his eyes had begun to water, just a bit. "No, that's fine," he said finally, shaking his head. "I can walk it down. The stroll will do me good." With this mission ahead of him, he stood up, folding the newspaper carefully as he did.

"I'll go with you," I said, taking his cup to the sink and adding it to my own.

He stopped folding the paper. "We both don't need to go," he said. "That would be overkill."

"I want to go," I said as casually as I could. "Besides, it's a nice day out."

He gave me a long, penetrating look. He had spent a few years in the early part of his career touring with a mind-reading act, but it didn't take those unique skills to deduce my ulterior motive for this mission. "You just want to gape like a lovesick schoolboy at the new landlady." He put a mischievous little spin on the word *lady*. "Don't think I can't see that. It's so obvious, you could see it from space."

"Guilty as charged," I admitted. "I'm going with you."

And that was that.

Presenting the monthly check to the landlord in person has been a Marks' family tradition for as long as I can remember. As a child I had enjoyed the privileged assignment of taking the check, sealed tightly in a plain white envelope, over to Mrs. Reinhardt, who lived in one of the brick apartment buildings on the other side of the movie theater. She always made a big fuss about my arrival and would encourage me to perform, for her and her cranky husband, whatever magic trick I was currently attempting to master. He matched her level of enthusiasm with his own dour nature and in his own, grumpy way he taught me a lot about dealing with a tough audience.

Now the tradition had moved from grandmother to grand-daughter.

It was a short walk from our door to hers. In addition to owning the strip of retail shops that took up half the block, and the old brick apartment buildings that took up the other half, Megan had laid a personal claim to the shop on the corner. For years it had served as our local drugstore, under the name Shenandoah Drug, an odd choice given how far away we are from the state of Virginia and the eponymous river. Over the years that corner shop had taken on other identities since the Targets and Walmarts of the world had driven nearly every corner drugstore out of business. Now it was owned and operated by Megan, with a new name that amused me every time I saw it—*Chi & Things*.

The inside of the store was about what you would expect for a store with a name like that. It was packed from wall to wall with New Age books, incense, crystals, natural oils and a large selection of teas; in short, just the sort of mishmash of items that would appeal to a wide spectrum of credit card-wielding spiritually-minded seekers.

Harry and I entered the store to find that, despite the early hour, numerous customers were already meandering through the cramped space, looking for just the right new age tchotchke to set them straight on the path to enlightenment or help them further tune their chakras toward nirvana.

While two young clerks roamed the aisles offering oil samples and answering questions, Megan stood behind the counter, merrily ringing up sales and chatting warmly with each customer. She looked stunning and, as is often the case with naturally beautiful women, seemed to have no idea of the visual impact she was making.

I tried to keep from staring, but it was hard not to. I was completely smitten. As we waited in line to give her the rent check, I surreptitiously tugged on Harry's coat sleeve. "Give me the check," I said in my best *sotto voce* whisper. "I want to give it to her."

Harry scowled at me. "What are you, five years old?" he said, not bothering to match my vocal volume.

"You gave it to her last time," I hissed through clenched teeth. "That makes it my turn. It's only fair."

"Well, if you want to talk about fairness, since I wrote the bloody check and it's coming out of my bloody account, I don't think you have any legitimate claim on its ultimate distribution." He waved the check in my face for emphasis and I snatched it out of the air just as Megan said, "And how can I help you today?"

I stepped forward, putting my body in front of Harry's and holding the check out to her. "Just your two favorite tenants, Eli and Harry Marks, with this month's rent," I said cheerfully.

She smiled and laughed, taking the check from me. "Well, thank you. You know, you two don't have to hand-deliver this every month. Pete's setting up a direct deposit system with the bank to make it easier for all the tenants."

"Oh, it's no bother at all. The walk does the old guy good," I said, gesturing toward Harry. "Plus, it's important to get him out of the shop from time to time," I added quietly. But not quietly enough it seemed, for a moment later I felt a sharp sting in the back of my right ankle where Harry had just kicked me.

Megan looked from Harry to me, and then slowly back to Harry again.

"Speaking of Pete," I said oh so casually, trying to turn her gaze in my direction, "I just saw him last night over at The Caves. I'm surprised you didn't come along...the show was right up your alley."

Megan shook her head as she stopped looking at Harry and leaned over to make a notation in a receipt book. "I had to give some readings last night," she said as she scribbled, then added quickly, "Although it would have been fun to re-visit the old caves and see how they've changed."

Before I could register a comeback, she tore out the receipt and handed it to me. I handed it back to Harry, who snatched it quickly out of my hand with nary a thought of the paper cut he could have given me.

"I hope Pete isn't becoming a pest at your store, Mr. Marks," she added, once again turning her gaze on Harry. I was beginning to feel like the Invisible Man. "He's really taken to the idea of learning magic."

"No, we love having Pete come into the shop," I answered quickly before Harry could respond. "He's a very enthusiastic student. Of course, I'm guessing we won't be seeing as much of him around here once the divorce becomes final."

"No, probably not," she said absently. She looked Harry directly in the eye.

"I hate to bother you with this, Mr. Marks," she said. "But there's a spirit over your right shoulder who is really trying to get my attention. The spirit says it has a message for you."

We both looked at her, surprised at the sudden change in subject, and then, without realizing we were doing it, simultaneously looked over Harry's right shoulder. I can't speak for him, but I didn't see anything out of the ordinary, except the evidence that both of us needed to find a shampoo that does a better job on dandruff.

"If you have a couple minutes," Megan added earnestly, "I'd love to sit down with you and do a reading. See what all the fuss is about." She looked at him expectantly and, to my surprise, he smiled at her.

"That would be delightful, my dear," he said sincerely. "I think a reading would be just delightful."

Megan arranged for one of the clerks to watch the cash register, and while she handled that, she pointed us toward the back of the shop. "Have a seat back in the reading area," she said excitedly. "I'll be there in just a moment."

"Why are you agreeing to this?" I whispered to Harry as we made our way through the cramped aisles toward a small table in a back corner.

"Nothing strange about this. I've historically liked to keep abreast of what's new in the field of parapsychology," he said indignantly. "Besides, you aren't the only one who recognizes how attractive she is."

Despite his advanced years, I was about to give him a solid smack across the back of the head, but was interrupted by Megan's arrival.

"Thanks for doing this," she said, gesturing Harry to a chair on one side of the small, linen-covered table, while she took a seat across from him. "I'm still learning how to effectively tap into my intuitive energy, so any time the spirits reach out to me I like to take the opportunity to practice."

"Practice makes perfect," Harry said in a sing-song voice and I once again had to restrain myself from striking the old man.

She opened a small black velvet bag and removed several crystals of various sizes, arranging them in two lines, one on either side of the table.

"I find that crystals sharpen the energy," she said by way of explanation. "The more I learn about my gift, the more I find a connection with crystals. Isn't that funny?"

Both of us nodded at once, almost perfectly in sync. We looked ridiculous.

"All right now. Sometimes the information from the spirit comes through very quickly," Megan continued, picking up a small pad and pen that sat on the table. "Many clients prefer to take notes, so as not to miss anything."

"Buster can take the notes," he said with mock efficiency, smoothly passing the items back to me. "Besides, it will give him something to do. Idle hands and all that."

There were only the two chairs, so I leaned against a nearby wall and prepared to take notes.

Megan had Harry place his hands flat on the tabletop, and then she placed the tips of her fingers so that they lightly touched his. She settled back and relaxed, shutting her eyes and sighing

THE AMBITIOUS CARD   51

deeply. She sat in this posture silently for several long moments, so long that Harry and I exchanged a quick look that said, "Is she asleep?" Then she suddenly opened her eyes and looked straight through Harry, as if reading a teleprompter from the other side.

"The spirit is not a blood relation, but is closely related. Perhaps a half-sibling. Do you have any step-brothers or sisters?"

"No." Harry shook his head but didn't offer any more information. This didn't seem to faze her for a second. She moved quickly over this psychic speed bump and continued. "Perhaps a spouse. Has your spouse passed?"

Harry dipped his head slightly in agreement with the question, but again didn't offer any additional help.

Megan nodded in agreement. "Yes, it's feeling very much like a spouse. And she passed several years ago, am I right?"

Harry shook his head.

"It was more recent, wasn't it?" Megan continued, plowing ahead unabated. You had to admire her spunk. I sure did. That and her hair, her eyes, her lips...

"Yes, I see that now, this is a relatively new spirit," she said, drawing me back to my note taking. "She went through a long, protracted illness, is that right?"

Harry shook his head again and he continued to shake it with increasing frequency for the next 20 minutes. I filled several pages of notes as Megan stumbled her way through the reading. If this reading had been a golf game, she would have shot one of the highest scores in history. If she had been bowling, she would have scored in single digits. Every path Megan went down found her hitting false turn after false turn, or, more often, yet another dead end.

To his credit, Harry remained cordial but at the same time he didn't give her an inch of assistance. It was painful to watch at times, like a stern lifeguard who refuses to throw a child a life-preserver while she's attempting to cross a treacherous stream.

After several minutes of this, Megan finally settled back into her chair. She looked tired but exhilarated. She looked great.

"Did any of the things I received from the spirit connect for you?" she asked Harry, as if hearing the word "no" forty or fifty times in a row hadn't already answered that question for her.

"Nothing hit like a lightning bolt, if that's what you mean," Harry said diplomatically.

"Well, they say that sometimes it takes a couple of days for all the pieces fall into place. You might be surprised."

Harry smiled. "Yes," he said. "I might be."

She stood up and Harry followed suit, reaching for his wallet as he got up. "How much do I owe you?" he asked softly as he opened the wallet and began sorting through the bills.

Megan waved away his question with one hand, resting the other casually on her hip as she pushed a stray strand of hair out of her face. "Oh, nonsense," she said. "I can't charge for connecting people to the other side. That just wouldn't be right."

A psychic who doesn't charge money. Harry gave me a look of surprise and wonder. I shrugged. Although it hadn't seemed possible, she just became even more attractive.

Megan began walking Harry toward the front of the store, with me tagging along. "I just saw that poor spirit over your shoulder," she continued. "Saw it the moment you came in, and it was just so persistent, I just had to help get its messages across."

"Well, thanks for that," I said before Harry could answer.

"You know, I'm amazed I could hear anything at all, what with all these new crystals I got recently," she said, gesturing toward a display case filled with various stones, gems, and crystals. "Crystals can be so loud sometimes, don't you think?"

Yes," I agreed, trying to sound sympathetic. "Yes they can. Rambunctious, even."

This produced a sidelong glance from Harry. I ignored it and drove forward, now that I had her attention. "I noticed that you've added a used-book section since I was last in."

"Yes," she said, looking over at the corner that housed several makeshift shelves of old paperbacks and hardcover books.

Two teenage girls were looking through the titles and exchanging conspiratorial whispers.

"That's working out well," she said with a hint of pride in her voice. "It's nice to be able to keep those books circulating to new souls."

"You know, I had an idea for a promotion that you could do," I said, gesturing to an invisible banner that could hang over that section. "You could have a banner that says, 'Used New Age Books— Any Book You Think You Read in a Past Life is Half Off.'"

She gave me a long, questioning look and then burst out laughing, giving my shoulder a playful slap in the process. "You're funny," she said, looking me in the eye—finally!—and then turning to Harry. "He's funny, isn't he?"

Harry was attempting to suppress a scowl and coming up short. "Hysterical," he said without humor, his flat tone speaking volumes.

"Could you be any more of a lovesick puppy?" Harry asked, not nearly as quietly as I would have liked.

Harry and I stood outside the front door of *Chi & Things* in silence for a few moments, making sure that Megan had returned to talking with customers and that we were well out of earshot.

"Me?" I squeaked, my voice hitting a higher range than I had intended. "What about you?"

I did my best impression of him. "I think a reading would be just *delightful*," I said, drawing out the last three syllables into about six. "You old phony."

He gave a harrumph and I harrumphed right back at him and then we turned and started heading up the street to the magic shop. I realized that I was still holding the small notepad Megan had given me. I absently flipped through the pages.

"Did she get even one solid hit?" I asked as I scanned my notes.

"Nada," Harry said.

"You'd think that mere chance would factor in and help her out with at least one hit."

"You'd think," he agreed, and then he stopped. "Wait, there was something. Something about dimes. She said it very quickly."

I paged through the notes until I found it. "Here it is. She said that your late wife is leaving you dimes. As reminders of her love."

I looked up to see that a cloud had crossed over Harry's face. "What?" I asked.

"It's just," he said, pulling on his beard thoughtfully. "When I first met your aunt, it was at a party. At someone's house, I don't remember whose. Anyway, at the end of the night I asked Alice if I could call her some time. And she said yes. She said yes, I could call her," he repeated, smiling at the memory.

"So? I don't get the connection to dimes."

"Hold your horses, I'm getting to it. At the end of the party, I shook her hand goodnight, which is what we did back then, not like your generation," he said pointedly.

"Yeah, whatever. Finish your story."

"Anyway, I shook her hand, and when I pulled my hand back, I found that she had slipped a dime into my palm." He grinned. "You see, at the time, a dime was the cost of a phone call."

"Well, that's sweet. However, that's not what Megan said in the reading." I looked at my notes again. "She said, 'Your late wife is leaving you dimes. As reminders of her love.'"

"Well, you see, that's just the thing," Harry said as he continued walking toward our store. "The last couple of weeks, or maybe more, I keep finding money on the ground."

He gestured to the sidewalk in front of us and I half expected to see some coins there.

"Now, pennies you find all the time. No one bothers to pick them up. I certainly don't. But I haven't found pennies. Nor nickels. Nor quarters. No," he said, reaching into his pocket. "I keep finding dimes. Like that one right there."

Harry stopped and pointed to a bit of silver, just visible in the dirt by the curb. I knelt down and picked it up, brushing it off on my pant leg. It was worn and scruffy, but it was a dime. I held it up and Harry took it from my hand, smiling at it. "Come on," he said as he dropped the coin into his pocket. "We're late getting the store open."

Still not entirely certain about what I had just seen and heard, I followed, lagging a few steps behind him.

Upon approaching our store, I was surprised to see a pirate leaning against the locked door. He was dressed in the full regalia, including three-sided black hat with a skull and cross-bones emblazoned on its side, eye patch, and a sword. I should clarify. I wasn't surprised to see the pirate. I was surprised that he was on time.

The pirate, Captain Magic to his young audience, is a kids' magician. He's also my friend Nathan, and anyone who knows him would consider him an odd candidate for the role of court jester to the kindergarten set. Perpetually depressed, he's lived his life under a dark cloud that follows him wherever he goes. He's a hell of a magician but I've never seen him get much joy out of that, either.

"Morning Eli," Nathan said in his slow, monotone. "Morning Harry."

"Good morning, Nathan," Harry said with extra cheer. Harry, like many people who know Nathan, was attempting to pull him away from melancholy by being just a little too cheerful himself. It has no effect on Nathan. Never has.

"Hope you haven't been waiting long," I said as I unlocked the door. "I've got everything ready for you."

"No, I just got here," Nathan said. "Found a parking place right out front, but I think I rolled over some broken glass, so I'll probably have a flat by the time we're done."

That sentence was Nathan in a nutshell. He could find the dark cloud under virtually any silver lining.

I let the three of us into the store. Harry immediately began his morning ritual, which included pulling open the blinds, turning on the lights, and removing the cloth covers from the display cases. Nathan and I made our way through the store, toward the basement.

Over the last few years, foot traffic in the store has dwindled considerably. We still did a brisk Internet business, with the tricks and devices Harry had invented throughout his career. And a couple items I had come up with were also starting to sell online. The basement housed our workshop, where we both had several projects in various stages of completion or abandonment, depending on our moods.

"I've tested it under a few different conditions so far, with solid results," I told Nathan as we made our way down the steep and creaky stairs. "Barometric pressure can be an issue, but I think I have a work-around for that."

"Just so you can stop the kids from crying," Nathan said with a plaintive edge in his voice. "I gotta find a way to make the kids stop crying."

Nathan's problem was one shared by just about any performer who employs helium balloons while working with kids. There's nothing that makes a kid happier than a helium balloon and nothing that makes them sadder than when they lose their grip and it floats up into the sky, never to be seen again. Even popping a balloon is not as traumatic, although I'm not really sure why. Perhaps the popping sound has some sort of primal catharsis built into it. But a single balloon that gets loose can turn a happy birthday party into a tantrum-filled nightmare scenario.

To solve the problem, I'd experimented a bit and found just the right combination of helium and oxygen so that a filled balloon will float, but won't go any higher than about six feet off the ground. It took a lot of trial and error and for days the basement was filled with hundreds of balloons, either caught in the ceiling or drifting lethargically several inches off the floor.

"Of course, finding the right mix was only the first part of the problem. The second was to make the process magical," I said to Nathan as I helped him remove his pirate coat. "And I think I've cracked that, too."

I handed him my invention, a cross between a large belt and a small corset, to put around his waist. It was a bulky fit because the back of the belt held a metal canister, like a miniature scuba tank. A tube with a small, custom nozzle on the end ran out of the canister.

I helped Nathan put his coat back on, taking care to snake the tube down the inside of his right sleeve. I gave the coat one final tug and then stepped back to check my work.

"That looks good," I said, gesturing for him to spin around so I could see him from all sides. "You really can't see anything out of the ordinary."

I crossed over to my workbench and opened a fresh bag of balloons, grabbing one and heading back to Nathan, who was looking at the nozzle on the tube in his sleeve. "Where'd you get this?" he asked.

I shrugged, handing him the limp balloon. "I cobbled it together from a couple different pieces. Here's how the gag works. You bring the balloon up to your face, just like you would if you were going to blow it up with your mouth."

Nathan followed my instructions as I talked him through the steps. "At the same time, you've palmed the nozzle at the end of the tube. You bring the end of the balloon to your mouth, but it's the nozzle that actually goes into the balloon. Your hands are covering it, so it just looks like you're blowing up a balloon normally. Once the nozzle is in place, just press the button on its side and the balloon will inflate."

I watched as he went through the steps and I was happy to see that it really looked like he was blowing up the balloon manually. When it reached the right size, he pulled it away from his mouth and quickly tied off the end. He then mimed handing the completed balloon to an invisible child in front of him. He let go of the balloon and it floated in mid-air right where he had left it. After a few seconds it began to drift upwards, but it didn't get any higher than six feet. The balloon floated around the room languidly. We both watched it, transfixed.

"That's cool," he said finally. For a second, he almost sounded happy.

Once I got Nathan's stuff all packed away and he headed off to his gig, I began to putter around the store, taking care of all the little chores that I never seem to get around to, but which always need to be done.

First I tackled restocking the gag gifts. It's a sad fact, but the few walk-in sales we do get all seem to come from that one rack in a back corner. Over the years, we've moved it around the store, to maybe six different spots. It doesn't matter where we put it, people always find it. It also doesn't seem to matter that the store is packed to the gills with some of the greatest magic illusions ever made. People are always drawn to the damned gag gift rack.

On that rack are all the staples for a classic gag gift: chattering teeth, fake dog poop, fake vomit, the coughing ashtray, exploding golf balls, joy buzzers, rubber chickens, and the ever-popular fart spray. We had actually sold out our supply of fart spray and I was just in the process of unpacking the new shipment we had recently received when I heard the tinkle of the bell over the front door, signaling that a customer had entered the store.

I set the fart spray aside and turned my attention toward the door, assuming it was Nathan returning with another question. One glance told me it wasn't Nathan. The guy was backlit by the late morning sun and he almost completely filled up the doorframe with his bulk. But I immediately recognized that big, dumb square head. It could only be one person—my ex-wife's new husband, Fred Hutton. Or, as I always referred to him, Homicide Detective Fred Hutton, because it annoyed him. Or, at least I hoped it did.

"Marks," he said in that raspy voice of his. That was the extent of his hello. I had discovered that Fred worked best with words of one syllable, or fewer if possible.

"Good morning, Homicide Detective Fred Hutton," I said. "What brings you by on this fine day?"

"This is not a social visit," he said, stepping into the shop. Another man—another detective I assumed—followed him in.

"Well, that's too bad," I said. "Because personally I don't think we socialize nearly enough."

"Yeah, right," he said, recognizing my subtle sarcasm and returning it in kind. For a moment, it was as if we had been transported back to the Algonquin Round Table, circa 1925. And then, just as quickly as we had gone, we slammed back to present day.

"I need you to come downtown," he said. He shifted his ubiquitous toothpick from one side of his mouth to the other, although to be fair it was unlikely he would have used the word ubiquitous.

"Is it about Deirdre?" I asked. The hairs on the back of my neck were beginning to stand on end. "Is she okay?"

"This isn't about her," he said. "It's about this guy named Grey."

"What about this guy named Grey?"

He scowled down at me. "There's this guy named Grey. And he's dead."

I certainly hadn't seen that coming. "How did he die?" I asked the question like I had a right to know.

"Stabbed. Through the eyes, among other places."

I tried to remain cool.

Fred stared at me for what seemed like a long time.

"So, you're ruling out suicide?" I finally asked dryly.

Chapter 6

The drive downtown was, mercifully, a quiet one.

Before leaving the shop I yelled up to Harry that I was going out for a few minutes. We were gone from the store before he had made his way down the steep stairs from his apartment on the second floor. I try to limit the number of times he has to go up and down those stairs in a day, but this additional trip couldn't be helped.

I was informed that I was, officially, a person of interest and was being brought in and held for questioning. If you read between the lines on that, which I was doing, it was pretty clear that Homicide Detective Fred Hutton was convinced that I had killed Grey. He was just waiting for me to break down and admit it.

I wasn't being charged, I was being *held*, which sounded like semantics to me, since either way I couldn't go home. However, he had the gun and the badge and all I had was charm and that was waning. So I kept my mouth shut and did what I was told.

Even though I wasn't being officially charged, I still had to be fingerprinted and had to surrender all my personal effects at the property desk before they put me in a room and began to beat me with a rubber hose. Or whatever they're using nowadays.

"Should we lock him up in some special way?" The uniformed officer in charge of processing me had addressed the question to Homicide Detective Fred Hutton, but he included a sidelong glance in my direction.

"What do you have in mind?"

"I don't know. He's a magician, right?"

Homicide Detective Fred Hutton responded with a disgusted grunt. "So they say."

"Well, I see these guys break out of jail cells all the time on TV. I'd hate to have something like that happen on my watch." The young cop stole another glance in my direction. "These guys are tricky."

He held out a large manila envelope and gestured that I should turn my pockets out and drop my belongings into the packet.

"I don't think we're dealing with Houdini here," Homicide Detective Fred Hutton said as I deposited my wallet, iPhone, keys, forty cents in change, and the deck of cards I always carry into the envelope.

"I think the worst he might do is fill the holding room with balloon animals." He chuckled at his own joke, but I refused to give him the satisfaction of a smile. Then I checked one last pocket and found three sad, flaccid balloons. I wordlessly added them to the envelope.

They put me in a small, airless room that held a table, two chairs, and a wooden bench that sat along one wall. For some reason, the room smelled of cheese, and old cheese at that. A digital audio recorder was permanently attached to one corner of the table. Homicide Detective Fred Hutton's partner, a vertically-challenged troll of a man who introduced himself as Homicide Detective Miles Wright, was handling the questioning while Homicide Detective Fred Hutton sat in the corner, glaring at me. Instead of Good Cop/Bad Cop, I was apparently stuck with Tall Stupid Cop/Short Angry Cop. Just my luck.

"So, Mr. Magician, how well did you know the victim?" Miles asked after flipping on the recorder and stating the time, date, place and participants involved in the interrogation.

"Not well enough to stab him through the eyes," I said, figuring what did I have to lose.

"So you know how he was killed? Interesting," he said, almost deciding to sit in the chair opposite me. He changed his mind at the last second and started a slow, circular trek around the table.

"Yeah, your partner told me all about it. I believe you were standing behind him at the time, but I wasn't sure if it was you or one of the neighborhood kids. He's a big guy."

Miles ignored this jab and continued. "You haven't answered my question. How well did you know him?"

I shrugged. "I've seen him around. I know him by reputation more than I know the man himself."

"And what was his reputation?"

"Depends who you ask."

"I'm asking you."

I leaned back in my chair and glanced over at Homicide Detective Fred Hutton, who was staring at me with an intensity that made me think he looked more confused than focused. "He was a fake psychic, a fraud, and not a nice guy. He made a lot of money being that way. I didn't know him well, but if I had I'm sure I would have thought even less of him."

"You have any reason to kill him?"

I shook my head. "Actually, it's just the other way around. After what I did to him last night, he had plenty of reason to want to kill me."

"Why's that?"

"Because I did a fairly good job of taking his act apart, piece by piece, and exposing him for the fraud that he is."

Miles didn't reply. He sat down and took a large, official-looking envelope out of the file folder he'd brought in with him. From that envelope he took a small, sealed clear plastic evidence bag. The label on the front of the bag, which was filled in with an illegible scrawl, blocked the contents of the carrier from view. Generating as much drama as he could muster, he slowly swung the bag around, revealing the contents.

"Can you identify this?"

Once the bag had made its 180-degree orbit, I could finally see inside. It was a playing card. The King of Diamonds, by the looks of it, but two things made it initially tough to identify. The first was that the face on the card had a large gash cut through it, but that wasn't the biggest problem. The real impediment was that the face of the card was smeared with what looked to be blood; so much blood that what had once been a stiff playing card was now nearly a mushy mash of pulp.

"It appears to be a playing card. A King of Diamonds."

Miles let the plastic bag continue to twirl as he held it up. "This card was found on the victim's body. To be more specific, when he was stabbed through the eyes, this card was over one of those eyes. The right eye." He set the clear plastic bag on the table and the card appeared to ooze a bit as it settled on the flat surface.

"What's interesting," he said, "is that the deck of cards you left outside at the property desk matches this design. And it's missing a King of Diamonds."

I thought this over before speaking.

"I'll ignore, for the moment, that you've gone through my personal effects, sort of nullifying the concept of *personal*," I said, looking from Miles to Homicide Detective Fred Hutton and back to Miles again. "I gave Grey that card at the end of my act last night. I put it in his breast pocket. Everybody saw me do it."

Miles was about to respond to that when the door to the room opened and the same, young uniformed cop from earlier entered. He made a point of not looking at me; instead, he handed a couple sheets of paper to Miles, turned on his heels and walked out. He looked like a man who was delivering bad news and didn't want to stick around to see it presented.

Miles paged thoughtfully through the report, taking his time. When he was done, he handed the papers over to Homicide Detective Fred Hutton and turned his attention back to me.

"Fingerprint report," he said, leaning back in his chair. "Seems your fingerprints are on the murder weapon. A letter opener."

"I remember it," I said, not liking this turn of events, but doing my best not to let that show. "I used it at the program last night. Two hundred people in the audience saw me handle it."

"Don't forget it was on television as well," Miles added. "The local PBS station."

"Well then, that's at least another hundred witnesses."

"And then someone used it to kill Mr. Grey." He looked at me for what felt like a long time and I did my best to hold his gaze. This stare down was interrupted when the door to the room opened again, but this time no one came in. From my position I couldn't see who had opened it. Homicide Detective Fred Hutton looked up, instantly jumped to his feet, and walked out of the room.

I heard some feverish whispering outside the door and a moment later Homicide Detective Fred Hutton returned. He moved to Miles' side and bent down to whisper in the small man's ear. Miles nodded and followed him out of the room, returning a second later to shut the door.

The room was quiet and I couldn't hear any sounds from outside. Perhaps it was soundproofed. I tapped my fingers on the table for a few seconds, enjoying the room's natural reverberation, and then noticed that the digital audio recorder was still in record mode, with its LCD time counter rolling forward. I glanced at the door and then started to hum a persistent song that had come into my head about an hour before.

After a few seconds I switched from humming to singing softly, and by the time I finished the second verse and was moving through the third I was almost to full voice. I drove, full-voiced, into the fourth and final verse and then listened to the reverb die down after I had finished singing. My timing was perfect, for at that moment the door swung open and Miles came back into the room.

"That's all we'll need from you today, Mr. Marks," he said in a practiced tone. "Thanks for coming down."

*   *   *

Ten minutes later I was walking down the steps into the echoing North rotunda of City Hall, toward the large and impressive Father of Waters statue, a marble monstrosity that completely overwhelms the lobby and makes you feel that you've just stepped into a Jason and the Argonauts movie. On any other day that might have been an appealing prospect, but at the moment I wasn't in the mood.

All of my personal effects were safely back in my pockets, with the exception of the deck of cards. Apparently the police wanted to hang onto it, perhaps for a card game later in the day, which was fine with me. Like any working magician, I have a case of cards in the basement and wouldn't miss that particular deck.

I was heading toward the glass revolving doors when I heard the distinctive sharp tip-tap of high heels approaching from behind. I got a whiff of the familiar perfume a nanosecond before she breezed past me, a short blonde whirlwind in a tight blue skirt and matching blazer.

"Meet me over at The Little Wagon," she said in a practiced whisper. "I'll be there in ten minutes." She made a sudden sharp right turn and headed down a corridor toward the east end of the building. I watched her go for a second and then pushed my way through the revolving door and out into the autumnal sunlight.

She had certainly picked a convenient, if not a particularly inconspicuous, destination. Just a block from City Hall, The Little Wagon is a downtown institution, perhaps not for its cuisine or atmosphere, but certainly for its longevity. It's gone through several owners in the past few years, but its location—walking distance from the government center, City Hall and the one remaining daily newspaper—makes it literally the hub of government and journalism in the city. Plus they make a Reuben sandwich that's almost worth going to jail for.

It was still a little early for the lunch crowd, but the place was not completely unpopulated. There were some well-worn regulars in the back corner. As far as I could tell, they were sitting exactly where they had been the last time I'd been here. That was probably two years ago.

At the bar, three guys were vigorously arguing the same side of a political argument, and a David Allan Coe song played through the sound system. I took a table near the wall and spared the ancient waitress, "Cora," the obligation of running through the specials, telling her I'd only need a cup of coffee—cream, no sugar.

As promised, Deirdre entered ten minutes later, taking off her sunglasses the moment she walked in. She stood in the doorway for a few moments, as her eyes adjusted to the perpetual dim light in the room. I gave an unnecessary wave, as there were only five customers in the place, and she headed toward my table.

While we were married, I had always referred to Deirdre as "my beautiful wife," and I kept up the practice even after the divorce, just altering it slightly to "my beautiful ex-wife." She certainly was that. A standout blonde in a land of blondes, she had an icy coolness that can be both attractive and off-putting, often simultaneously. I'm sure when we were married, people wondered how a no-nonsense gal like Deirdre had ended up with an all-nonsense guy such as me.

I've often pondered that myself.

"Sorry about that," she said as she sat down, a little breathless. She waved to Cora and gestured to her empty coffee cup. Cora, looking up from her crossword puzzle, made a quick erasure on the newspaper, then headed toward the coffee urn.

"Sorry about what?" I asked.

"Fred sort of jumped the gun back there," she said, pulling her hair back out of her eyes and depositing her sunglasses into her purse. "I mean, bringing you in and all that."

"Perhaps he was trying to avoid the appearance of favoritism," I suggested. "How would it look if the Assistant DA's ex-husband was given preferential treatment? I'm sure there was nothing personal in it," I added without a trace of conviction in my voice.

She looked up, concerned. "You didn't call him that name, did you?" she asked tentatively.

"No, I was able to restrain myself."

"Good. He hates that name and using it isn't going to make things go any easier for you."

Ah, yes. *That* name. Let me explain. Once Deirdre's tawdry and clandestine affair with Homicide Detective Fred Hutton had come to light, followed quickly by our divorce and her subsequent remarriage—where Deirdre Sutton took on the hysterical...at least to me...hyphenated name of Deirdre Sutton-Hutton—I had begun the habit of referring to her new beau not simply as Fred, but instead as Mediocre Fred.

The fault is not entirely my own. I blame my Uncle Harry and his love of comedy albums. Throughout his career, Harry had made a point of tracking down the record albums of those comedians he had had the pleasure of performing with, from the well-known to the truly obscure. Harry had worked many of the top nightclubs during the sixties, so as a result he had a truly massive and impressive comedy album collection. Victor Borge, Shelly Berman, Woody Woodbury, Mort Sahl, Henny Youngman, Rodney Dangerfield, even Bill Cosby and Bob Newhart, were artists I listened to over and over again as a child. And, of course, The Smothers Brothers. One song of theirs in particular was a personal favorite of mine, a charming ditty entitled *Mediocre Fred*.

Given the emotionally painful conditions under which I first met Homicide Detective Fred Hutton, there are a plethora of other names I could have assigned to him. Under the circumstances, he could have done a lot worse than Mediocre Fred. Apparently, though, he disagrees and it's been the primary sore spot among many sore spots between us.

"So am I an actual suspect in Grey's murder?" I asked, changing the subject and cutting to the chase.

Deirdre saw that Cora was approaching, so she held off speaking until after the unsmiling waitress had filled her empty coffee cup, topped off mine, and then returned to her crossword puzzle across the room. Deirdre spoke in a quiet voice, one I hadn't heard in a good long time, as many of the final conversations of our marriage had been pitched at a considerably higher decibel level.

"They don't have enough evidence to charge you, at least not yet," she said. "There's no clear motive and this particular victim was not particularly well-liked, in either the real estate world or the psychic world. So holding you now could potentially hurt the case, particularly when you consider the personal connection between you and the arresting officer —"

"— and the Assistant District Attorney," I said, completing the triangle.

"Yes," she said. "There is that."

"So, who else do they suspect?"

"Well, now that I've taken you off the short list, at least for the time being, they're beginning to widen the net. We've watched the tape of last night's performance for leads, and they've already talked to Grey's assistant from the show. Apparently, several witnesses saw them having quite the screaming argument in the parking lot around eleven."

"Which one?" I asked.

"Which parking lot?"

"Which assistant?" Once it registered, the question nearly made Deirdre do a spit take with her coffee. Which, admittedly, would have been a great sight gag, but since I was sitting directly across from her, I'm glad she was able to control the spew.

"What do you mean, which assistant?" she said, coughing a bit and wiping her mouth with her napkin. "I watched the tape. There's just the one, the scary dark-haired chick."

"Nova," I added. "Yes, she was on-stage with him. But he clearly had another assistant working backstage. Grey was wearing some sort of hidden earpiece and receiving information during the show.

How do you think he did the magazine and book bit? Second sight?"

"I don't know," Deirdre shrugged. "Mirrors?"

"Tsk, tsk," I said, wagging a finger at her. "And you, the ex-wife of a magician, falling for an old routine like that."

Deirdre rolled her eyes as she grabbed her purse. She hurriedly burrowed through it and pulled out her cell phone, hitting the speed dial. "It's me," she said to whoever answered, although I have a pretty good idea who it was. "Grey had two assistants, not just the one. Yes, someone backstage." She glanced over at me, then turned her attention back to the phone. "I just know, that's all. There's another assistant."

She ended the conversation by closing the cell phone, although I think I detected a small voice still coming out of the phone as it was snapped shut.

"I think you cut him off," I said, holding back a smile.

"Yeah, probably," she said as she tossed the phone back into her purse. We were both silent for a moment, just looking at each other. I can't say for sure what she was thinking, but I couldn't help wondering what it was that had gotten us to this point, and what I could have done earlier that would have changed the outcome.

"So, they stabbed him in the eyes," she said, breaking my train of thought. "That's a little weird, don't you think?"

"Perhaps they were making a point," I suggested. "Something about his second sight."

"Perhaps," she said, taking another sip of her coffee. "Or perhaps the killer was referencing the card trick you did. With the knife through the King of Diamonds' eyes."

"Perhaps," I cautiously agreed.

She set the cup down and gave me a hard look. "I'm not kidding around here, Eli," she said firmly. "And neither is Homicide. You're a legitimate suspect, until..." Her voice trailed off.

"Until I'm not," I said.

"That's right," she said. "Until you're not."

She finished her coffee in one gulp, then set the cup back in its saucer and pushed it away. She stood up to leave.

"One last question," I said. "The audio recording of the interrogation I just went through. What happens to that?"

She grabbed her purse off the corner of the chair and began to dig through it. "They burn it to a disc and then have it transcribed," she said.

"And then?"

"Then the interrogating officers sign off on it and it goes into the file. If it's needed in court, they pull it out and send it over."

"So the interrogating officers read everything that was on the recording?"

She had found her sunglasses. "They're supposed to," she said. "Why do you want to know?"

"No particular reason," I said casually. She gave me a puzzled look and then turned and headed toward the door, disappearing out of the dim room into the bright sunshine on the street outside.

I sat back and sipped my coffee, smiling with the understanding that, at some point in the near future, Homicide Detective Fred Hutton was going to read a transcript of me, singing all four verses of The Smothers Brothers' song, *Mediocre Fred*.

You can't buy satisfaction like that.

Chapter 7

"A murder suspect?" Harry said again, this time more indignantly than the first.

"The term they used was 'Person of Interest,' but I think it comes down to the same thing."

"Bunch of imbeciles," Harry mumbled as he pushed another length of rope and a printed receipt into a box and slid it across the worktable to me.

We were in the back room of the magic shop, filling Internet orders for one of Harry's most popular and bestselling illusions, a self-tying rope trick. I taped the box shut and added the address and return address labels, and then tossed it in a bin that I'd take to the post office later. It was mindless work, but for some reason I really enjoyed it.

I'd loved doing it as a kid, when Harry gave me five cents per order while he regaled me with stories of the magicians he'd worked with in his career. And I still enjoyed doing it as an adult, when just as often it was now me giving him an account of some recent stage triumph. Or sometimes we'd work for hours and barely say ten words. It was still fun.

We packaged a few more of the self-tying ropes and were moving on to his equally popular Screaming Dice when we heard the bell ring on the other side of the wall in the shop. Neither one of us made a move to get up.

"It's your turn," I said finally as I added labels to a sealed box.

"Like hell it is," he snapped back. "I got the last three, and two of those times it was that terrible student of yours."

"Pete's not all that bad."

"He's a wretched, graceless magician. If he were a dog, I'd have him put down to take me out of my misery."

"I'll go," I said, getting up. "We really can only handle one murder suspect in the family at a time."

I parted the red velour curtain that separated the back room from the store and stepped into the shop, surprised to see Clive Albans, the British writer I'd met in The Caves. Although Halloween had come and gone, you wouldn't know it by looking at Clive. Flared bell-bottom pants and a silk shirt were covered by a long, flowing raincoat, a London Fog knock-off in a deep violet hue. It made me think of Willy Wonka.

"Hello."

"Ah, yes, brilliant," he said, looking up from one of the glass display cases he had been peering into. "Eli, isn't it?"

"Yes," I said. "Clive?"

"Spot on," he said. "Impressive memory. You must teach me your method sometime."

"No trick, really. You say your name, I remember it. That's really all there is to it."

"Clever bit, that. Well done."

"Yes." There was a pause just this side of pregnant. "So, how can I help you, Clive?"

"Yes, well, the interview? With yourself. And your uncle, if he's so inclined." He took a few steps toward me, removing his rich, red leather gloves and placing them on the display case. "I believe I mentioned the article I'm doing for the *London Times*, on charlatan psychics."

"Yes," I said. "You did."

"Your uncle, being as renowned as he is in the field, would be the ideal candidate. Nothing extensive, mind you. Just a few juicy quotes. His thoughts on the current state of the field, that sort of thing." He had taken out his notebook and flipped it open to a blank page. He pulled out a pen from his inside breast pocket and gave it a click, then made a quick jot on the paper to ensure its viability.

"Let me check and see if Harry is interested in taking part," I said as I turned back toward the red curtain.

"Not interested," came Harry's reply from through the thick fabric before I had walked two feet. I turned back to Clive.

"I'm afraid that my uncle isn't currently available for an interview," I said. "Perhaps another time."

"Fat chance," was Harry's muffled response.

Clive was certainly a pro, because Harry's curt reaction didn't faze him for a second.

"Well, perhaps I could get *you* to talk on the record," he said, turning his attention toward me. "What has your experience been with charlatan psychics? I saw how you dealt with the late Mr. Grey last evening...terrible business, that, by the way," he added, clucking his tongue sympathetically. "Grisly stuff. Anyway, is that how you usually deal with them, give them a bit of their own medicine, a bit of the hair of the dog, that sort of thing?"

He lowered his tall frame onto one of the stools in front of the display case, not-so-subtly signaling that we were going to have a conversation of some duration. I sat on the other stool.

"Well, in that particular instance," I said, "I was dealing with a performer who was doing, as I mentioned at the time, a very traditional mentalist routine, which is in many ways part and parcel with what magicians do in their acts. With other types of psychics...palm readers, astrologists, healers, spoon benders, and that sort...you have to adjust your techniques in order to uncover their methods."

I was feeling tongue-tied and remembered how much I hated being interviewed.

"Excellent," he said as he made some indecipherable notes about my blathering on his pad. "Now then," he said. He leaned back as far as he could on the stool and bit down thoughtfully on the tip of his pen.

"Back in the day of Houdini, it was not uncommon for highly-educated people to be completely taken in by paranormal charlatans. Even Arthur Conan Doyle himself was famously fooled by two teenage girls and their fake fairy photos," he said, hitting the alliteration hard as he spoke. "Do you think people are, as a rule, more sophisticated today?"

"Well, yes, I'd like to think that people are better educated and less susceptible to sham—"

I was cut off by Harry, who burst through the red curtain like a freight train. He had his head down, a man on a mission. He didn't look in our direction as he spoke. "Nonsense. People never change. They are the same today as they have always been," he declared as he ducked behind a counter and stooped down to open a drawer. I could hear him digging through the drawer as he spoke, his disembodied voice bellowing up from behind the display case. "They aren't any more sophisticated and neither, for that matter, are the psychics who consistently fool them. And it's the very fact that they think they're more sophisticated that gets them into trouble in the first place. Take it from me...people are idiots."

He popped up from behind the counter holding three boxes of Screaming Dice, looked at the boxes, glanced at us for a split second, and then disappeared back behind the red curtain. I suppressed a smile, because I knew for a fact that there were four cases of Screaming Dice in the back room sitting on the worktable.

I looked back at Clive, who sat frozen for a moment. Then he jerked into action and began to furiously jot down what Harry had just said.

"Excellent," he murmured as he scribbled.

"So, what spurred the idea for this article?" I asked while he wrote, hoping to turn his attention away from me. "Is it just some kind of an assignment or is there a more personal reason for your interest?"

He stopped writing and looked up at me. I couldn't read the expression on his face and a moment later I didn't have to, as his countenance had returned to his earlier bright, smiling appearance.

"Oh, it's a freelance piece, to be sure," he said, offhandedly. "I've had a couple run-ins with the psychics back in London, in Belgrade Square, but nothing to speak of. Just always interested in the topic and thought there might be a story in it."

"So the article isn't what brought you to the U.S.?" I asked.

"Oh, no, I've been here for years, on and off. I'm afraid I'm a bit of a whirligig. I file reports from all over. It suits me."

He looked back at his notes and then spoke again before I could interject another question. "So what is it about magicians and psychics? Harry Houdini railed against them in his time. And your uncle's work is, in a word, legendary. Why the antipathy? I mean, aren't you all basically the same when it comes right down to it? You're both just fooling people, isn't that so?"

"Well, not exactly," I said. "The difference is —"

"The difference is," Harry said, once again bursting out of the back room, "that a magician stands in front of an audience and tells them, in effect, 'Everything I'm about to do is a lie.' We are, at our core, honest about our contract with the audience. The psychic, on the other hand, stands in front of his crowd and says, 'Everything I'm about to tell you is the truth.' And then he proceeds to lie to them. It's as different as night and day."

As soon as he finished speaking, Harry realized that, in his enthusiasm, he hadn't established a sufficient ruse for coming out of the back room. He looked around the immediate area. He finally spotted a paper clip on a nearby counter.

"There it is," he said with fake relief as he picked it up and pushed his way back through the red curtain.

I looked at Clive, who was smiling as he scribbled. He finished, adding a flourish to the last word, and looked up at me. "So, Eli, have you ever experienced a paranormal event personally? An occurrence you couldn't explain with your traditional methods?"

I looked over at the back room, expecting another dramatic, exasperated entrance from Harry, but the red curtain remained strangely motionless. I waited a couple of seconds, and then turned back to Clive.

"Well, I certainly have experienced odd coincidences," I said finally. "I think everyone has at some point."

"Like the phone ringing and you know who it is before you pick it up?" he offered.

"Well, that's not a paranormal experience," I said. "That's just Caller ID." Clive laughed politely, which in my world is more painful than no laugh at all.

"But, seriously," he continued, "you must have had experiences that you, as a person and as a magician, cannot adequately explain."

"I'm sure I have," I said. "But I'm a skeptic. I'm not a debunker. I don't make the presumption that every supernatural occurrence has been faked in some way. As a skeptic, I am more inclined to look for a natural explanation before leaping to a supernatural conclusion."

"Would you like to encounter a true, paranormal experience?"

"Sure," I said. "Who wouldn't? It would be cool. But that desire doesn't cloud the part of my brain that first looks for the rational explanation. How about you?" I asked, turning it back on him. "Have you ever experienced something you couldn't explain?"

He smiled and shook his head. "I've yet to find anything that has completely mystified me, with the exception of your Electoral College. But hope springs eternal, doesn't it?"

That seemed to conclude the formal part of the interview, but at his request, I spent the next few minutes giving Clive a tour of the shop. In addition to demonstrating some of the most popular illusions, I also took care to point out a few of the classic effects that Harry had created.

I also indicated the photos of Harry with celebrities that had been taken over the years. Clive seemed genuinely interested in everything he saw and he spent a long time examining the old framed photos that hung on the walls.

"Magic is fascinating, isn't it?" he said. "Like that trick you did last night, what was it called, The Returning Card?"

"The Ambitious Card," I corrected. "Yes, that's a classic routine with literally hundreds of variations."

I stepped behind the counter, picked up a deck that was lying there and did a quick version of the routine, with one card continually returning to the top of the deck.

"Amazing," he said, studying my actions closely. "Simply amazing. How long would it take a person to learn that trick?"

I thought this over. "Well, in its simplest form, it still requires a couple of sleights that do take a bit of practice," I explained. "I don't think this is the ideal trick for a beginner."

"And what trick would be ideal for a beginner?" he asked, leaning down to peer through the glass top on the cabinet.

I scanned all the display cases quickly, finally settling on the perfect effect for him. "I think this is what you're describing. It's a little coin trick called Scotch and Soda."

"Oh, I like it already," he said. "Sounds like something that could come in handy with my mates in a pub."

"Absolutely. This is an easy one that works anywhere at any time," I said as I pulled a small, sealed Scotch and Soda package off its place in the display case and opened it up. "It involves a little transposition with a couple of coins," I explained as I demonstrated the trick for him.

"You see here, we have an American half dollar and a Mexican centavo. As you can see, the half dollar is just a tad larger than the centavo." I placed the larger coin on top of the smaller one and gestured for Clive to open his hand. I placed the two coins on his open palm. "Now close your hand and without opening it, see if you can reach in with your other fingers and find the smaller coin."

Clive did as instructed, looking up at the ceiling with great concentration as he felt inside his closed hand for the smaller coin. "Got it!" he said.

"Great, let's see it."

He pulled the coin out and his jaw dropped when he realized that, instead of holding the centavo, he was now holding a quarter that has appeared out of nowhere. He opened his closed fist to reveal the half dollar, but the centavo had completely vanished.

"Bloody hell," he said, examining both coins closely. He insisted that I perform it for him again and then one more time after that, howling with delight each time he was left with the half dollar and the quarter.

"How in God's name are you doing that?" he asked, examining the coins closely after my final performance.

"A professional magician never reveals his methods," I said grinning back at him. "But just this once I'll reveal the secret." I proceeded to show him how it was done, which produced the inevitable post-trick letdown that frequently occurs when the curtain is pulled back and the process revealed.

"Well, that's bloody simple when you know how it's done, isn't it?" he said, examining the coins in a completely different light. "Fiendishly clever but absolutely simple."

He reached for his wallet. "I'll take it."

I waved away his money. "This one's on the house," I said.

He looked up from the coins in his hand, delighted. "Brilliant," he said.

He was still marveling at the trick and my generosity as I walked him to the door and closed it behind him. I sighed and shook my head as I walked through the shop. Potentially the only sale of the day, and I had given it away for nothing.

I returned to the back room with Harry, packaging up mail orders in silence for a long time, each of us in our own little thought bubble. Once we finished all the orders for the Screaming Dice, we turned our attention to the Card-Presto, a device I had created for keeping a deck of cards flat. It's not a sexy item, but if you make your living doing card tricks, it can increase the lifespan of each deck of cards by a factor of five.

I thought we might close out the afternoon in silence, but then Harry began to speak.

"The reason I didn't want to talk to the reporter was simple," Harry said without looking up at me. "I'm still a skeptic through and through, that hasn't changed. But for the first time in my life, I really want it to be true. I'd like to believe that there is something on the other side."

He looked up at me. His eyes were just a bit watery.

"I finally have a reason to want to believe in all this nonsense, not to fight it," he said, "but frankly I don't have the strength to do either."

He pushed the last of the orders across the worktable toward me. "I think I'm going to lie down for a bit," he said as he moved across the room and through the curtain.

I heard him slowly climbing up the stairs, and then I heard him open the apartment door and move through his kitchen and living room. Finally there was the sound of his bedroom door closing, and then all was quiet again.

Chapter 8

"Ah, the Prodigal Nephew," Abe Ackerman said, looking up from the perpetual card game that absorbed the greater part of the Minneapolis Mystics' time.

He's used that same line every time he's seen me since I moved back into my apartment above the store. And although I don't find the line particularly funny, I give him credit because like any good performer, he makes it sound brand-new each time he says it.

In his day, Abe was a top mentalist, although he insists that The Amazing Kreskin stole most of his prime material, along with his best, and most attractive, assistant. It's still a sore subject with Abe and a conversational minefield that is best avoided.

"Hi, Abe. Hi, guys," I said to the group, which today numbered four. The others just glanced up from their cards and grunted a collective greeting.

I had stepped into the bar next to Chicago Magic expecting to find Uncle Harry seated in the back and he did not disappoint. Once my eyes adjusted to the dim light provided by the dirty 40-watt bulbs and the illuminated beer signs that lined the walls, I'd had no trouble spotting Harry and his cronies seated at their regular table at the far end of the long, narrow room.

Nowadays we have friends, acquaintances, and Facebook buddies, but in Harry's world you had cronies. The group has suffered some attrition in the last few years, but that's inevitable in any group whose members' average age is seventy-five. The club formed when they were in their teens and just on the cusp of their respective entertainment careers. Officially they call themselves The Minneapolis Mystics, but ever since I was a kid I've called them by the name that Aunt Alice lovingly bestowed on them: The Artful Codgers.

I put a hand on Harry's shoulder. "I'm headed off to the memorial service," I said. "So I've locked up the shop until you're done over here."

"I might as well be done, with the miserable cards I've been getting. I'm out," Harry said, tossing his cards on the table in disgust. He looked at the current dealer, Sam Esbjornson.

"I'd accuse you of cheating, Sam," Harry growled, "if I didn't know for a fact that you're the worst card man west of the Mississippi."

"East of the Mississippi as well," chimed in Abe. "He's got incompetence covered, coast to coast."

"Not to mention incontinence," Harry added.

"Aw, stick it in your ear," Sam grumbled as he peeked at his cards. Sam was primarily a coin magician, and his alleged inability to handle cards was a consistent source of amusement for the group. However, if you wanted to witness a perfect rendition of The Miser's Dream—a magician producing a seemingly endless shower of coins magically from his fingertips—Sam was your man.

"Did you say memorial service?" asked Max Monarch, who like many in his age bracket was perpetually interested in who had just died or was suspected to be approaching the end. Unlike Sam, Max was a card magician, one of the best, and so all eyes were trained on him like lasers whenever it became his deal. If he did cheat, my guess is that even at his advanced age they'd never spot it.

"Yes, a memorial service," I repeated. "No one you know," I added, before he could raise the question.

"It's that fake medium who was murdered," Harry explained to the group. "And my nephew here is the prime suspect," he added with a hint of pride in his voice.

"Is he now?" Max asked earnestly.

"Hardly the prime suspect," I said, making my tone as jovial as possible. "Probably not even in the top ten."

"Don't be so humble," Harry said. "They took him in for questioning," he said, turning back to the group. "An interrogation, actually."

They all nodded in appreciation at this new, juicy bit of information.

"I've got a nephew, been arrested plenty, let me tell you. Every other day, he's in or out of jail," Abe said.

"For jaywalking, most likely, and other petty offenses," Harry said, waving it away with his hand. "This is serious business. A capital crime."

"So, you're a suspect and you're going to his memorial service? What's the sense in that?" Max asked, and the others all made grunts of agreement. "Seems a bit on the crazy side, if you ask me."

"Of course he has to go," Harry said, raising his voice above the general hubbub of the group. "How else can he get a handle on the other suspects and clear his name? That doesn't happen if you're just sitting at home on your tush...a person has got to burn a little shoe leather when you're the top suspect in a murder."

This comment miraculously turned the direction of the argument, with everyone now agreeing that attending the memorial service was, after all, the most prudent course of action.

"The actual murderer always turns up at the funeral," Sam said definitively. "I've seen it happen a hundred times. On TV."

"Yes, you just keep your eyes peeled and you'll nail him, clear as day," Abe agreed.

"But you keep on your toes, Buster," Max added. "How many times has the prime suspect ended up being the second victim?"

"You're right. Ninety-nine percent of the time that happens," Sam agreed. "It catches me by surprise every time." He looked up at me. "You be careful, Buster. I mean, what's the point of clearing your name if you just end up dead?"

I patted him on the shoulder. "You make a good point," I said, trying my best to not sound patronizing. "So, let me make sure that I understand how I should approach this...I need to keep my eyes peeled for the actual killer." I looked around the table and received expressions of agreement all around. "But at the same time, make sure I'm not the next victim. Is that it?"

"Bingo," Abe said. "And, if you have time, you should also try to get yourself laid."

They were all still laughing when I left.

The memorial was held at a church that stretched the term nondenominational to its breaking point. Sitting high on a hill overlooking Lake Harriet, and nestled in a funky little neighborhood of high-income, well-intentioned liberals, vegans and soccer moms, the silver-domed church had evidently gone through multiple incarnations over the years. Currently it was stripped of all vestiges of Christianity inside and out, with the obvious exception of two impressively large stained-glass windows depicting scenes of Jesus and his disciples.

Although I had no trouble finding a parking space, I was surprised to find that the main floor was packed when I arrived. Informed that there was no seating available downstairs, I was directed upstairs to the small two-row balcony that overlooked the sanctuary.

That someone as universally loathed and repellant as Grey could command a sell-out crowd for his final send-off struck me as a hopeful sign for anyone who has worried about the attendance numbers at their own memorial service. It certainly made me feel better about my own funereal expectations.

The leader of the service—an exceedingly calm and painfully soft-spoken man in his early forties—was dressed in khakis and a turtleneck and sported long brown hair and a beard. I don't know if he was consciously trying to look like Jesus in the stained-glass windows, so as to justify the windows' continued existence, but the resemblance was uncanny.

He was in the midst of a guided meditation as I made my way down the length of the balcony to the one remaining seat, a wobbly folding chair that had seen better days.

It was tough getting past the others seated in the row, as most had their eyes closed and some were rocking back and forth to the melodious sound of the leader's words that echoed through the church's surprisingly up-to-date sound system.

"You're on the river of love," he said in a voice like warm caramel. "Floating in the flow, in the moment, in the now. You are embraced, enveloped, and encased in love."

Once seated, I scanned the room below me, taking advantage of the fact that most people were in full meditation mode, with their eyes closed. Based on the few recognizable faces I spotted, the local psychic community was out in full force.

Although they may not have liked Grey in life, they were certainly coming together as a group behind the idea of his passing.

I inspected the crowd again and recognized a face—or, to be more accurate, given the angle I was at—the side of a face, some hair, a nose and a right ear that looked familiar. I was pretty certain that it was Megan and I strained to get a better view without toppling over the railing. If the railing was in the same shaky condition as my chair, I realized that I would be wise to not put any weight against it.

I peered as best I could from the relative safety of my seat and my suspicion was confirmed in the worst possible manner.

The person next to my potential Megan chose that moment to adjust his position in the pew and I recognized him as Pete, her soon-to-be ex-husband.

I swore under my breath, but apparently not far enough under for the woman seated next to me. Her eyes snapped open like a window shade with an overactive spring and she raised an accusing eyebrow in my direction.

I settled back in my seat and put on my best look of repose. Once her eyes were closed again, I continued my long-distance scrutiny. It certainly looked like Megan and it was absolutely Pete. I couldn't tell for sure from this distance, but they might have even been holding hands.

I didn't like the looks of that at all.

"Thank you, everyone," the leader said, speaking softly into a microphone on a stand at the center of the altar. "And now, in conclusion, we will celebrate Grey's life with affirmations of his spirit. We'll open the floor to any of you who desire to step forward and express your feelings for Grey, for his energy, and for the tranquility of his spirit in the next world.

"And," he added with a tone that sounded a bit too upbeat for the proceedings, "your affirmations of Grey will be supported, musically, by harpist, full-body healer, medical intuitive, and aura photographer, Arianna Dupree."

With that introduction, a large, dramatically dressed middle-aged woman stepped out of the congregation and toward the harp, which was situated off to one side of the altar. She wore a bright, multi-colored caftan and on her head sat a turban that looked distinctly African, although the woman herself couldn't have been more white. She settled her bulky form behind the harp and the large instrument seemed to disappear into the folds of her caftan.

Even from the balcony I was amazed at the delicate sounds she produced from the instrument with her large, doughy fingers.

The leader took a seat, Arianna continued to play, and we all waited for the first mourner to step forward and present their tribute to Grey.

The tranquil sound of the harp and an occasional light cough were the only sounds in the church for several moments. After a few more moments with no volunteers stepping forward, people began to fidget nervously in their seats. The sound of their rustling was misinterpreted by others as the sound of someone getting up to speak.

People craned their necks and peered around, and one or two popped halfway up out of their seats like prairie dogs to see who was taking the plunge. But the truth was, no one was stepping forward.

Arianna moved gracefully from one tuneless song to the next and still we sat, waiting for someone—anyone—to break the silence, which had gone past uncomfortable and was now well into the realm of sort of creepy.

Then, from my vantage point high above, I saw a lithe figure rise and move down a pew, gently stepping past congregants who shoved their legs aside as best they could within the tight quarters of the bench.

As soon as she hit the aisle, I recognized her. It was Nova, Grey's assistant.

She was dressed all in black, as she had been at the show, but this outfit was a lighter, more casual version of her show attire. She stepped into the aisle and moved silently toward the altar and the microphone.

The leader, seated off to one side, gestured toward her, as if to say, "Yes, I believe you're next. Go right ahead, dear."

Nova stepped gingerly up to the microphone and barely looked at the crowd, her long dark hair surrounding her face. She cleared her throat and then stepped back for a moment, looking like she was about to reconsider the notion of being up there. Then she stepped forward and began to speak softly. Her low volume was not an issue, though, as everyone was leaning forward in rapt anticipation.

"Grey was a son of a bitch," she said in a surprisingly girlish voice. This statement produced an audible gasp from the group—it didn't appear to come from any one person, but rather from the entire group en masse.

"He was hurtful and hateful and I for one am glad he's dead." She stepped back from the microphone, seemingly finished, and then stepped forward one more time. "Plus he was bad in bed."

With that final statement, Nova gave a quick nod and moved away from the microphone. With her head lowered, she glided back down the aisle to her pew. Everyone made room for her to pass and in a matter of moments she was back in her seat and the church was once again quiet, with the exception of Arianna's monotonous plucking on the harp.

The leader looked around the church hopefully, as I'm sure Nova's speech was not, in his mind, the ideal closing act. No one else stepped forward, so he finally got up and returned to the microphone.

"Thank you," he said, smiling in Nova's direction, "for sharing your feelings. And for those of you who enjoyed Arianna's performance on the harp, she wanted me to remind you that her CDs are available out in our lobby, at her shop, Akashic Records, and at the Akashic Records website. And finally, before we conclude, I want to remind you that a reception will take place, starting immediately, just down the street, at the home of Dr. Maurice Bitterman."

That name rang a bell with me. A few years back there had been a football player with the Minnesota Vikings named Maurice Bitterman. There had been a lot of confusion during his arrival in the Twin Cities, because he insisted that his first name be pronounced using the British pronunciation, Morris.

It seemed unlikely that there would be two identically-named men in the same city, but it seemed just as unlikely that a former Viking defensive end would be attending Grey's funeral.

On the main floor people began to get up and shuffle toward the exit. The folks in the balcony were filing out even more slowly, so I stood and watched the crowd below as they made their way out of the sanctuary, trying to see if there was anyone large enough to be a former football player. As they walked down the main aisle, it was now abundantly clear that the woman I thought might be Megan was, in fact, Megan. And Pete was Pete.

I was just stepping back to get clear of their line of sight when Pete spotted me. A big smile washed across his face and he waved up to me, then turned to Megan and pointed me out to her. It was too late for me to step out of sight, so I waved wanly at them.

Pete used some rough sign language to indicate that we should meet outside the building. I bobbed my head in agreement, trying to appear happy about it. From that distance, it might have even looked convincing.

Although I felt like I was stalling, and in many ways I was, it really did take a long time to get out of that skinny balcony and down the narrow, twisty steps to the church's foyer. By the time I made my way down, most of the crowd had exited the church and the remaining attendees were standing in conversational groups of two and three right outside the front door on the concrete steps leading to the sidewalk. I quickly scanned the groups before I spotted Pete and Megan standing on the sidewalk, talking to a small, bird-like woman. Once again Pete noticed me before I could duck out of view. He gave me an enthusiastic wave and I waved back as I headed down the steps toward them.

I hadn't seen the two of them together very often, but when I had, I was always struck with the same, cruel thought: How did such a doughy, average-looking guy like Pete hook up with a woman like Megan?

It wasn't that Pete was unattractive. It was that his bland averageness was put into sharp relief whenever he was standing next to Megan. On the other hand, I realized, people would probably be saying the same thing about me if Megan and I were a couple.

"I'm surprised to see you two here," I said. "Really surprised."

Pete shrugged. "Megan's trying to get more involved in the psychic community, and I thought I would just tag along. To be supportive."

I smiled and looked toward Megan, who was of course stunning, in a light winter coat over a dark blouse and skirt combination. Then I noticed that her smile seemed even more forced than my own. There was an awkward silence and then Megan quickly filled the gap by turning to the tiny, gray-haired woman next to her.

"Eli, do you know Franny? Franny Higgins? This is Eli Marks."

"I don't believe we've met." I turned and put out my hand to the woman, who was at most a speck over five feet and probably in her late sixties.

She seemed to take no notice of me, but instead rummaged in her purse. She finally found what she was searching for and wrestled it out of the bag. It was a pair of glasses with almost comically thick lenses. She pulled them onto her face and peered up at me.

"So, you're the one they say killed Grey?" she stated more than queried in a thin, raspy voice. She had a sharp, pointed nose and the glasses magnified her deep blue eyes, throwing them out of proportion with the rest of her face.

Before I could answer, she had taken my outstretched hand, but not in a handshake. She grabbed my fingers roughly and began to knead them like a pile of bread dough, rolling my fingers around in her tiny hands while looking up at the sky thoughtfully.

After a few moments, she clucked her tongue and shook her head. "No, no. It wasn't you. You didn't do it."

She patted my hand warmly and then released it, turning her attention to Pete and Megan. "I'm hungry. Are you two going to the reception?"

The sudden change of topic seemed to take them by surprise. They looked at each other, obviously with no pre-arranged game plan in place.

"Yes," Megan said without assurance. "I was going to go. It's just down the street. I thought I'd walk."

"That sounds nice," Pete said. He looked to Megan for confirmation and her non-reaction was taken as assent.

"Too far for my old feet," Franny said, turning back to me. "Are you going, and more importantly, are you driving?"

"I could go and I could drive," I said. "I'm parked just over there," I added, gesturing to the lot directly across the street.

"Rock star parking. I like you better already," Franny said, giving me a slap on the arm as she turned and headed toward the corner. She spun back and looked at Megan and Pete. "We'll see you there."

She started to cross the street without waiting for me. I looked to Pete and Megan.

"I guess I'll see you there," I said, as I hurried to catch up with Franny, who moved with remarkable speed for someone who was both old and tiny.

"Does this thing have heated seats?" Franny asked once she had settled into the front passenger seat.

"Yes, yes it does," I said. "But we're only going a block…"

"Crank it up," she said, cutting me off. "I've been chilled since my mid-forties."

I started the car and turned the seat warmer on for the passenger side, and then turned the car's heater to high for good measure. She settled back with a sigh as the warmth began to seep through the upholstery.

"Nice," she said with a satisfied sigh. "I could get used to this."

I shifted the car into gear and we moved out of the parking lot, following the small parade of cars that had chosen to drive the short distance to the reception.

After a few moments, we passed Pete and Megan, walking together down the sidewalk. Pete's hands were stuck deep into his pockets, while Megan was looking up at the houses they were passing. I watched them for just a moment too long.

"I'd stay away from that pair," Franny said suddenly. "They're doomed."

"Pardon me?" I turned my attention back to my driving. "Who's doomed?"

"That couple. The end is near. You can feel it on them, like a stink."

"Really? So, is that a psychic prediction?" I asked, trying to sound light and conversational.

"Simple intuition. Plus I've been married three times, so I recognize the signs." Franny put her hands up in front of one of the air vents and let the warming air envelop her fingers. "I saw the way you looked at her. It's only going to end in tears my friend, only going to end in tears."

She began to fiddle with the radio knob. "Do you have satellite?"

"No, sorry."

"That's a shame. They say it helps the resale value of the car," she added. "This car warms up quick, though. I'll give you that."

"Good thing, since it's supposed to snow tonight."

Franny shook her head. "No snow. Not tonight."

I glanced over at her as she adjusted the vent that was pointing at me, turning it so that it blew in her direction. "The weatherman said we're getting a big snowstorm," I said. "Six to eight inches by morning."

Franny shook her head again. "Not going to happen."

"Even the National Weather Service predicts a big storm," I added, not really knowing why I was being so adamant about the weather forecast.

"Like they've never been wrong before?" she said, turning her hands over and warming the other sides.

We had arrived at our destination and now it was just a matter of finding a place to park. I slowed my speed and began to look for an opening.

"There's a space right around the corner," Franny said.

"No, I've seen a lot of cars turn there, I don't think so."

"Trust me, there's a parking space."

It was such a definitive statement that it was hard to ignore, so I did as instructed. Just as I had suspected, there weren't any spots. And then a parked car suddenly pulled out into the street, leaving a prime parking spot in its wake. I glanced over at Franny, who shrugged.

"Told you," was all she said. "Now let's get something to eat."

The second I stopped the car she shoved open the passenger door with a surprising amount of gusto and moments later had moved quickly toward the house. I hurried to catch up with her.

Chapter 9

The house was massive, too big for the lot it sat on. Like an increasing number of houses that overlooked Lake Harriet, it was a McMansion—a smaller house that had been purchased and renovated so that not only did it no longer resemble its former self, but it actually looked a silly when compared to the surrounding homes.

Whoever had renovated this house had gone all out, building up and out, pushing the footprint to the very edge of the lot. It might at one time have been a charming two-story colonial-style home, but so much glass had been added—along with porches, decks and balconies—that it now resembled a house designed by MC Escher on a bender.

Although not everyone from the memorial service had made their way down the street for the reception, there were still a healthy flow of people streaming in as Franny and I made our way up the stone steps to the main door.

As we approached I could see straight through the mostly-glass structure, from the front through the back to its view of Lake Harriet and the downtown skyline beyond. We worked our way into the stream of people and as we entered the two-story foyer, I looked ahead into the wide, open living room, which was lined on three sides with floor-to-ceiling windows.

Suddenly a shadow fell across me and my view was entirely obscured by something very large and dark blue. A hand fell upon my shoulder, nearly making my knees buckle from the impact.

"Eli Marks, isn't it?" a deep, booming voice said. I looked up to see the smiling face of Maurice Bitterman, an impressively large, beautifully-groomed black man. He stood about six-foot five and must have tipped the scales at over two hundred and eighty. He was wearing an elegantly-tailored dark blue suit, with a white pressed linen shirt open at the neck. Gold bracelets adorned both wrists and at least one tooth in his smile appeared to be gold as well. He was completely bald.

This was a man who made a stunning first impression.

"That's me," I said, shifting my weight to help maintain my balance. "And you're Maurice Bitterman, right?"

His smile, which was large to begin with, grew even wider, possibly because I had pronounced his first name correctly.

"Guilty as charged," he replied, and then his hand flew up and covered his mouth in mock surprise. "I'm sorry. Perhaps the wrong choice of words to use around you, under the circumstances. No offense, I hope."

"None taken. No charges have been filed and I'd like to keep it that way."

"I'm sure you would." His gaze moved from me to something next to me, even closer to the ground. I followed his eyes to see that he was looking down at Franny. "Franny, don't even ask. The food is in the kitchen, down that hall to your left."

She darted away without a word and bulldozed her way through the crowd toward the kitchen, quickly disappearing from sight. Maurice wrapped a mammoth arm around my shoulder and guided me toward the living room. "Let's talk for a minute," he said.

A bar had been set up on one side of the immense living room and Maurice ordered two beers from the bartender. He waved away glasses and instead effortlessly clasped both bottles in one large hand. He offered one to me as he directed me toward a huge couch that offered a beautiful view of the lake.

The couch was occupied, but by the time we had crossed the room, everyone who was seated there had found a reason to go sit somewhere else. Maurice didn't seem to notice and I suspect that it was a common occurrence for a man of his size and commanding presence.

I settled in and looked out at the view. The day was at the tipping point between dusk and darkness. Most of the leaves had fallen from the trees and it was beginning to look and feel like November. A couple of die-hard runners plodded past on the leaf-strewn path below, while a flock of ducks out on the water decided at that moment to decamp and perhaps head toward a warmer climate. The glass walls made you feel like you were sitting outside, although the new-age music playing on the invisible sound system and the hubbub of multiple conversations in the room reminded me that we were, in fact, very much indoors.

"I saw you on television," Maurice said, settling into the comfy sofa and putting his feet up on a matching ottoman. "That trick you did at the end, with the knife through the card, that's a good one. You'll have to show me how you did it some time."

"I think I may retire the knife trick," I said. "At least for the foreseeable future."

"Prudent choice," he agreed, taking a long sip from the bottle.

I took a sip from my own and then got up the nerve to ask the question that had been bugging me for the last thirty minutes. "So, what's a former All-Star football player doing at the memorial service for a well-known, if somewhat dubious, psychic?"

He stopped mid-sip and for an instant I thought I might have taken a potentially dangerous conversational turn. But then he broke into that wide, bright grin again and I relaxed, at least for the moment.

"That, my friend, is an interesting story." He took his feet off the ottoman and leaned forward. "It started because I couldn't get a good night's sleep. For love or money, I couldn't. I'd wake up exhausted. I was two years out of the game, still trying to find my feet, career-wise. I didn't want to end up as a casino greeter or worse, and man, I was floundering. Or foundering. Which one is it?"

"In the context that you're using it, I think they both mean roughly the same thing," I said helpfully. "Although I'm sure there are people who would argue the point."

"The same thing? Like flammable and inflammable?"

"Same thing."

"Well, that's just stupid."

"Yes. Yes, it is."

"Anyway, I couldn't get a good night's sleep. I tried everything." He leaned back in the chair, tapping the side of his beer bottle thoughtfully. "Let me tell you, a man doesn't appreciate sleep until he can't."

"You don't know what you've got 'til it's gone."

"Amen, brother." Another sip, followed by a thoughtful sigh. "Anyway, someone recommended hypnotherapy and, at that point, I figured what the hell. I called the guy and went in for one session with no level of enthusiasm. And within one week I was sleeping like a baby."

"Because of hypnotherapy? Interesting."

He surprised me by shaking his head. "Nope. The hypnotherapist took one look at me and said I probably had sleep apnea. It's common in men with large necks, which you may have noticed I have."

I nodded. His neck was roughly the same diameter as my thighs, combined.

"But something about hypnotherapy intrigued me, so I started looking into it. And it turned out I had an aptitude for it. Two years of schooling later, I was Dr. Bitterman, which would have thrilled my mother no end, God rest her soul. Then I got turned onto past life regression, via our mutual friend, the late Mr. Grey. That's our primary business now."

"Our?" I asked.

"Yeah, I have clinic out in Wayzata and two satellite clinics, one in Rosemount and another one downtown. We've got a staff of about twelve people. And then of course there's the online component, which is, frankly, the lion's share of our business. People are endlessly fascinated about their past life experiences, and there are thousands out there willing to drop $29.95 a pop for a little insight. It adds up, let me tell you; it adds up mightily." He looked past me and his smile widened to twice its size. "And speaking of past lives, here's one of my favorite clients, past, present, or future."

I turned to see Megan moving through the crowded room toward us, with Pete in tow. Pete was holding two clear plastic cups full of some form of alcohol, while Megan was balancing a couple small plates layered high with exotic-looking appetizers.

Megan's smile rivaled Maurice's in intensity, and when she arrived at our couch, she and the good doctor exchanged as much of a hug as they could, given the cargo she was carrying. Maurice half pulled, half lifted her over me, placing her gently between us on the couch.

Having nowhere else to sit, Pete sat next to me, balancing awkwardly on the arm of the couch, a slightly forced smile on his face. He raised one of the plastic cups in a mock toast toward me, and then handed the other cup to Megan.

"Eli, I didn't know that you knew Dr. Bitterman," Megan said to me as she took the drink from Pete. "Isn't he the best?"

"Actually, we just met about five minutes ago. We were talking about past life regressions," I began, but she cut me off, grabbing onto my leg with her free hand to demonstrate the intensity of her excitement about the topic.

"Oh, you have to have him do you," she said. "I've had about eight sessions so far, and the stuff we're finding out is just phenomenal. Mind-blowing stuff, really."

"Past lives?" I asked, consciously tempering any ironic or sarcastic tone in my voice. "Really?"

"Oh, I know what you're thinking," she said. "Most people think it's about finding out whether or not you were Cleopatra or Joan of Arc or Jack the Ripper or somebody famous in a past life, but it's not about that at all, is it?" She turned to Maurice for support and he patted her on the shoulder, clearly relishing her level of enthusiasm on the topic.

"Yes," he said, "it's a common misconception. We were never someone else in a past life. You're always yourself, always the same *you*, but just in a different form. Each time we come back to this corporeal world, we're simply working on perfecting a different facet of that *you*. We're all on a journey of perfection, and each lifetime is our opportunity to continue to smooth off the rough edges."

He took a quick sip of his beer and continued. "Past life regression, at its core, is just a way of looking at how far each of us has come on our journey and to gain some insight into what problem or issue is our primary focus for this particular lifetime."

"You can't tell where you're going until you know where you've been," Megan added.

"That's what we say," Maurice agreed. "Although I always prefer the way it sounds coming out of your mouth." They both laughed.

"So that's how you met Grey," I said to Maurice, turning the conversation back. "Through the psychic community?"

Maurice finished his beer and then shook his head. "Actually, he was my realtor first. He helped me get this place," he added, waving his free arm at the house. "And he was a huge help when the neighborhood tried to block the remodel. They took me to court, there were lawsuits. Ugly stuff. Grey absolutely pulled some strings for me on that nonsense. He really knew how to work the system, let me tell you. We were going to have lunch next week, in fact. He had another scheme of some kind he wanted to discuss. But, I guess now that won't be happening."

We all lapsed into what appeared to be a respectful silence, which Maurice finally broke. "However, deep down, we all know he was, in fact, a world-class dick."

Megan was momentarily shocked by this, and then she burst out laughing, nearly doing a spit take and slapping Maurice on the knee. "Oh, Dr. Bitterman, what a terrible thing to say."

"Did you know him?" he asked her.

"No, I didn't, but still —"

He cut her off. "But nothing. Trust me, there is a Karmic wheel that guides the souls on this planet, and it does go 'round. Grey got his ass kicked by the Karmic wheel and probably for good reason."

"I guess he's got his work cut out for him in the next life," I suggested.

"I would say the next several lives," Maurice added with a smile.

There was another conversational silence and it began to sink in how awkward our seating situation was. I had Megan on one side of me, and Pete balancing uncomfortably on the armrest on my other side.

As much as I wanted to spend time talking to Megan, it was becoming increasingly clear that this was neither the ideal time nor place. I stood up and stepped away from the couch.

"You know, that food looks great," I said. "I'm going to go grab myself some."

Pete wasted no time and slid off the armrest into the spot next to Megan.

"Dr. Bitterman, it was great to meet you." I put out my hand. He reached up and grasped it, which disappeared within his grip.

"Nice to meet you, Eli," he said with genuine warmth. "And, remember...Hypnotherapy. It's good for what ails you."

"Unless what ails you is sleep apnea."

He laughed. "Yes, you've got me there. But I've got that under control."

I nodded toward Megan, but she had immediately pulled Maurice close and they were already deep in conversation. I gave Pete a wan smile, which he gave right back to me in spades.

"How's your Hindu Shuffle coming?" I asked.

He shook his head. "I've dropped more cards on the floor in the last two weeks than I think I have in my entire life. At this rate, I'll never advance to something really hard, like a Faro Shuffle."

I nodded and chuckled along with him and then watched as he glanced over at Megan. He looked very sad.

And then a surprising feeling hit me and it hit me hard.

I was suddenly struck with an obvious thought that had, up until that moment, eluded me. If Megan started to feel about me the way I felt about her, I would become a Fred in Pete's mind. I would be Mediocre Fred to him and, as much as I didn't want to admit it, I would deserve that nickname.

I was no longer hungry, but I headed toward the kitchen just to get away from the trio and clear my head.

"Stay away from the seafood," a voice barked at me as I picked through the large, catered spread that covered the entire center island in Maurice's mammoth kitchen. I looked over to see Franny leaning against a polished wood cabinet.

She was using a torn scrap of a bread roll to clean the surface of the plastic plate she was holding. She popped the bread into her mouth and chewed contentedly.

"Which fish?" I asked, gesturing to the shrimp salad, which was next to the scallops, which were next to a large plate of artfully-displayed clams.

"All of it. It's a good general life rule...stay away from the seafood. I'll take hormones in beef over mercury in seafood any day. Of course, in the end, it's all poison."

"The real killer is sugar," another voice added. "Processed sugar. And don't get me started on corn syrup."

This opinion had issued forth from Arianna, the harpist from the memorial, who was standing across the center island from me. Her plate was piled high with two dark chocolate brownies, several variations of cookies, and a heavily-frosted piece of cake. She was daintily adding two small carrot sticks to the pile when she looked over at me and laughed a high, girlish giggle.

"Do as I say," she said, "not as I do."

"I'm a big believer in moderation in everything," I said. "Including moderation." I picked up two cookies and added them to my plate.

"I like the way you think," she said as she extended a fleshy hand across the counter to me. "You're Eli Marks, right?"

"Yes I am," I said, as I shifted my plate from my right hand to my left to free up a hand for her to clasp.

"He didn't do it, Arianna," Franny said in a bored voice. "I did a quick reading. He's clean."

"There's nothing wrong with getting a second opinion, Franny." Arianna held my hand for a long moment as she stared blankly at the ceiling.

Her hand was warm and moist and just a little bit sticky. She squinted for a moment and then furrowed her brow pensively. She released my hand and returned to her meticulous process of adding more layers to the small mountain of food on her plate. "Yes, I agree. He didn't do it."

"I'm glad you both concur on that," I said, as I surreptitiously wiped my right hand on my coat before I picked up my plate again. "What I don't understand is why you both seemed disappointed to come to that conclusion?"

"Well, I can't speak for Franny," Arianna said. "But if you were the one who killed Grey, I'd want to shake your hand. Good riddance to bad garbage, as my mother used to say."

"Hear, hear," Franny added. "Arianna, I love your bracelet."

Arianna paused her hunting and gathering for a moment to look down at the large silver bracelet that fit snugly around her wide right wrist. She held it up to the light.

"Isn't it delicious? I found it online and just had to have it. It took a lot of cleaning, but in the end it was worth it." She admired it for another long moment, then returned to picking at the food options on the counter.

"Does anyone know if these olives are pitted or not?" she asked the room at large. She didn't wait for a response, but instead scooped several olives onto her plate, ignoring the one or two that evaded capture and ended up on the floor. She held up one of the green olives she had just plucked and looked over at me.

"They say the green ones are aphrodisiacs," she said slyly before popping it into her mouth. Her eyes sparkled with a slightly naughty twinkle.

"I believe you're thinking of M&Ms," I said as tactfully as possible. She considered this for a moment, then shrugged and continued chewing.

"Whatever." She took her completed plate, grabbed a fancy napkin off a stack and breezed out of the room. I watched her go and then noticed that Franny was watching me watch her.

"Careful of that one," Franny said dryly.

"How do you mean?"

"Trouble follows her like kids following an ice cream truck." She clucked her tongue. "I'd like to do a reading of you someday," she said, deftly changing the subject.

"I thought you already did that," I said, returning my attention to the amazing spread of food in front of me.

"That was a quick scan. I mean something more in-depth. You might be surprised by what we find."

"I'm sure I would be. Where do you work and how do I make an appointment?"

"I only do phone readings these days. They're more conducive to my lifestyle," Franny said, moving to the center island and picking at the tray of cookies until she found one she wanted. "Lifestyle being a euphemism for 'sitting around in my bathrobe all day.'"

"That's a lifestyle I can get behind."

"It's one of the benefits of age, of which there are precious few," she said with a weary smile. She handed me a card, which held only her first name and phone number. "Thanks again for the ride. And don't worry...Tonight there will be no snow."

With her chosen cookie in hand, she gave me a smile and a wink and headed back into the living room.

*   *   *

In order to keep my distance from Pete and Megan, I took my time contemplating my food options.

The crowd in the kitchen had thinned out and I could now see that the far end of the room opened out into a glass porch. A couple was standing out there and from their body language and the muffled sounds coming from the room, it was apparent that they were in the throes of a serious argument.

I was about to look away so as not to appear a voyeur, when I recognized the woman in the pair and she recognized me.

It was Nova, and when she saw me she immediately stopped the argument and broke into an excited smile. She waved me over and then appeared to laugh when I looked around to make sure I was, in fact, the one she was waving at. She smiled and waved again, so I finished filling my plate, grabbed a fork and napkin and headed toward the porch.

"Settle a bet," were the first words out of her mouth when I stepped out onto the porch.

I hesitated for a moment, because not only were the walls all glass, but I was also surprised to discover that the floor was transparent as well. This provided a vertiginous view of the patio two stories below and the lake beyond.

I gingerly stepped into the room, which was basically a floating transparent cube jutting from the house. In order to steady my walk across the small room, my hand instinctively reached out to touch the wall, as if driven by some primal force. I did my best not to look down.

"I will if I can. What's the bet?"

Nova was standing next to a beefy guy in his late twenties. She held a nearly empty glass of what looked like red wine in her hand. The guy was holding a large can of beer in his. He was wearing a loud Hawaiian shirt, which helped to mask a bulky frame that looked to be the result of many, many nights of holding large cans of beer. His head was covered with stringy blonde hair that barely hid a rapidly-receding hairline.

"That one thing you did the other night, where you used all of our psychic powers to find specific cards," she said. "That's really a psychic experiment and not a card trick, right?"

Her companion shook his head derisively. "It's a stupid card trick," he grumbled.

She looked to me for contradiction. "Let him say."

I shook my head sadly. "Sorry to burst your bubble," I said. "But it's a card trick, and, yes, not a very sophisticated one at that."

"You don't use psychic powers in your act?" she asked quietly.

I shook my head again. "Not that I know of."

"And neither did Grey," the guy said, building off my comment. "And that's my point, know what I mean? In three years I never saw him do anything that wasn't a sham or put-on. When are you going to face facts on that?"

"I don't think we've met," I said, having a pretty good idea who this guy was. "Did you know Grey?"

He grunted a response that sounded like "Did I ever."

"This is Boone. He and I worked for Grey," Nova said, picking up the introductory slack. "Although Boone was with him a lot longer than I was."

"Were you working with him the other night?"

"Yeah," Boone said. "That was going to be my last show with him, know what I mean? And, as it turned out, it was." He chuckled in a humorless manner.

"You were going to quit?"

"I figured I might as well before he fired me, know what I mean?"

I was marveling at his ability to turn virtually any statement into a question when I glanced down and realized I had an untouched plate of food in my hand.

I extended the plate to Boone and Nova. "Anyone want some?" I asked.

She passed on it, but Boone didn't hesitate, taking the entire plate from me in one quick movement.

"I got the sense the other night," I said, looking sadly at my now-empty hands, "that there was some friction between you and Grey during the show. You were on the other end of his earpiece, during the book and magazine bit, right?"

"That was me," Boone said, and he began to snicker. "Grey got pissed off because I started demanding a raise, right in the middle of the show. Which might not have been as professional as he would have liked," he added with a grin, "but it was a great time to put the screws to him, know what I mean? You know what they say, 'When you have them by the balls...'"

"'Their hearts and minds will follow.' Yes, I can see that mid-show would make for a perfect time to renegotiate one's contract."

"Aw, I knew he'd never go for it," Boone said, licking his fin-gertips and then taking another quick swig of beer. "I just wanted to screw with him one last time before calling it quits, know what I mean?"

"Why did you want to quit?"

Boone shrugged, which I soon realized was his go-to form of communication.

"I dunno," he said finally. "I was getting really tired of sitting in a cramped little room listening to Grey screw with people. And he was a pain in the ass. Plus my DJ business is really starting to take off."

"Boone is an amazing DJ," Nova added.

"It seems like a lot of people didn't like Grey," I said.

"You got that right," Boone agreed, taking one final gulp from the beer can and crushing the empty in his fist.

"Do you think anyone disliked him enough to kill him?"

Boone gave me a long look.

"Well, yes, Columbo," he said. "Obviously one person did. That's why he's dead. Know what I mean?" He snorted and shook his head contemptuously.

"Can I get you some more wine?" I asked Nova, deftly changing the topic away from just how stupid I was. She smiled and held out her glass.

"That would be sweet," she said. "I think this was a Shiraz. But, you know, whatever."

Before I could take the glass, Boone had moved in and cut off the exchange, taking the glass from her. "You've had enough," he said curtly.

"No I haven't," she said, trying to pull the glass back. "I've only had two."

"You've had four by my count."

"And how many beers have you had?" she asked, still struggling to regain ownership of the wine glass.

"Me and the amount of beer I've had are not the problem," he said. "I don't get stupid when I drink beer."

"That's because you start out stupid," she said. "In fact, I think the beer actually makes you smarter."

I started backing away.

"I'll just let you two discuss this on your own," I said, although I'm not sure either one of them heard me. The volume of their voices was still on the upswing when I shut the glass door, and the muffled sounds continued to reverberate in the glass cube as I made my way to the kitchen.

I considered grabbing another plate of food, but that same idea must have occurred to a lot of people simultaneously, because the counter that held the catering was now surrounded two-deep on all sides.

I squeezed my way through the kitchen and was turning to head back to the living room when I slammed into a woman who was just coming around the corner.

"Oh, excuse me," I said, jumping back to let her pass. It was then that I realized it was Megan.

"There you are," she said. "You went to get food and you never came back. Are you avoiding me?" She gave me a playful slap on the arm.

"Yes," I said, a bit tongue-tied. "I mean, no. I ran into some other people. Back there. On that porch-thing." I pointed vaguely in the general direction of the porch and nearly poked a passing woman right in the eye. "Oh, sorry."

Megan and I each squeezed back against our respective walls to let the woman through. The woman gave me a careful stare as she wiggled between us on her way to the living room.

"Oh, I love that porch. Isn't this house just wild?" she said, smiling widely. "It's so open and clear."

"Yes, but you know what they say about people who live in glass houses."

"They go through a lot of Windex?"

It took me a second to realize that she was joking with me, and then I recognized the humor in what she had said. I laughed and she joined me. Then I immediately realized that the laugh I had emitted might have been out of proportion to the quality of her joke.

In fact, I was sure it was. So I throttled the laugh down and then it petered out awkwardly. We stood there quietly for a moment as people struggled to get past and around us.

"Maybe we should find someplace else to talk," Megan suggested. "Where we won't be in the way."

Without waiting for a response, she turned and headed back toward the living room, but where everyone else was turning left, she veered right. The flow of traffic prevented me from following her immediately, and it was all I could do to not get pulled into the undertow that was sucking people back into the living room.

As I struggled to follow Megan, I recognized Clive Albans across the room. He was surrounded by a group of young women and it looked like he was demonstrating Scotch and Soda for them. They laughed and applauded his efforts when he finished the trick.

He spotted me and gave me a smile and a wink. I smiled back at him and continued to work at making my way through the throng.

I finally broke through the pack and turned right down a short hallway. By the time I finally caught up with Megan, she was seated comfortably on one of the clear Plexiglas steps that led to the second floor. She patted the space next to her invitingly and I sat down.

"So, how did your uncle like his reading?" she asked.

"Oh," I said, surprised by the question. "It was great. He loved it. Very informative." I hope that my response sounded more truthful than it actually was.

She sighed and visibly relaxed. "Oh, good," she said. "I'm so new to this, and completely clueless as to whether or not my psychic gifts are in any way helping people. So, I'm glad he was happy with what I saw."

"Yes," I agreed, trying desperately to come up with something positive he had said about the experience. Finally it came to me. "The dimes," I said quickly. "The thing about Aunt Alice leaving him dimes as a symbol of their love. That was dead on. He was very impressed by that."

"Oh, good, good," she said. "That was such a persistent image, stronger than any of the others. I'm glad it had meaning for him."

"Yeah, it really did," I said honestly. "So, where's Pete? Networking?"

She smiled. "No, he went back to the car to get me some ibuprofen."

"You have a headache?"

She shrugged. "Sort of."

We sat there for a few moments, listening to the music from the other room. "So, did you and Pete enjoy the memorial service?" I asked.

She sat quietly for what seemed like a long time before speaking. "I don't know. It's weird. He wanted to come, to be supportive and all."

She shook her head and looked down at her feet. "We're in such a funny, in-between place right now." She looked up at me. Her eyes were amazing, blue and literally sparkling. "You've gone through a divorce, so you must know what it's like."

"Yeah," I agreed. "I'm sure in some ways every divorce is different and in some ways they're exactly the same."

"So, how did you make that final break, to not being a couple anymore?"

I thought about this for a few moments.

"Well," I said, "it helped that my wife was sleeping with someone else. And then she moved in with him. Those two things really made it easier to call it quits."

She saw me smile and then she laughed and gave me another playful slap on the arm. "You're very funny," she said.

"You're not so bad yourself."

"I don't know about that," she said quietly.

Then the most amazing thing happened. She leaned against me. Not her full weight, but enough. Just the right amount, her shoulder against mine.

I sat perfectly still and for a few moments she leaned against me and it was the nicest thing I had felt in a very long time. And, for at least that instant, I stopped feeling like I was a Mediocre Fred.

She was separated, practically divorced; I had not come between them. I wouldn't be breaking up anything that wasn't already broken. And she was leaning against me.

If you can live a lifetime in a moment, I did. And then I heard the following five, amazing words:

"Can you take me home?"

I was stunned for a moment, frozen, unable to respond. And then it began to dawn on me that Megan had somehow said those five words without moving her lips. Plus she had altered her voice. And made it sound like her voice was coming from in front of me. Then, much later than I should have, I realized that someone else had said it.

We both looked up to see Nova standing in front of us. She had been crying. Running mascara had given her the look of a very attractive Goth raccoon.

She stood there sniffling, her slight shoulders heaving up and down, and then she spoke again in one continuous run-on sob. "I want to go home and I shouldn't drive because obviously I've had too much to drink and I'm not that stupid to drive myself and Boone won't take me because he's an ass and the booze is free and he wants to stay until Dr. Bitterman shuts down the bar and it's been a long day, a long week, a long fucking year, and I shouldn't drive and I want to go home, so will you drive me?"

I looked from Megan to Nova and back to Megan, who was staring at the girl with a real sadness in her eyes.

"Of course he will," she said softly.

"Of course I will," I echoed immediately.

"Eli will get you home safely," Megan added.

"Absolutely," I concurred.

"Thank you," Nova said, using her sleeve to wipe her nose.

I pulled a handkerchief from my pocket and offered it to her and then stood up. I looked down at Megan, who was smiling at me.

"Well..." I said, not sure how to bring this moment to a conclusion.

"I'll call you sometime," she said.

"That would be great," I said.

And then Nova blew her nose loudly into my handkerchief, effectively killing any romance that might have been building in the moment.

Five minutes later, we were in my car and pulling away from the house. Nova's crying had turned to sniffling and she looked very small in the passenger seat.

I gave the bizarre glass home one last look as we headed away down the street. The lights were on in every room and you could see people moving about, like little ants in a multi-million dollar ant farm.

Within the crowd, I recognized one lone, still figure. Boone was standing on the glass porch, another beer in his hand.

He appeared to be watching my car with great intensity as we drove away.

Chapter 10

"It's that house over there. The one on the right. No, left. It's on the corner." Nova pointed a long, thin finger as I drove, and I noticed that not only were her fingernails painted black, but also that tiny, sparkling stars were visible in that blackness. She saw me glancing at her nails and smiled proudly. "It's a special nail polish, I made it myself. I call it Infinite Universe. The stars actually glow in the dark. Cool, huh?"

"You should market that," I said, as I pulled the car into a parking space across the street from the unlit house that her incessant, if imprecise, stream of verbal directions had led us to.

"I will, someday, when I get around to it. But who has the time?" She opened the passenger door and stepped out, turning back to me as she did. "Will you come in until I get the lights on? I don't like going in without the lights on."

She didn't wait for a response, but closed the car door and was across the street, and halfway up the front steps, before I had even gotten myself unleashed from my seatbelt.

I got out of the car and looked around, not entirely certain where we were. I knew we were somewhere in the Prospect Park neighborhood in Southeast Minneapolis, a tangle of curved streets that encircle Tower Hill Park and border our sister city of St. Paul. Standing by the car I looked up and I could see the small light atop The Witch's Tower, a water tower at the top of the park. The peak of the tower, which really did resemble a witch's hat, was visible from just about anywhere in the Prospect Park neighborhood, but it wasn't a particularly helpful directional landmark, because you couldn't tell by looking at it which side of the park you were near.

It had been an informative, if a bit tiring, twenty-minute drive from Dr. Bitterman's house across town.

I don't know if it was due to the alcohol, but Nova talked nearly nonstop. I learned all about her living situation—currently without a permanent address, she was something of a professional house-sitter, moving from assignment to assignment; her boyfriend troubles—the most current being Boone, with Grey right behind that, and someone named Dewey before that; the quality of sex with said beaus—just okay with Boone, boring with Grey, transcendental with Dewey; and finally her deeply-held beliefs about her own, unique psychic gifts—a natural intuitive, she was best at communicating with animals and could also commune with fairies when the stars were properly aligned.

When all that information was jumbled in with her inexact driving directions—"Go left here...no wait, not here. Where are we?"—suddenly the low-grade headache I was experiencing made perfect sense.

Plus, on top of that, I realized after we left the reception that I had not actually ever gotten anything to eat.

It was just that kind of night.

By the time I reached the top of the steps, Nova had unlocked the front door and was standing back from it, apparently waiting for me to step into the darkness and search for the light switch.

"I probably should have left some lights on, but the sun was still out when I left."

"And yet, here it is, nighttime and it's dark. Tough thing to plan for." I looked at her and saw that my sarcasm was completely wasted. She was peering into the house, squinting.

"I think the light switch is on the left. No, the right. No, left."

I stepped into the house, placed my right hand on the right wall just inside the door and found the light switch—in the same spot you might find it in perhaps ninety-nine percent of the homes in America. I flipped the switch and the lights popped on, which produced a slight "Ooh" from Nova, as if we were witnessing a small and sadly unimpressive fireworks display.

"There you go," I said, standing back from my handiwork. "You're all set."

"Can you come in and help me check the house?" She waited for me to go in ahead of her.

"Check the house for what?"

"Strangers."

"Do you often get strangers?"

"I don't like to stay in an unfamiliar house at night until I've checked to make sure that no strangers have gotten in." Her tone was emphatic. I stepped into the house and she followed me, shutting and locking the front door behind us.

It was a pleasant, homey living room in what appeared to be a pleasant, homey house. The neighborhood was favored by professors at the nearby University of Minnesota campus, and this definitely felt like an educator's home. Two walls of the living room were lined with bookcases, while another held a large tapestry of Mexican origin. The hardwood floors were covered by worn but clean oriental rugs. A staircase just inside the foyer ran up to the second floor and a hall straight ahead of me appeared to lead into the kitchen. The far end of the living room was open, probably leading to a standard dining room. No strangers were in sight.

"Where would you like to start?"

"First we check this floor."

I shrugged and made my way through the living room, into the predicted dining room. I turned on the lights without requiring directions on light switch placement, and then made my way through the dining room into the adjoining kitchen. Nova followed noiselessly, three paces behind me. I switched on the light in the kitchen, glanced down the hall back toward the living room and foyer and then turned to Nova.

"So far, so good. Now what?"

"Make sure the back door is locked."

I walked over to the door and gave it a cursory check. It was, in fact, locked and bolted. "Ground floor is secure, ma'am," I said.

She smiled nervously. "Now the basement."

"Of course," I said. "The basement. A favored hiding spot for serial killers and lunatics."

"Don't make jokes," she said seriously, sounding more sober than she had in the last hour. "Check the basement."

The door to the basement was down the hall, between the kitchen and the front foyer. I stopped at the door. Nova stopped three steps behind me. I opened the door and turned to her.

"So even though movies have cautioned us for the last forty years to not go into the basement," I said with mock seriousness, "you're asking me to ignore all those warnings and go down there?"

She didn't even pause to think this over. "Yes," she said quickly. "And check the entire basement, including under the stairs and that creepy room in the back. And there's a trunk down there. Look in the trunk."

"Any job worth doing is worth doing well," I mumbled as I flipped on the light to the basement and headed down the stairs into the murk and beyond.

Once I reached the bottom, I looked up to see Nova, silhouetted in the doorway. I considered doing the old reach-your-own-arm-from-around-behind gag and drag myself further into the basement, screaming, but I realized that such an action would probably have put the poor thing into cardiac arrest. So I simply turned and continued into the basement.

The lighting was dim, even by basement standards, but I could see all four corners from where I stood and I saw no other creatures, humanoid or otherwise.

The footprint of a large, octopus-style furnace system was still visible on the floor, but it had been replaced with a slimmer, more modern version, which was tucked neatly in one corner.

A door hung halfway open across the room. I crossed to it and opened it completely, revealing a small pantry that once held pickled and stewed food supplies, but which now sat dusty and empty.

A quick check under the stairs revealed a pair of his and hers bicycles that had not seen sunlight for quite a while and three folded lawn chairs that has also seen better days.

I gave one last look around the basement and was about to head back upstairs when I remembered that Nova had mentioned a trunk. I turned and scanned the room again, finally spotting it on the other side of the furnace. Upon closer inspection, it hardly qualified as a trunk, and if someone were hiding in it, they couldn't be much more than three feet tall. But my mission included opening the trunk, so I stepped forward and flipped the two rusty latches, half expecting a demented jack-in-the-box to spring out. Sadly, nothing that exciting emerged. Instead all I found was a stack of musty *Life* magazines, along with the obligatory pile of *National Geographics*.

My mission accomplished, I returned to the stairs and headed back up to the first floor. "All clear. Now, onto the second floor?" I suggested as I turned off the basement light and shut the door.

"First check the back door."

"I did that already."

"We need to check it again."

I looked at the door and then looked at her. "Did you unlock it while I was downstairs?"

She shook her head categorically.

"Did you touch it in any way?"

Another head shake.

"Did anyone else come in here and touch it while I was in the basement?"

Head shake.

"But you still want me to check it again?"

She nodded. I sighed.

"Let's check the back door," I said cheerfully.

I walked the eight steps to the door. It was, in fact, still completely secured and locked. I jiggled the door handle for verisimilitude.

I looked to her and she turned and gestured down the hall toward the front door. I passed her and headed down there wordlessly. Without being asked, I double-checked the front door, which was also still locked. Nova had followed me. She gave me a smile of thanks and then looked up the stairs.

"Have you ever considered that house-sitting might not be the ideal occupation for you?"

"I love it during the day."

Unable to refute that train of logic, I headed up the stairs, with Nova three steps behind me.

The second floor consisted of a single hall with two doors on the left side, one door on the right, and one door at the far end. All the rooms were dark. "Which one shall we check first?" I asked as I turned to Nova, who stood motionless three steps below me on the staircase.

"First my room, then go clockwise."

"Clockwise."

"It works best that way."

I took a deep breath. "Which one is your room?"

"The first door. On the —"

She gave up trying to discern right from left and pointed to the first door on the right. I stepped in and found the light switch. I flipped the switch, which turned on a lamp on the bedside table.

This was clearly the master bedroom, with a large queen bed taking up most of the room. Without requiring direction, I inspected the closet and under the bed, and then stopped at the mirror over the dresser. I leaned forward and peered into it.

"What are you doing?" Nova asked from her position in the doorway.

"Checking the other side of the mirror."

"The other side?"

"Yeah. To make sure no one is there, on the other side."

Nova stepped forward tentatively and joined me. We both peered into the glass. I glanced over at her to see her earnestly staring into her reflection, and for a second I felt like a real ass.

"I think we're good," I said. "Keep an eye on it while I check the other rooms." She continued to stare into the mirror while I made my way out of the room and into the hall, shutting the door behind me.

Obediently moving clockwise, I checked the other two bedrooms, both of which were blissfully devoid of strangers. One was a home office—the other was a guest room that was now overrun with unwanted items from the rest of the house. I checked the small bathroom as well, including pulling back the shower curtain, and then headed back down the hall to the master bedroom.

"All clear," I said as I opened the door and walked into the room. I stopped dead in my tracks.

She was naked. Of course she was. Why wouldn't she be? Standing in the center of the room. Completely naked. I should have seen it coming.

"Oh my," was all that came out of my mouth.

She was stunning, of course, I expected that, but I had not anticipated the tattoos. She had a lot of tattoos, starting on her shoulders and moving, in varying patterns and illustrations, all the way down to her ankles. They meshed perfectly with the curves of her body, seeming to be a part of her, as natural as her skin. One design in particular—a half-moon, directly beneath her left breast—was exceptionally captivating, almost eclipsing the breast itself.

"What's this all about?" I finally said.

"I don't like to sleep alone," she said, sounding almost shy. I mean, for a naked person.

"And yet you insist on banishing strangers from the house."

"What?"

She was, admittedly, not my best comedy audience. I took a different tack. "Thanks, but I don't think so."

"You don't find me attractive?"

"On the contrary. Just the opposite."

"And you're not married."

"Yes, I'm not married."

"Do you have a girlfriend?"

"Sort of," I hedged.

"You do? Or don't?" My hedging confused her. To be honest, I was a little confused myself.

"I have someone I'm interested in."

"So that means you can't sleep with me?"

"In my world, yes."

She shook her head and nearly giggled, holding one hand up to her mouth. "You're weird."

"Hello, pot. Kettle's waiting for you in the lobby."

"What?"

"Never mind."

She turned and headed toward the bed, completely unselfconscious. She pulled the covers off. "I'm going to go to sleep."

"Then I'll be on my way," I said, moving toward the hall.

"No, no, no, no," she said plaintively. "Can't you stay until I fall asleep? I'll fall asleep faster if you stay."

I stood in the doorway for a long moment while she climbed into bed and got herself all comfortable and arranged. She smiled at me and gestured toward a high-back chair near the bed. Realizing there was no other gracious way out of the house, I made my way across the room and settled into the chair.

"Tell me a story," she said, as she reached over and flipped the switch on the table lamp, returning the room to darkness. The only light in the room came from the streetlight out the window. In the dim light I could barely see her as she laid her head on the pillow and closed her eyes.

"I don't know any stories," I said.

"Then do something magical."

"I can't work magic in the dark."

"Oh, I bet you could." This was followed by a wicked little laugh. "Come on. It will help me sleep."

"So, you want to fall asleep?" I said. "Let me see. I'm sure there's something in my act that fits that bill." I thought for a few moments and then an idea came to me. "Okay, here's one. My friend Nathan does this trick all the time. He's a kid's magician."

"I love kid's magicians," she said softly.

"I want you to pick a number between one and nine."

"Twelve," she answered quickly, and then giggled.

"Pick a number between one and nine and don't tell me what it is."

There was a long moment while she thought this through. "Got it," she said finally.

"Okay, take that number and multiply it by nine."

"Multiply it by nine?" Another pause. "Okay, I got it."

"Okay, now whatever that answer is, add those two digits together."

"Together?"

"Yes. Like, if you had 27, you'd add two and seven together."

"Oh. Got it."

"Now, whatever that total is, subtract five from it."

Her voice was very quiet. "I'm subtracting five."

"Now it gets fun."

"It's fun already."

"Okay, it gets more fun. Take the number you got when you subtracted five."

"Okay."

"And find the corresponding letter of the alphabet. Like, if you had one, that would be 'A," if you had two, that would be 'B."

"Okay." Another pause. I could see her lips moving silently in the light from the street lamp. "I've got the letter."

"Okay, now think of a country that starts with that letter."

There was a long silence and then she finally said, very softly, "I've got one."

"Now take the second letter in the name of that country and think of an animal whose name starts with that letter."

"Okay." Her voice was sounding very far away.

"Now think about the color of that animal."

"I've got the color." Her voice was just above a whisper.

"Using my magical powers, I can tell you that the country you were thinking of was Denmark."

"Yes. It was. It was Denmark." I could actually hear the smile in her voice.

"And the animal you were thinking of was an elephant."

"It was an elephant. A big elephant."

"And the color you were thinking of was—"

I stopped in mid-sentence, silently cursing myself. This is a very standard trick that always played out the same way. And I had stupidly forgotten the nearly inevitable outcome. The country was always Denmark. The animal was always elephant. And the color was always—

"And your color was...gray."

I waited for a reaction from Nova, and after what seemed like a very long time, she gave me one. The only sound in the house was her steady breathing. She had fallen asleep.

I sat for what felt like a long time in the dark, still room, enjoying the quiet, with only the sound of Nova's breathing breaking the silence. I had no immediate desire to get up. I had nowhere I needed to be, it had been a long, strange day, and the chair was more comfortable than it had first appeared.

I reviewed the events of the day, re-ran conversations through my head and tried, as best I could, to sort things out. In the end, answers eluded me.

My reverie was broken by a slight chirp from my iPhone, signaling the delivery of a text message. I glanced over at Nova, hoping that the soft sound had not awoken her, and was glad to see in the faint light that her eyes were still closed. I flipped off the ringer to forestall any future beeps, chirps, or actual ringing.

I didn't recognize the phone number from which the text had been issued. The text read, simply, *"Did u get the drunk girl home ok? M."*

I ran the initial *M* through my mind quickly and then it hit me. Megan. Texting me. At night. Would wonders never cease?

I texted back, making as little noise as possible so as not to rouse Nova. *"Yes. Safe and sound."*

Moments later a response came. *"Fun talking 2 u 2day."*

I hit the keys quickly and quietly, recognizing that the abbreviations Megan was employing might speed things up and yet opting against them. *"Me too. Good time."*

Her response was almost instantaneous. *"Again sometime?"*

I thought about the correct response for a long moment, weighing content and word choice. I settled on: *"Absolutely. Maybe lunch?"* I hit send and although I can't be certain, I may not have actually taken a breath until the response came.

"Sounds Gr8. Later in the week?"

I cheered silently and almost got up to dance around the chair, but then thought better of it. I didn't have enough material to get Nova back to sleep. Instead, I carefully typed and sent my reply. *"Yes."*

A reply came back through the ether with remarkable speed. *"Talk later. Sleep well. Gnight. M."*

I typed my response. *"Good night."*

I held the phone for a long time, happily scrolling back and forth through the text exchange. Then I shut the phone's screen off and set it in my lap, closing my eyes for what I thought would be a short rest before getting up, leaving the house, getting into my car and driving home.

When I opened my eyes, sunlight was streaming in through the bedroom windows and my iPhone was vibrating insistently against my leg.

Chapter 11

I looked down at the screen on my vibrating phone. It was Deirdre, although at some point in the past I had set the Caller ID so that it read, *"Ex-Wife (Probably Pissed)."* I looked around the room. Nova's bed was empty and the sun was clearly up. I considered my options for a long moment, and then pressed the answer icon.

"Good morning."

"Where the hell are you?"

"I'm fine, thanks, how are you?"

"Eli, I don't have time to play around," she said, the level of agitation in her voice at a peak I hadn't experienced recently. "I've been calling you since 6:30 this morning, the police are looking for you at your apartment, your uncle has no idea where you are, and Fred is about to issue an APB, listing you as a fugitive from justice."

If I had been groggy twenty seconds ago, I was now fully awake. "Why? What? What's going on?"

"What's going on is that Dr. Maurice Bitterman is dead."

For a split second I considered correcting her pronunciation of his first name and wisely thought better of it. "Dead? How dead?"

"What do you mean, how dead? Completely dead."

Now it was my turn to be agitated. "I meant, how did he die?"

"We can talk all about that when you get down here. Your options are to come in on your own or Fred will send uniformed officers to bring you in." She paused, her tone warming just a bit. "Personally, I would recommend the former."

"I'll be right there," I said and she broke the connection. I sat in the chair for a few more seconds. The house was completely still and quiet, with the exception of an odd hum coming from the floor below.

I stood up, feeling a bit rubbery in my legs, and headed toward the door and down the stairs.

The odd hum turned out to be Nova, who was seated in what looked to be a very uncomfortable yoga position in the center of the living room floor. Her eyes were closed and her mouth was open in the shape of an O. All of her hair had been pulled up into a tousled bun atop her head.

She was wearing more clothes than the last time I had seen her, but not by much. She stopped humming when she heard me come down the stairs but didn't open her eyes.

"Hey, sleepyhead, you're finally up. Want to go out to breakfast? Or I could make something. I'm a vegan but I make a mean poached egg."

There was an odd domesticity in her tone that I found surprisingly inviting. "Um, no thanks. Some other time. I've got to head out."

"That's cool," she said, her eyes still closed. "Maybe next time. Thanks again for the ride. And everything."

"No problem," I said, turning to the front door and flipping the deadbolt. "Do you want to get up and lock this after I go?"

She tilted her head quizzically to one side, but still didn't open her eyes. "Why?"

"No reason," I said. "No reason at all."

The room was once again filled with humming by the time I closed the door behind me.

As I approached my car I was surprised to see that absolutely none of the snow that had been so feverishly predicted by the weathermen had materialized.

Franny had been right yet again.

*   *   *

Fifteen minutes later I found myself seated in the sunny, glass-walled conference room in Deirdre's workplace. Deirdre and Homicide Detective Fred Hutton were in a deep, hushed conversation just outside the room. He stood a head taller than her and yet his current posture somehow gave the impression that she was standing over him, whacking him with a ruler.

They reached some sort of impasse and Deirdre marched into the conference room, setting a small stack of file folders on her side of the large, deeply polished table that took up the lion's share of the room.

"I feel like I'm spending way too much time trying to keep you out of jail lately," she grumbled as she flipped open one of the folders, took out her reading glasses, and quickly scanned the first document.

"Do you feel that I should be in jail?" I asked cautiously.

"No, I don't," she said flatly. "Which is why I'm working so hard to keep you out."

"So Dr. Bitterman is dead and somehow you...or, more to the point, Homicide Detective Fred Hutton thinks I'm involved?"

"In a word, yes."

"And what has led him to that conclusion?"

"We'll get to that in a minute. I'd rather keep you two apart for as long as I reasonably can." She continued to page through her documents, almost as if I weren't in the room.

"Did the transcript of my interrogation come back?" I finally asked.

"Yes, Eli, it did," she answered without looking up.

"And he read it?"

"Yes he did."

"The part at the end? Where I sang the song?"

"The entire thing."

"Anybody else read it?"

She sighed deeply and looked up at me, peering over the top of her reading glasses. "Eli, everybody read it. In fact, the MP3 of you singing nearly crashed the server, it got e-mailed around so much."

"Oh." I sat silently while she finished the report.

She set the papers down, sat back, and took off her glasses. She glanced over at the glass wall behind me and gave her head an almost imperceptible nod.

A moment later, Homicide Detective Fred Hutton entered, followed by his partner, Miles Wright, carrying a manila folder. They both sat on Deirdre's side of the table, looking at me coolly. Homicide Detective Fred Hutton looked particularly icy.

"I want to open by saying that this is all preliminary," she said. "Eli, as I'm sure I've said to you many times in the past, the office of the District Attorney works closely with the Minneapolis Police Department on major crimes. We have the responsibility and authority to direct the police on investigative issues and we make recommendations on charging decisions, because after all, we will be responsible for prosecuting those charges. You are here for questioning today because you are directly linked to the deaths of Walter Graboski, also known as Grey, and now to the death of Dr. Maurice Bitterman."

"How am I linked? Can you define 'directly?'"

"I'll get to that in a moment," she said. "Here's what we know so far. At around four-thirty this morning, Dr. Bitterman was found dead by his personal trainer, who apparently was in the habit of arriving at that hour for Dr. Bitterman's exercise regimen.

"He found the doctor unconscious in his bed. Paramedics were dispatched and pronounced him dead at the scene. The Medical Examiner's initial ruling is death by poisoning, but as I said, this is all preliminary."

"Poisoning?" I repeated.

"Yes, we believe so."

"But what about everyone else at the reception? There were at least a hundred people there, all eating. Even I—" I stopped in mid-sentence, realizing that I had, in fact, not eaten anything at the reception. I decided to hold onto that tidbit for the time being.

"There have been no other reports of illness or death resulting from food or drink ingested at that reception. I will say, though, that since there was no official guest list, we're having no small amount of trouble locating all of the other attendees."

I looked from her to Homicide Detective Fred Hutton, who was burning holes through me with his stare. "But if there was a mass poisoning of a hundred people, you would have heard something by now," I offered.

"We agree. And in fact, we believe that Dr. Bitterman wasn't poisoned via the food, but was in fact poisoned while he slept." She let that sink in. "What do you know about sleep apnea?"

"Not a lot. I know that Bitterman suffered from it."

Homicide Detective Fred Hutton raised one eyebrow at this statement and sat up a little straighter in his chair. Deidre made a point of not looking at him.

"And how did you come by that information?" she asked.

"He told me. Yesterday. At the reception."

She considered this, then put on her glasses and skimmed the notes. "Dr. Bitterman regularly used a device called a CPAP machine, which stands for Continuous Positive Airway Pressure. The device was in operation last night. As I understand it, the patient straps a mask to his face, covering his nose and mouth. This mask is connected by a small hose to the machine, which administers a continuous, pre-determined level of air pressure into the patient's mouth and nose while he sleeps. This air pressure, in theory, prevents the patient's airways from constricting while asleep, which is the primary cause of sleep apnea."

She looked up at me, again peering over the top of her glasses. "It's also effective at controlling snoring, in case you're interested. Unless you've outgrown that." She returned to her notes.

"One of the features of the CPAP machine that Dr. Bitterman owned is a small, removable water storage reservoir, which holds about a cup of water. When the machine is operational, a heating element under the reservoir warms the water, which moisturizes the air being blown at the patient's face."

"Like a miniature humidifier," I offered.

I regretted making this comment as soon as it came out of my mouth. Homicide Detective Fred Hutton had continued to stare at me, but now glanced down and made a brief note on his pad. I decided it would be best if I didn't offer any further comments on the operation of the CPAP machine or sleep apnea in general.

"Yes, like a miniature humidifier," she repeated. "We believe at some point a capsule containing poison...we suspect cyanide...was introduced into the reservoir. When the machine was turned on, the poison was released into Dr. Bitterman via his respiratory system. Death would have occurred very soon after he fell asleep."

"Cyanide?" I said. "Where would someone get cyanide?"

"It's not as difficult as you might think. It's commonly used to clean precious metals, and also frequently used to kill rodents and other pests."

She looked up at me, to see if I had any comments to offer. Recognizing I had none, she continued.

"We suspect," she said, "that Bitterman used the machine every night, which means that the poison capsule would likely have been introduced into the water reservoir at some point yesterday. Perhaps during the reception."

She took off her reading glasses, closed the folder, and leaned back in her chair.

The three of them looked at me for what seemed like a long time. I got the impression that it was my turn to talk.

"So, let me see if I understand," I said, choosing my words with care. "You think someone at the reception snuck up to Bitterman's bedroom and slipped a poison capsule into his CPAP machine."

They looked at me without expression. Deidre gave me the slightest of nods.

"Given that there were at least a hundred people at that party, and that I had never even met Bitterman before yesterday," I continued, "I'm not entirely certain why you feel I am linked...directly or otherwise...to this crime."

"You make a good point," Deirdre said. "And with only those facts, you wouldn't be. However, as part of the investigation, the police bagged the CPAP machine and were preparing to send it down to the lab for fingerprint analysis and other tests. When they picked it up, guess what they found attached to the bottom of the machine?"

I shrugged. I literally had no idea.

Deirdre turned to Homicide Detective Fred Hutton, who turned to Miles. Very slowly and deliberately, Miles opened the manila folder on the table in front of him and picked up a clear plastic evidence envelope. He held it up. Despite the indecipherable writing on the front of the packet, I could see the contents quite clearly.

It was a playing card.

The King of Diamonds.

"This playing card directly connects this homicide to the murder of Grey," Deirdre said dryly. "A crime to which you are...to some degree or another...still inexorably linked." She paused for a long moment. "Do you care to posit any idea on how the card got there?" she finally asked.

I shook my head.

"All right," Deirdre said, starting to wrap things up. "There is a certain degree of disagreement between the District Attorney's office and the Homicide division as to the next best step to take with you. Our position is that there is not enough evidence to hold you or to charge you with a crime."

"Currently," Homicide Detective Fred Hutton added, speaking the only word he said thus far.

"Yes, currently," Deirdre agreed. "When that changes, we will certainly be in touch."

"So I'm free to go?" I asked.

"Eli, you've always been free to go," She answered. "Try to keep it that way."

I gave the trio one last look. They stared back at me like three-quarters of Mount Rushmore, but without the sense of madcap fun the monument provides. I stood up and headed toward the door.

And then I had a thought.

"I'm sure this has occurred to all of you," I said as I reached the door and turned back to face them, "but don't you find it interesting that the psychic who made his living with his *second sight* was murdered by being stabbed through the eyes, and now the psychic who's a hypnotherapist has been murdered in his sleep? That's sort of an odd coincidence, isn't it?"

Judging by the way they stared back it me, it became immediately clear that this idea had, in fact, not yet occurred to them.

Someday, perhaps when I'm very old, I'll learn to keep my big mouth shut.

The interview, which five seconds earlier had been officially concluded, instantly resumed. They didn't have many more questions, but for some reason they felt the need to ask the same ones over and over again.

Nearly ninety minutes later I left Deirdre's office and was halfway through the building's exit door when I heard a muffled voice calling my name. I looked over and saw Clive Albans on the other side of the revolving door, on his way into the building. He gave me a wave and a big smile.

I waved back, continued pushing the door and stepped out of the building. Clive revolved with the door and a moment later joined me on the front steps.

"Are they done with you?" he asked breathlessly.

"For now," I said. "How did you know they were talking to me?"

"The walls have ears," he said, waving his hands in what I guessed was supposed to be a spooky manner. "Two murders, both psychics, very bizarre, don't you think?"

"Sure," I said, trying not to stare at his outfit, which today consisted of a pale blue leisure suit from the late seventies. He wore shiny black boots that made him even taller than usual.

"This has taken my writing project in an entirely different direction," he continued. "Fake psychics is one thing, but fake dead psychics can put one on the bestseller lists."

"So you're no longer just writing a newspaper article?"

"I think this is a book now. It feels like a book. This will be big." He cocked his head toward the building. "I've got to run. I've come here to see what I can find out from the local constabulary. But promise me this, Eli."

"What?"

"If you're the killer, be a dear and give me an exclusive."

He was so off the charts that I couldn't help but smile. "Clive, you can count on it."

"That's a good fellow." And with that he stepped back into the revolving door and disappeared into the building.

I parked my car in my spot behind Chicago Magic and entered via the back door. As I closed the door behind me, I could hear Uncle Harry out front with a customer, in the midst of a familiar diatribe.

"Yes," I could hear him saying in an exasperated tone, "I'll happily sell you this illusion. But not until you demonstrate mastery, or at the very least proficiency, in the most recent item you bought. Which I believe was just two days ago, if I'm not mistaken."

I quickly stepped into the store to find Harry behind the counter and Pete in front of it, at a retail impasse.

"Hi guys, what's going on?" I asked nonchalantly. Harry, upon hearing my voice, immediately abandoned his discussion with Pete and headed over to me.

"Buster, where have you been? The police were here. They wouldn't tell me why."

"Not a big deal," I said reassuringly. "Just my ex-wife's new husband with his undies in a bunch."

Harry was instantly relieved. "Oh, thank God. This morning, when I saw that you hadn't come back from that memorial service, I started to fear the worst."

"That I was the next victim?"

"No, that you had a chance to get laid and you blew it."

Harry might not believe in psychics, but he was oddly clairvoyant at times.

I decided to change the subject. "Hey, have you had lunch yet?"

He shook his head, his mind now completely off his conversation with Pete. "No, not yet."

I gently took him by the shoulder and steered him toward the stairs. "Why don't you go up and get lunch started and I'll finish up down here and then come join you?"

"That's fine," he said, starting up the steep stairs, grasping onto the handrail for support. Then he turned and stated emphatically, "But I better not hear the ring of the cash register while I'm up there." He very pointedly did not look at Pete as he returned to his climb.

"When it comes to not making sales, Uncle Harry, I'm your man," I called after him.

He responded to this with a grunt and a harrumph and then disappeared from sight.

I turned back to Pete. "Sorry about that. Harry can be something of a hard-ass when it comes to learning magic."

"So I discovered," Pete said. "All I asked for was a Rubik's Cube illusion that I saw this morning on YouTube and thought was kind of cool..."

I put my hand up, signaling that he should lower his voice. "Oh, Lord, you didn't use the word 'YouTube,' did you?"

"No," he answered, matching my whispered tone.

"Good." I gently steered Pete down to the end of the counter.

"You have to understand that in Harry's day...hell, even when I was a kid...you'd never show anyone an illusion, particularly another magician, until you had completely mastered it. I made the mistake of showing him a clip of something on YouTube, a guy in Japan who's got this amazing act. When the clip was done, he started clicking around, seeing all those videos uploaded by goofs who get a trick in the mail one day and then next day are broadcasting it on the Internet. He was apoplectic...I thought he was going to have a stroke."

"I don't know how you deal with him," Pete confided. "He scares the hell out of me. It's like he can see into my head and knows what I'm thinking."

I smiled. "Well, if it's any consolation, you're not alone in that. He once made Uri Geller break out in hives."

"So let me see if I understand this...I have to be one hundred percent perfect with one trick before he'll sell me another one?"

I shrugged. "It's not a hard and fast rule. He does it on a case-by-case basis. If you're a kid looking to change a nickel into a quarter, he'll give you a pass, but he'll probably also sell you a book on magic. But once you begin playing with the higher-end stuff, new rules start to apply."

"Eli, I'm a realtor, just looking for something I can impress my clients with. Something to make me memorable."

"Isn't selling their house enough?"

He shrugged and leaned on the counter. "Depends on the market. Anything that gives me an edge, I have to pursue it. Plus, it's fun. I did that cut-and-restored rope thing to a client a week ago, and two days later his brother called to give me his business. Was it the magic trick? Who knows? But I bet it didn't hurt."

"And now you want the magic Rubik's Cube?"

"Yeah, the little one. You know, so I can carry it around in my pocket."

I glanced upstairs, where I could hear Harry banging around in the kitchen. Assured that he wasn't on his way back down, I slid open the back panel on one of the display cases and pulled out the cube—a neat little gimmick that goes from a normal-looking Rubik's Cube to a completely solved one in the blink of an eye. Again making sure that we weren't about to be interrupted, I handed it to Pete, who took it happily.

"Cool." While he examined it with one hand, he reached into his coat and pulled out his wallet with the other. "How much do I owe you?"

I held up my hand quickly to quiet him.

"Sorry," he whispered. "How much do I owe you?"

I shook my head. "Let's not push our luck. Pay me some other time." I headed toward the front door, hoping that he would follow me. He did, but not nearly at the speed I would have preferred. He kept eyeing different items on the walls and the shelves and in the display cases. I stood by the front door, waiting for him. My phone beeped, and I pulled it out of my pocket.

"You know what's weird," he said as he finally made it to the front door.

"What?" I asked as I looked at the text that had come in.

It was from Megan. It said, simply, *"Lunch? 2day? MayB now? M."* I read it twice and didn't hear Pete's next comment. I looked up at him, tilting the phone so that he couldn't see the screen.

"I'm sorry, what did you say?" I said.

"I said, it's weird that I feel so guilty."

All I heard was the word 'guilty.' I was instantly afraid he had somehow read that look on my face. "Excuse me?"

"When I do a trick for someone," he continued, "and I fool them, I start to feel guilty, like I'm lying or something."

I quickly transformed my sigh of relief into a feigned sigh of compassion. "That's the bane of the magician's existence," I agreed as I opened the shop door. "In order to master our craft, we have to master lying. But it's in pursuit of a higher cause. As Harry always taught me, 'Don't sweat it...just pull the rug out from under them.'"

Pete considered this for a moment.

"I suppose you're right," he said. He stepped into the doorway. "I've got an open house to get to. That will give me some time to work on this." He patted the pocket where he'd put his new Rubik's Cube trick. "And I promise I won't show it to anyone until I've mastered it. Or until tomorrow...whichever comes first."

We laughed and as he headed toward his car, I locked the door and turned the open sign around. I re-read Megan's text and quickly sent a reply, choosing my words carefully.

Then I went upstairs to break the news to Harry that I wouldn't be joining him for lunch.

"I'm so upset about Dr. Bitterman," Megan said after we had placed our order and the waitress had disappeared.

We were in a back corner of Pepito's, the very fine Mexican restaurant two doors down from Chicago Magic. It was the end of the lunch rush and the crowd was beginning to thin out.

"He was still so young, so vibrant. Do you know if they have any idea what the cause of death was?"

"They're considering a number of different scenarios," I said tactfully. There was an awkward pause, one of those moments when you realize how little you know about the other person and aren't sure where to head conversationally. We were saved, temporarily, by the quick return of the waitress who delivered Megan's glass of red wine. She set it on the table and, being an excellent waitress, disappeared without a word.

"Are you sure you don't want something to drink?" Megan asked again as she unclasped a bracelet from around her wrist.

I shook my head. "Too early in the day for me," I said.

"It would be too early for me, too, if I hadn't discovered amethyst." She took her bracelet and dipped it into the glass of wine, as if it were a teabag that happened to be made out of silver and crystals. She looked up and smiled at my expression, which I imagine was on a spectrum somewhere between amused and confused. "Amethyst detoxifies alcohol, so that you don't get drunk. In Greek, the word amethyst means 'not drunken.'"

"That actually works?" I asked.

"I don't know, but after a couple of glasses you tend to stop caring."

She used her napkin to dry off the bracelet and then took a sip of wine, smiling contentedly. "So, everybody seems to know you here," she said with a touch of amazement. "The hostess, the waitress...even cooks were waving at you from the kitchen when we walked in. Do you come here a lot?"

I shrugged. "On and off. Not so much anymore. But I spent a lot of time here in my late teens and early twenties. I worked here."

"Were you a waiter?"

"No, I did magic. Table to table."

"You were the house magician? That is adorable," she said, smiling broadly. "What sorts of things did you do?"

"Oh, the typical stuff. Some card work, some coin work. Cut and restored a rope. Make your watch disappear. Perfectly timed to cover the duration between when the order was placed and the food arrived."

She leaned forward, excited. "Do something for me now."

"What, right now?"

"Please. Please, please."

I patted my pockets, which may have looked like a show business move, but was actually designed to see what I might have on my person to create a spontaneous performance. "I can't believe that I've violated the one rule I religiously tell my students... Always travel with a pack of cards."

I looked around the table to see what might be handy. "Well, it's sort of a stupid trick," I said as I grabbed the saltshaker, "but it will have to do in a pinch."

I slid the saltshaker back and forth smoothly across the top of the table a few times, and then deftly covered it with my napkin. Megan watched closely, her eyes following the movement of the covered shaker as I danced it around the tabletop a couple more times.

"These restaurant tables may seem solid," I said, improvising some patter, "but they all have a weak spot...a point that isn't nearly as strong as the rest. With a little testing, and practice, you can actually locate that spot. In fact, I think I've found it, right here."

With that, I suddenly slammed my hand down, hard, on the covered saltshaker, flattening the napkin against the table. At that same instant, there was the distinct sound of something hitting the carpet beneath the table. I lifted up the napkin off the tabletop to reveal that the saltshaker was now gone.

Megan's hand had flown to her mouth, her eyes wide. Then, almost in unison, we both leaned over and peered under the table. There, sitting on the floor, was the saltshaker. I reached under the table and picked it up.

"Holy crap," Megan exclaimed, barely squelching a yelp. "I love it. Don't tell me how you did that. I don't want to know."

"It's magic," I said, replacing the saltshaker and putting my napkin back in my lap. "So, if your grandmother owned this block, how come I never saw you around here when I was younger?"

"We lived in Michigan," she said, taking another sip of wine. "Sometimes we'd visit, but we didn't hang around here so much. She had property in St. Paul where we'd go play and stuff, but we didn't hang out in Minneapolis much at all."

"And now you're in charge of all that property?"

"Well, it's not all that much, really. She sold a few things before she died. Pete's helping me get rid of the rest. With the exception of this block, of course. I wanted to stay here. There's just something special about it."

"Well, I agree," I said, taking a couple of the tortilla chips from the basket on the table. "I've had the chance to travel quite a bit, both as a kid with my uncle and as a working magician myself, but I am always drawn back to this particular spot."

"Speaking of your uncle, here's something I've been meaning to ask you... Why does he call you Buster?"

I shrugged as I munched on the chip. "Well, that's a short and not-too-interesting story."

"Tell me anyway. We need to talk about something until our food gets here. I don't want to fill up on chips." She pushed the basket of chips away, out of her reach but well within mine.

"All right. Well, in addition to being my uncle, Harry is also my godfather. Here's what you need to know about Harry Marks... He's a student of the history of magic. Years ago there was another magician named Harry that you might have heard of...Harry Houdini."

Megan nodded, her eyes sparkling as she listened. "Everyone's heard of Harry Houdini. He was a great magician."

"Actually, he was a so-so magician, but a phenomenal promoter and showman. If you're looking for an amazing magician from that era, look at a guy named Howard Thurston." I realized I was getting off track. "Anyway, Harry Houdini's godson was a kid named Joseph Keaton...he was the son of a couple Vaudeville performers Houdini had worked with. When the kid was quite small, Houdini nicknamed him Buster...there's several different versions as to why...and the name stuck. Then the kid grew up and became famous himself."

Megan thought through the story so far and finally put the pieces together. "Buster Keaton," she said.

"That's right," I said. "Buster Keaton. Somehow, in Uncle Harry's twisted brain, it made sense to nickname me Buster, which he did and it's stuck. At least with him. My aunt always called me Eli."

"And they raised you?"

"Mostly, from about age ten, after my parents died." I looked up to see that the waitress was approaching with our food. "And, speaking of death, here comes one of the deadliest, hottest tamales you will find this side of Guadalajara. Consider yourself warned."

The waitress set our food in front of us and conversation ceased for a few moments. "So, yesterday," Megan began between mouthfuls, "we started to talk about divorce."

I chewed for a moment before answering. "Yes, we did."

"Do you ever regret getting divorced?"

"Well, to be honest, I didn't really feel like I had a choice. It was over; it was that simple. The divorce was just the paperwork."

We continued to eat quietly for a few moments.

"How about you?" I ventured. "Are you having second thoughts?"

She immediately shook her head. "I know it's the right thing," she said. "I mean, I know in my heart. Plus, I went to two completely different psychics, and they both said that divorce was the right move. Independently," she added.

"Sounds like you've got it covered."

She nodded in agreement. "I guess it's just a matter of slogging through it."

"Is Pete making it hard?"

"No, not at all. He's been really good about it. I mean, he's dragging his feet a bit, because I think he's still holding out hope. But that's normal, right?"

"I guess so. I mean, if we were married, I'd be very hesitant to let you go."

This produced a smile from Megan that bordered on shy. The restaurant was now nearly empty and the waitstaff were cleaning tables and getting things set for dinner. Faintly on the sound system I could hear what sounded like a Mexican version of "Seasons in the Sun," all in Spanish. In case you're wondering, it didn't sound any better in that language either.

After we finished lunch, we walked slowly down the sidewalk, toward our respective retail establishments. It was cloudy and chilly, with a real snap in the air that let you know with no uncertainty that winter in all its glory was just around the corner, thank you very much.

We stopped in front of Chicago Magic, neither one of us certain what the correct protocol was for ending this, our first quasi-date.

Megan looked from me to the items Harry had put on display in our small front window. For Halloween he had arranged a couple of jack-o'-lanterns, each with a white stuffed bunny popping out of it. In the background were two skeleton cutouts. It wasn't exactly Macy's at Christmas time, but it looked nice.

Megan turned to me suddenly. "I know what I wanted to ask you," she said a little breathlessly. "It's been driving me crazy." She stepped closer to me, in classic close-talker mode.

"I'm all attention," I said.

"You know, down there, on the parkway," she said, pointing vaguely over my left shoulder. "It wasn't here the last time I came to visit my grandmother, and now it is, and it's the weirdest thing."

I waited patiently for her to land on a noun. "What are you trying to say?" I finally asked.

"What's the deal with that rabbit?" she blurted out at long last.

"Oh," I said, comprehending. "The statue. Of the rabbit." I nodded along with her. "Actually, no one knows for sure. It just showed up one day. Out of the blue."

I shrugged and looked at her with complete seriousness. She cocked her head to one side and then gave my arm a hard but playful slap.

"You got me," she said. "You completely got me on that one."

Then she took me completely by surprise by leaning in and giving me a warm but impulsive kiss, right on the lips. She tasted soft and sweet and oh-so-slightly of chilies. And then, just as quickly, she turned and headed down the sidewalk toward her store.

"See you around, Buster," she said without turning back.

I stood there, watching her go, and I realized that—although I had never had occasion to use the word or even say it out loud in my entire life—I was now, at this very moment and for the first time, gobsmacked.

Completely, utterly gobsmacked. And it felt great.

Chapter 12

"They *still* think you're a murderer? Well, that's a load of malar-key."

"Actually, now they think I'm a double murderer."

"Double malarkey, then."

Harry and I were having breakfast in his kitchen and I was bringing him up to speed on the death of Dr. Bitterman and my current standing with the Minneapolis Police Department, which could best be defined as just to the right of iffy. I cleared the plates and came back with the coffee pot for refills all around.

"So what's your next move?" he asked, adding fake sugar, which he's allowed to have, and real cream, which is forbidden. The action instantly turned the coffee from rich dark brown to ashen white.

"I don't have a next move," I said, replacing the coffee urn and returning to my chair. "Unless you count doing my darnedest to stay out of jail for a crime – two crimes, now – that I didn't com-mit."

Harry shook his head. "You need a next move. Times like this call for action, not complacency. You've got to be, what's the term they use nowadays," he said, searching for the word and finally finding it. "Proactive. Grab the bull by the whatever."

I considered this. "So, what steps are you recommending that I take, pro-actively?" I asked, pouring the rest of the cream into my cup to help deaden the coffee's acidic taste.

"Oh, the usual," he said brightly. "Revisit the crime scenes. Interview the witnesses. Evaluate the evidence. Create a hypothesis and then take steps to prove or disprove it. Basic scientific method."

"But that could take all morning," I whined.

"Don't be a smart ass," he said in a grave tone. "That ex-wife of yours can only keep the wolf at the door for so long, and then you're going to have to pay the piper."

"Metaphor police," I called out. "Metaphor police."

"Oh, joke all you want," he grumbled as he sat back and took a long sip of the beige coffee. "I'm just saying, no one on the police force is looking out for your best interests and if your name is going to be cleared, odds are you're the one who's going to have to do it."

We sat in silence for a few moments. "Actually," I said finally, acquiescing, "there are a couple of people I'd like to talk to. Just to clear up some of the questions in my own mind."

"Excellent. That's the spirit," Harry said as he got up to take his cup to the counter. This new sense of purpose seemed to take ten years off his normally measured movements. "I'll go with you. Help you make sure that no stones are left unturned."

He set his cup in the sink and began to rummage around in his pockets. "Now where are my keys? Oh, my, I forgot about these." He pulled two coins out of his pocket and held them up for me. "These are just since yesterday morning," he said.

"What do you mean?"

"I mean, I found two more dimes. Since yesterday morning. Just walking down to the mailbox on the corner. Can you believe that?"

"Well, that is interesting. You should hang onto all the ones you find."

"Oh, I'm already doing that."

He moved past me, toward the stairs, and as he did he deposited the two coins in a small Mason jar that sat on a small knick-knack shelf near the doorway. He bent down and straightened the worn, braided throw rug that sat at the top of the staircase, then headed down the stairs.

"Let's get a move on," he said as his voice disappeared down the narrow, steep stairway into the shop below.

"I'll be right there," I called after him, taking my own coffee cup over to the sink, but never really taking my eyes off the Mason jar. The cup deposited, I made a beeline to the jar and studied it for a long moment.

I'm terrible at those "Guess How Many Jelly Beans Are in the Jar" contests, and so I had no real idea how many dimes were in the Mason jar. But there were a lot of them—they covered the entire bottom of the jar. How many was that? More than ten, for sure. But thirty? Possibly. More than thirty? Also possible.

I picked up the glass jar and gave it a gentle shake, listening to the coins as they danced around inside, then set it down and headed to the shop.

The official opening time for Chicago Magic is, at best, a moving target. I can safely say that it occurs at some point in the morning, Monday through Saturday, but you'd be foolish to set your watch.

In fact, there was one quiet day without a single customer when—at closing time—we went to close up shop and discovered that we'd never actually unlocked the front door. When I pointed out this oversight to Harry, he was sanguine on the topic, reasoning that anyone who really, really wanted to come in only had to knock.

I was reminded of this as I descended the steps from Harry's apartment into the store, because I was greeted by the sound of someone knocking on the front door in a manner that could only be described as lackluster.

At first, I wasn't even sure that it was an actual knock. It was as if the very act of raising one's arm and striking one's hand against the door was simply too exhausting and that attitude was reflected in the knock itself.

"Nathan's here," Harry said as he took down his coat from the hook by the back door. "Sounds like he's in a good mood, too," he added.

Harry was correct on at least one point. It was Nathan, who stood morosely outside the front door with two large shopping bags, one in each hand. He was not dressed as a pirate today, but instead in torn jeans and a t-shirt that I believe was the same one he was wearing when I first met him fifteen years earlier. Over this ensemble he wore a leather bomber jacket, another piece of his clothing that never looked new yet never seemed to age.

"Morning, Nathan," I said cheerfully as I swung the door open.

"Yes, it is that," he agreed flatly as he passed me in the doorway. "No getting around it."

He hefted one of the bags up and set it atop the first display case. The other one he set on the floor. It made a distinctive *clank* when it connected with the tile floor.

"I brought back the balloon gag," he said and he bent down and opened the top of the bag, pointing out the items within. "The tank, the belt, the hose and nozzle, and all the leftover balloons."

"Great. How'd it work with the kids?" I was anxious to hear if it had produced the desired effect.

"Oh, it went okay. I think it went okay," he droned in his emotionless intonation, his head bobbing rhythmically as he spoke. His manner made it sound like it had been a massive bomb, but then everything he described sounded that way, so in my mind the jury was still out.

"And..." I said, prodding him for more information.

"Well," he said, considering his words, "when I finished the first balloon, I let go of it and the air circulation in the room picked it up and it just gently floated over to the birthday kid. Right to him...it looked like it was planned, you know. It was like out of a movie. It just drifted over to him, just above his head, and sat there. Kids started cheering, moms were crying, dads were asking for my business card, so yeah, it worked pretty good."

"That's great," I said, picking up the paper bag and carrying it toward the back of the store. "Let me know when you need it again and I'll make sure that the tank is refilled."

I sat the bag down in my "To Do" area, which still included restocking the gag gifts. The carton of fart spray sat opened and untouched from several days earlier when I had begun that task. I picked up the carton and set it atop one of the display cases, taking out a couple of the cans to act as a visual reminder of what still needed to get done.

"Yeah, that's what I wanted to talk to you about," Nathan said, leaning one elbow lazily on the counter next to his other shopping bag. Seeing that our departure was, for the moment, delayed, Harry sat on a stool by the back counter.

"I've got a gig next week," Nathan continued. "A birthday party, about twenty kids, out in North Oaks. Turns out it's the same date as my cousin's wedding in Park City, out in Utah. I was wondering if you'd like to cover for me? I brought all the stuff," he said, gesturing to the bag he'd placed on the counter. "Nothing too difficult, nothing out of your league."

"Me? Be a kid's magician?" I asked in mock amazement.

"Hey, trust me, it's a lot harder than it looks," Nathan replied.

"Of course it is," Harry echoed from the back of the shop.

He got off his stool and headed toward us. "It's a fine and noble tradition, that of the children's magician. You see," he said, moving into lecture mode, "the primary difficulty with children's magic is that...to a child...everything is magic. You put bread in a toaster and out pops toast. That's magic. You put a plastic card in a machine at the mall and out pops money. That's magic."

"Harry's right," Nathan said. "Kids aren't impressed with magic. What impresses kids is when you screw up. And then screw up again. And then you get it right. They eat that up."

I considered what he had said. "Screw up, screw up again, and then get it right?" I repeated.

Nathan nodded.

"I can do that," I said confidently. "Hell, that's basically a description of my act."

I got the details of the upcoming kids' show from Nathan, and he showed me the pirate costume and the other props that he'd packed into the shopping bag, having anticipated that I would agree to cover the gig for him.

Then Harry and I locked up the store, which to that point had only essentially been open for about five minutes.

After an amiable drive during which Harry continued his lecture on the purity of children's magic, we found ourselves in front of Akashic Records, a funky store on the south edge of downtown Minneapolis.

The store was visible from the freeway, and although I had driven by it on that same freeway for years, this was my first attempt at finding it via side streets. This involved a couple of wrong turns and the sudden and surprising appearance of a one-way street, but eventually we found the store, parked the car in the adjacent lot and headed toward the entrance.

A sign on the store's front door declared 'This establishment bans dangerous weapons,' which immediately produced a hearty chuckle from Harry. "But I'm guessing that non-dangerous weapons are welcomed with open arms," he said wryly as we pushed open the door and stepped into the shop.

The first thing that hit us was the smell, followed immediately by the smell.

Of course there was patchouli, but that was the least of it. In fact, for once the patchouli was almost refreshing.

Imagine that your grandmother had spent the last forty years assembling every smelly, putrid, flowery candle on the face of the earth. And we're not talking candles with complementary odors. These are candles that were in a fighting mood, all elbows and attitude. And then imagine that your grandmother had stored all those candles in one cramped closet and one day your overweight, mean-spirited, pimply cousin locked you in that closet for an hour. That comes close to describing the intensity of the olfactory assault, but not entirely.

It was clear that the store sold candles, we had determined that by the wall of stench that had bombarded us at the door, but the rest of the inventory was a bit mind-boggling and perhaps even schizophrenic.

Incense, rock posters, jewelry, political posters, meditation tapes, wheat-free muffins and cookies, fresh-ground coffee and shade-grown beans, children's toys and games, books on spirituality, funky clothing, more jewelry, hand-woven bags and shawls, and finally CDs and DVDs.

And, oddly enough, bins full of something I had not seen in quite a long time.

"Vinyl records," Harry said in a hushed, almost religious tone. "Oh my Lord, look at them." And with that he was gone, headed over to the rows and rows of bins stuffed with new and used vinyl records.

Several customers roamed through the sprawling store, but I didn't see anyone who looked like they worked there. Not that I was clear on what a clerk at Akashic Records would actually look like.

After several moments of searching, I found the lone cash register and positioned myself near it, figuring that action would tag me as someone interested in a transaction of some kind. Moments later that gambit paid off.

"Have you been helped?" a voice asked. I turned and found myself face to face with perhaps the most beautiful man I'd ever seen. He was in his late twenties and was wearing a crisp white shirt. He had thick black hair and a dark complexion, making me think he could be Greek or Italian or just really tan. With his perfect teeth, classic day-old beard stubble and high cheekbones, he looked like he had just stepped off the pages of GQ. He was so good-looking it was all I could do not to squint when I looked at him.

"Yes," I said. "I'm here to see Arianna Dupree."

He gave me a long look and then tapped a few keystrokes into the laptop next to the cash register. "Arianna is in session right now," he said as he studied the screen. "Do you have an appointment?"

"No, do I need one? I just have a few questions for her. It won't take long. I was just in the neighborhood..." I was making this up as I went along and it sounded like it.

"Can I tell Arianna what this concerns?" His tone made him sound like the maître d' at a five-star restaurant instead of a retail clerk at the local head shop. I decided to fight fire with fire.

"Yes," I said with gravity, "I'm here to discuss the murder of Walter Graboski, also known as Grey, and the murder of Dr. Maurice Bitterman."

That got his attention. "Who should I tell her...?" He let his words hang in the air like the balloon effect I had created for Nathan.

"Eli Marks," I said.

"One moment, please." He discreetly closed the laptop and disappeared through a beaded curtain into the back of the shop.

I glanced around the store and finally spotted Harry, who was happily sorting through old albums, occasionally pulling one out and examining it more closely. I heard the jangle of beads and turned to see the handsome male clerk returning.

"Arianna will be with you in a minute," he said, all the frost now melted from his voice. "Can I get you a cup of green tea and some mango slices?"

I shook my head. "No thanks."

"Would you care for a quick hit off the oxygen bar?" he suggested, gesturing toward one counter that was set up with small oxygen masks, tubes and tanks. "It's great for clearing out the negative ions."

"No thanks, man," I said. "I'm cool."

"Well, don't hesitate to ask if you need anything."

"Actually," I said as he began to walk away, "I did have a question. For you."

"Yes?" He turned back, clearly trying to put on an expression of interest and concern on his face. It wasn't really working.

"Did you know Grey and Dr. Bitterman?"

"I've met them both, yes. When I decided to get into the intuitive healing arts, I made a point of meeting all the top people in the Twin Cities. The best, of course, being Arianna."

"So you didn't know them personally?"

"I've interacted with both of them at social gatherings. And I did one past life reading with Dr. Bitterman, which was, at best, disappointing, and at worst unprofessional."

"Really?"

"I'd prefer not to go into it."

"Were you at the memorial service for Grey? And the reception that followed?"

His eyes narrowed at me. "Yes. I helped Arianna set up her harp before the service. I also went to the reception, but I arrived later than most of the others."

"Why was that?"

"Not that it's any of your business, but Arianna didn't want her harp to sit in the car during the reception. Cold weather can warp it, or so she says. So I took it back to her apartment for her, and then came later to the reception." His stare had turned to ice. "Is there anything else?"

I shook my head. "That's it. Thanks."

"Fine. Arianna will be out in a moment."

He walked away again, stopping at a nearby counter to straighten a small display that didn't need straightening. I could tell that he was keeping an eye on me.

"Eli! How nice to see you again." Arianna parted the beaded curtain and skillfully maneuvered her large frame through the narrow doorway. "I had a feeling that our paths would cross again and I was right. Score one more for the psychics."

She moved with remarkable speed and grace for a person her size, and before I realized what was happening, she was nearly on top of me. She was wearing several flowing layers of billowing pastel silks and scarves, looking like Mama Cass as dressed by Stevie Nicks.

She deftly planted an air kiss on each cheek and then turned around and headed back toward the doorway, just in time to greet a thin, sad-looking woman in her twenties who was making her way through the beads.

"Now, Virginia, remember what I told you," Arianna said to the woman in a cooing, soothing voice. "The mind, the body, the spirit are all one. If one is damaged, they're all damaged. If one is cured, they're all cured. We made a lot of progress today, but this was just another small step on what may prove to be a long and strenuous journey. However," she continued, placing a hand gently on the woman's back, "it's a journey that we'll be taking together. You'll never be alone. Do you understand that?"

"I do," she said softly. "I'm just so worried about everything, and I think that's what's making me sick. My job, my finances, my cat. It's kind of overwhelming."

Arianna smiled sympathetically. "Yes, of course it is. But the key thing to remember is that you're not alone. The universe is there to support you. And, don't forget, I'm here as well. Okay?"

The woman smiled, just a bit. Arianna moved in closer and took her hand. "I'll see you at the same time the day after tomorrow, but you call if you need to talk before then. Promise me you'll call?"

The woman nodded. "Good girl," Arianna said. "Now go talk to Michael and he'll settle up today's charges." She gently pushed the woman toward the handsome clerk, who had noiselessly returned to his position at the cash register.

He looked to Arianna, who gave him a subtle shake of her head. He began to flip through some screens on the laptop. The woman was opening her purse as she approached him.

"You know, Virginia, it looks like you overpaid last time, so there's no charge for today."

She looked up, surprised. "Really?"

He consulted the computer again. "That's what it says here. You're all set."

"Oh, okay. Great. I can use the money." She closed her purse and smiled at him, clearly pleased at this turn of events. "I'll see you next time."

She headed toward the door and Arianna watched her go. When she had left the store, Arianna turned and gestured toward me to follow as she moved back toward the beaded curtain. Michael called after her.

"Dewey, don't forget that your eleven o'clock wanted both the full body work and the aura photos."

Arianna nodded at him as she sailed through the store.

"I'm between sessions," she said, glancing back at me, "so if you want to talk, you'll have to walk." She laughed as she disappeared into the back room and I followed. And then I stopped.

He had called her Dewey. It was pretty clearly a nickname based on her last name, Dupree, but something else about it sounded familiar.

I turned to check on Harry one last time. He was still standing by the used bins in vinyl bliss, so I pushed the beads aside and stepped through the doorway.

I wasn't sure what I would see when I walked through the curtain.

Straight ahead was a small photo studio, set up with a digital camera, lights, a laptop, and printer. The backdrop for the studio was a bit puzzling—the left half of the wall was painted bright white, while the right half was painted black. Arianna saw my reaction and smiled.

"That's where I do my aura photos. Some people's auras photograph best against a white background, some against black. Even after doing it for years, I can't tell which will work better until I get them in front of the camera."

She turned left, into a small room, while I stopped to look at the framed photos on the wall. They were all portrait shots, like you'd get from a professional photographer. The difference was that each person had a colorful glow surrounding them. The colors varied—some were surrounded by blue light, others by yellow, while a small number were bathed in red.

They reminded me of the old days, when we shot photos with film and the last photos on a roll would have an odd glow to them, because the film had been exposed to extra light before developing.

"So, what can I do for you, Eli?" Arianna called from the room she had disappeared into.

One photo caught my eye. It was of a young woman, with long dark hair, and although I didn't recognize her, she did remind me of someone. And then it hit me. "Nova," I said out loud.

"What's that?" Arianna called from the other room.

Nova had told me that one of her past beaus had been named Dewey. I had assumed that Dewey had been a male, but most of my other assumptions about Nova had been wrong, so there was no reason why this one couldn't get in line to join them.

"Nova," I repeated as I rounded the corner and stepped into the small room. It was a therapy room of some kind, with a couch and chair. It was lit entirely with candles, some of which Arianna was in the midst of switching out for her next client. "Do you know a girl named Nova? She worked for Grey."

"And before that she worked for me," Arianna said with just a touch of bitterness in her voice. She lit the final two candles and stood back to assess her work, then turned to me. "A sweet girl and a lovely spirit. We did not part well. I blame Grey for that. He took a perverse pleasure in destroying things, like relationships." She turned and looked at one of the candles for a long moment. It may have been a trick of the light, but I think I saw a tear in her eye. "She was a very special girl and he took her from me. In every way."

"I'm sorry to hear that," I said.

She shook her head, breaking her reverie. "Yes, well, now I have Michael and all is as it should be."

"I must say, you have a rare gift for hiring stunning clerks."

"What can I say, I have a thing for beauty," she said, giving me a playful tap on the arm. "Some people are addicted to drugs, some to cigarettes, some to sex. Me, I'm addicted to beauty."

She stepped out of the therapy room and moved toward the photo studio, flipping on the lights to fully illuminate the backdrop.

"So that was the therapy room, where I do readings and full-body healings," she said, gesturing expansively around the space. "This is the studio for aura photography, and over there," she said, pointing around a corner to a long, tall bench with bright lights positioned above it, "is where I do jewelry repair. If I've learned anything in this life, it's that success is all about diversification."

"Did you ever confront Grey about what he did to your relationship with Nova?" I asked as I followed her.

She turned on the final light and looked at me. "You mean, did I kill him?"

"Well, yes, if you want to cut to the chase."

She smiled wickedly and shook her head. "No, I didn't. But I certainly thought about it. A lot. Fortunately, someone beat me to it." She gave me another wicked smile and began fiddling with the camera on the tripod, adjusting the controls while she looked at the image on the small screen on the back of the camera.

"Do you have any idea who beat you to it?"

"Hon, do me a favor and stand in front of the camera. On the 'x' on the floor." I obliged and moved in front of the camera. There were two marks on the floor, one on the white side and one on the black side. "White or black?"

"Let's start with white."

I stood in front of the white portion of the backdrop, but the moment I got settled she called from behind the camera. "Oops. Wrong. Dead wrong. You need the black background."

I moved over to the black side and waited patiently.

"You have a very inquisitive aura," she said, her face still hidden behind the lens.

"You can see that through the camera?"

"Honey, I saw that the moment you walked in. So you're playing detective now, in an attempt to clear your name?"

"Something like that."

"Well, I love that. And I love your aura."

I heard the click of the shutter, followed immediately by a second identical click.

Arianna's head popped up from behind the camera and she turned toward the laptop on the stand next to the camera. She began tapping away on the keys.

"Unfortunately, I'm afraid I won't be of much help to you. Not only is the list of people who hated Grey as long as my arm—" She looked around dramatically, pretending that she was making sure that we were alone. "But, to be honest, I don't want whoever did it to get caught. Unless they're planning on giving that person a medal."

"You said as much at the reception."

"And I meant it. The world is a hard enough place as it is without bastards like Grey making it worse."

She hit another key on the keyboard and a moment later a piece of paper began to come into view from the printer. She smiled knowingly as it emerged. "Very interesting," she said slowly. "Very interesting indeed."

She picked up the completed print and brought it over to me. It was the photo she had just taken of me, but my body was surrounded by a rainbow of colors: blues, reds, yellows and a thin layer of sickly green that hung close to my body.

"Wow," was all I could say after looking at the photo.

"Obviously there's a lot going on here. If you have a minute," she said, "There are a few things I can tell you about your search, based on your aura."

*   *   *

I'll spare you the details of Arianna's exhaustive reading of my aura.

Suffice it to say that my aura was in conflict. My Chi was completely out of whack. My chakras were jumbled up like a crash test dummy after a serious wreck.

Consequently, she explained, this was not a good time for new relationships or existing relationships. And, if one could believe my aura, whatever trouble I was in was likely to get worse. Basically, my aura, my Chi, and my chakras were suggesting that my wisest course of action would be to take to my bed and stay there.

By the time we emerged from the back room, Uncle Harry was completing the purchase of a small stack of records. Michael had rung up the total and was just processing Harry's credit card.

"Oh, Buster, you have to see these. I got some choice records to add to my collection," Harry said as I made my way through the beaded curtain. "Stanley Myron Handelman. Corbett Monica. Woody Woodbury. Even a Rusty Warren that I was missing."

"My uncle collects comedy albums of performers that he worked with at one time or another," I said by way of explanation to Arianna. "He's a magician."

"So it runs in the family," Arianna said, smiling broadly.

"Arianna, this is Harry Marks, my uncle," I said. "Harry, this is Arianna Dupree. She's the proprietor of Akashic Records, among other skills."

"A fine establishment," Harry said as she took his hand in greeting. "And what are your other skills?"

"I travel along a wide spectrum on the astral plane," she said, still holding onto his hand. "But my primary gift is that of a full body healer, using the art of Johrei."

"Which means what?" he asked, as he seamlessly switched into his avuncular inquisitive mode.

"It means," she said, caressing his hand slightly as she studied it closely, "that my gifts allow me to diagnose and treat illness of the mind, body and spirit. For example, I'm intuiting that you're currently suffering from a bit of arthritis." She looked him right in the eye.

Harry shook his head, but continued to smile benignly. Arianna quickly moved ahead without skipping a beat. "Or actually, it feels more like a rheumatoid condition." Another gentle shake of the head from Harry. Arianna set down his right hand and took up his left.

"A respiratory ailment, something in the chest, on the left side." She looked at Harry questioningly. He smiled and shook his head. She released his hand. "Harry, you seem to be in fine shape."

"Knock on wood," he said, giving the wooden portion of the counter a solid rap.

"Harry's not a big believer in the intuitive arts," I said, feeling that someone had to state the obvious. I was surprised that the only person to raise an objection to this was Harry.

"On the contrary, I often look to the intuitive arts to help me plan for the future," Harry said, turning back to Arianna. "In fact, I'm a big believer in Clidomancy, Gyromancy, and Tiromancy, to name only three."

"I don't think I'm familiar with those," Arianna said, a puzzled expression on her face.

"Oh, they're the art of divining the future by, respectively, dangling keys, walking in a circle until you become dizzy and fall down, and my favorite, Tiromancy, whereby you tell the future by means of a piece of cheese."

Arianna looked at him for what seemed like a long time, and then her lips began to form a wry smile. "Harry, you're having fun with me, aren't you?"

He returned the smile. "Yes, I am, just a bit."

She put an arm around him and pulled him close, enveloping him within her massive bosom. "Eli, I like this man."

I could barely see Harry's face, but what little I saw told me that he liked her right back.

* * *

When we got out to the parking lot, I discovered that I'd forgotten my iPhone in the car and that someone had left me a message.

I turned on the engine to get the heater going, and while Harry cooed over his cache of albums again, I checked my voicemail. It was an unfamiliar number and a slightly familiar voice, but she got my attention right away.

"Hello, Eli," the voice on the recording said. "This is Franny Higgins; we met at the memorial service? Sorry to bother you, but I thought we should talk. I just got a phone call from someone. He wanted a psychic reading. And the thing is, he said he thinks that he was the one who killed Grey."

Chapter 13

"Are you hungry? You must be hungry. I've made lunch." These were the first, breathless words out of Franny's mouth when I arrived on her doorstep.

I had dropped Harry off at Chicago Magic, because he had insisted he wanted to open up the shop. In reality I knew he was itching to put his records on the turntable and take a leisurely trip down memory lane.

Consequently, I was flying solo when I arrived at Franny's small bungalow on the edge of Richfield, a suburb that is itself on the edge of Minneapolis. Hers was a perfectly nondescript house nestled among other post-war bungalows, each unique only in their color and trimmings, as they were all otherwise exactly the same.

For someone who couldn't have weighed more than a hundred pounds, it was clear that Franny seemed awfully interested in eating, as demonstrated by her all-consuming interest in food at the reception. And upon arriving I was immediately ushered into her tiny but immaculate kitchen and greeted by enough food for a small battalion. Franny walked ahead of me, although *flitted* would be a more accurate description.

The primary color in the kitchen was yellow, with the secondary colors being variations on yellow, making the room feel buttery. The kitchen table was not exactly overflowing with food, but the spread was pushing the edges of what the tabletop could hold. She picked up an empty plate and handed it to me.

"First we eat," she said with finality. "Then we'll talk."

Eight and a half minutes later, with the shattered remains of a terrific roast beef sandwich in front of me, and the last bite of a classic German Minnesotan potato salad hovering on a fork in front of my mouth, Franny resumed our aborted conversation. She set her napkin down and pushed her chair a few inches away from the table.

"So I got a phone call," she said in a very businesslike, just-the-facts manner. "About nine-thirty this morning, which is early for me, but I was up and about, so I took the call."

I finished chewing the potato salad and was contemplating another small helping, but I didn't want to plunge us back into silence. "You don't take every call that comes in?" I asked.

She shook her head. "Oh, I couldn't. I'd be on the phone 24/7."

"Really? I had no idea there was that much demand for phone psychics."

"Well, I can't speak for the others, dear, but there's that much demand for this one."

Her lack of humility on that one topic made me smile. "So, where do you advertise?"

"Oh, I don't, really. I have a lot of regulars. Most of my new clients come via word of mouth. My nephew set up a nice little website for me, so that might be helping, but I don't really know."

"How long have you been doing this?"

"Well, I've had the gift since I was a child, but I didn't really start to put it on a paying basis until about fifteen years ago."

"But you don't take calls at any time of day?"

"No, I try to run it like a business and keep business hours, like ten to six on weekdays. Some Saturdays I'll take calls, if there's nothing else going on. Otherwise, I turn off the phone and turn on the machine, which tells them to try back during business hours. Most of them do. They just keep coming back."

"Franny, there are a lot of businesses that would kill for that level of customer loyalty."

"Well, my philosophy has always been that when I work, I work. And when I'm not working, I'm not working. It's pretty simple, really." She saw me eyeing the potato salad dish and gave it a gentle nudge in my direction. "Hardly enough left to bother wrapping it up. Why don't you finish it?"

"So, anyway, you got a call around nine-thirty this morning..." I prodded as I scooped the last dollop of potato salad on my plate and then snagged a pickle as well.

"Yes, a call came in and I answered it. It was a man. I asked for his access code..."

I interrupted her, even though I was in mid-bite with the pickle, which was crisp and tart and most likely homemade. "Access code? What's that?"

Franny sighed as she scraped the remaining morsels of potato salad off the serving dish and onto my plate. "Well, to simplify billing, I belong to a national psychic network. A customer goes online and buys a certain number of credits, which they can use with any psychic in the network. When I take a call, I put the client's access code into the system on my computer and it deducts it from their account and gives me the credit. Much easier than the bother of taking credit card numbers over the phone, writing down all those numbers and all that nonsense."

I nodded and she continued. "Anyway, I put his access code in the computer, which said he had an hour of credit available and we started chatting. I asked him if he had any question in particular or if he was looking for a general reading."

She had moved the now-empty potato salad bowl away and slid a plate of brownies into its spot. Not wanting to appear rude, I took two. "Which did he want?"

"Well, he said he wanted a general reading," she explained, "but I could tell from the tone of his voice that he had a particular question in mind. You get so that you can sense that after a while and eventually they always get to the specific question, so it hardly matters. So I gave him a general reading."

"And what did that entail?"

"Fairly typical stuff, really, nothing too surprising. He's in his late twenties or early thirties, he's a bit lost, has a bad relationship with his parents, there's trouble with his current romantic partner, he's got some serious issues concerning money. Lost one sibling in his teens, nearly drowned himself when he was four, allergic to shellfish, misplaced his car keys last week, stubbed his toe this morning. Standard stuff."

"He told you all of that?"

She gave me a long look, shaking her head like I was a dim child who was not paying attention. "No, dear. *I* told *him* all that."

"Really? And it was all correct?"

"Of course. Why else would I say it?"

It took me a few moments to process this. "So, how did you know all that stuff about him?"

She reached over and patted my hand. "Do you not understand the concept of psychics?"

"Yes, I get that part. It's just that I've never met one with, let's say, that level of reliability."

She shrugged. "Well, as the saying goes, your mileage may vary."

"So, anyway, did he get to the specific question?"

"Yes, well, he hemmed and hawed a bit, and then he asked if I could see any recent violence around him. I asked him what sort of violence he was concerned about, and then he just let it all spill out. He said that he's been drinking a lot lately and on occasions has suffered blackouts—he'd wake up and not remember how he got home the night before. He said that someone he knew had been murdered recently, that I'd probably read about it in the news, and that he wasn't at all sure that he hadn't done it, and then there'd been another murder and he was very much distressed."

I had trouble believing I was about to ask this question, but since she had been correct on so many other things I figured it couldn't hurt.

"So, what did your…" I wasn't sure what word to use. "What did your powers, your intuition, your gift, what did it tell you?"

She took a sugar cookie off the plate on the table and leaned back in her chair. She nibbled on it for a moment, and then brushed some fallen grains of sugar off her brown polyester slacks.

"It wasn't altogether clear," she said slowly, choosing her words with care. "I got a sense of intense anger and hostility from him, those feelings were apparent right away. And there was violence…something fatal, I think…but to be honest, I couldn't nail down whether it had already happened or was about to happen."

"You can't tell the past from the future?"

She shrugged. "Sometimes you can, sometimes you can't. It's like when you close your eyes and spin yourself around, you lose your bearings and you're not sure which direction you're pointed. So I wasn't able to give him a definitive answer."

"But you think this might be our guy?"

She pursed her lips. "I do. He emanated a level of anger and fury that was right below the surface but very powerful. I found it very unsettling."

I finished the first brownie and could feel the sudden jolt of the sugar racing into my system. "So why tell me and not the police?"

"It's simple…I don't think you killed Grey, or Bitterman for that matter, and I understand they think you did. And I know from experience that they're not going to listen to me. And I suspected that you might." She smiled at me broadly. I returned the smile.

"Okay, I'll check him out. What's his name?"

She got up and started to pick up our plates. "Oh, I have no idea what his name is. That's your job."

"He didn't give you a name?"

She shook her head. "I told you. Just his access number."

"And you couldn't, you know…" I gestured vaguely with my hands. She gave me a quizzical look.

"Couldn't what?"

"You know. Do the psychic thing."

She laughed. "'Do the psychic thing?' You have so much to learn." She shook her head as she sat down across from me again. "Names are transitory, something we're using in this incarnation. They're not attached to our spirit. It's like when you give a dog a name and then you give the dog away and the new owner changes the name to something else. It's still the same dog, but the name is different. The name is transitory. If you want, dear, I could lend you some of my books to read up on it. You've got a lot of catching up to do."

"Maybe later. But, this network you belong to, they would certainly have a record of his name, right?"

She smiled patiently while I spoke. "Yes, dear, but let's think it through, shall we? If he actually is a killer, I doubt he'd have much compunction about also stealing a credit card number and lying about his name. Don't you think?"

I nodded in agreement. "Good point." I sat back in my chair, trying to think of a good next move and coming up short. Franny returned to the sink and added more dishes to the pile, then turned and leaned against the counter.

"There was one other reason I called you," she said tentatively.

I looked over at her. She seemed a bit nervous. I waited for her to continue.

"When I was doing the reading, and I got the image of violence, another image came up as well."

"What was that?"

"I saw you. An image of you. It was very unnerving." She let this sink in. "If you don't mind, I think it would be best if I did a complete reading of you, as well. Do you think you would be up for that?" Although her voice was quiet, it had a real strength and intensity behind it. I nodded slowly, not really sure why I was agreeing to this.

"Good," she said. "Let's get started."

* * *

"I feel stupid," I said. "Is this really the only way it works?"

"Sorry, dear," Franny said, her voice sounding tinny through my cell phone. "I'm a phone psychic. I work on the phone. If you want, you could go sit in your car."

"No, I'm okay."

I was sitting on a creaky wooden swing in Franny's back yard, my cell phone to my ear, wishing that I had thought to bring my jacket along when she thrust me out of the house for the reading.

I folded my arms close to my chest and stamped my feet on the green and brown lawn in a vain effort to warm up. The swing rocked lazily in response to my movements.

Looking around the yard, I noticed it was full of curious knick-knacks. On my left was a small flock of plastic geese that lined the garden on one side. A series of wind chimes, in various colors, shapes, and sizes hung from the eaves, providing a constant tinkling sound in the background. At the corner of the swing sat three ceramic frogs, looking up at me quizzically. I returned the look and turned toward the back of the house, where I could see Franny, a cordless phone in her hand, looking out at me from her yellow kitchen. She gave me a little wave and I waved back without enthusiasm.

I looked at my hands—they were starting to turn pink from the cold.

"Are you ready?" she asked. I nodded. "I said, are you ready?" I looked back at the window and saw that Franny had turned away.

"Yes," I said, trying to keep my teeth from chattering. "All set."

"Okay." There was a long pause, and I could hear her breathing softly through the phone. Finally, her voice came through again. "I think I've got you, but let's make sure that I'm focusing in on the right person," she said. "It's always embarrassing to do a reading and find out that you've got the wrong person."

"Yes," I agreed. "I can see how that might be awkward."

There was another pause, and then she sighed, a soft and sad sigh. "Oh, your parents died. When you were ten. I'm sorry, Eli."

This took me a little by surprise. "Thanks," I said, not really sure of the proper response in this situation. "It's okay."

"The first thing I see is a new opportunity," she continued, "a way to rejuvenate your enthusiasm is coming up very soon. Does that make any sense?"

The only upcoming opportunity I could think of was filling in for Nathan at a kid's birthday party, which I didn't foresee as being a particularly rejuvenating event. "It does," I said, "maybe."

"Good. Now, let me see..." Another pause, during which all I could hear was her soft breathing. "As I mentioned at the memorial service, I don't see you directly involved in Grey's death or the death of Dr. Bitterman, although you are connected. Connected but not involved, if that makes any sense."

Another long pause. Although I was cold, what I was hearing was so intriguing that I had almost forgotten to shiver.

"I also see more connections coming up...a connection to something violent. And you're standing right next to it." She paused again and for several seconds all I could hear was her light breathing through the phone and the sound of the breeze through the wind chimes.

"And darkness," she said finally. "I see darkness. And I hear...I think it's munchkins. Isn't that strange? Munchkins. How funny." Another pause. "That's all I've got. Does any of that make sense?"

I wasn't sure how to answer because I really had no clue what anything she said meant. Before I could mumble any sort of response, she spoke again. "Oh, one more thing. I see a romance. A new romance. It's coming to me in the form of a light, but it's odd. It's like one of those neon signs. It's flashing on, then off, then on. I'm guessing that would suggest ambivalence on someone's part. Does that make sense?"

"I suppose so. In fact, I think I can point to ambivalence as a prevalent theme with most of my past romantic partners." I waited to see if there was more coming, but she was quiet. "Can I come in now?" I asked.

"Yes, dear. Of course. You must be freezing out there."

A cup of hot tea later and I was back to normal, temperature-wise. Franny insisted on wrapping up a couple brownies to go and she was just showing me to the front door when she stopped suddenly, her hand resting on the doorknob.

She stared at the far wall in her living room for a long moment, a look of deep concentration suddenly appearing on her face. I looked where I thought she was gazing, but saw nothing amiss.

The living room was small and comfortable and the furniture, like Franny herself, had a certain ageless quality to it. The far wall was decorated with two long shelves that were lined with presidential plates. It appeared to represent every American president since FDR, but on closer examination I noticed that both Richard Nixon and George Bush (the second) were noticeable in their absence.

"I just remembered something," she said. "About the caller this morning."

This jolted my attention away from the plates on the wall. "What was it?"

She chewed on her lower lip for a moment before continuing. "He had an odd way of speaking. He ended a lot of his sentences, practically all of them really, with the phrase 'know what I mean?' It was like a verbal tic of some kind. 'Know what I mean? Know what I mean?'" She looked up at me, searching my face to see if this tidbit was of any assistance. "Does that help you at all?"

"Yes," I said, knowing exactly what she meant. "As a matter of fact, it does."

Chapter 14

They say you can find just about anything on the Internet, and in this particular instance they were right. As soon as I returned to my car, I Googled the words 'Boone' and 'DJ' on my iPhone and after just two clicks I was on his website, which was a garish display that touted him as the Midwest's Premier Party Machine. The site was rife with misspellings and fuzzy photos, including some shots of female partygoers that were just this side of *Girls Gone Wild.*

I scrolled past those and found his contact information and in a few more clicks I had cross-referenced his phone number and tracked down his address. As it turned out, he was just a couple miles away, at an apartment complex on Cedar Avenue, a stone's throw—assuming you have a good arm—from the massive Mall of America shopping complex.

Finding Boone's building was no problem. He lived in a tired and worn three-building red brick compound grouped around a massive, pothole-pitted parking lot, which at that time of day was only about a quarter full. And finding his vehicle was even easier, unless there was more than one person in the complex who owned a piece-of-shit gray van with magnetic signs on the driver and pas-sengers' doors that read, 'The Midwest's Premier Party Machine.'

I pulled my car a discreet distance away and put it into park as I tried to come up with something that resembled a plan of action.

I rejected my first two ideas and was forming a third when I looked up to see someone exiting the building and heading toward the van. It was Boone, his bulky frame covered in a dark wool over-coat. A black baseball cap was pulled down, shading his eyes. His stringy blonde hair stuck out from under the cap and he appeared unshaven and tired. Even at this distance he looked like a poster boy for disheveled.

He started the van and pulled out of the lot. Since I had no real plan of my own, I put my car into gear and followed him.

As it turned out, it wasn't a long trip.

Barely two blocks later, he pulled the van into the parking lot of the International House of Pancakes, which sits directly across a busy street from one of the multiple entrances into the Mall of America. I watched as he parked and shambled into the restaurant, which appeared to be in the midst of a mid-afternoon lull. Moments later, I spotted him again, this time through one of the restaurant's windows as he took a spot in a booth and began to examine the multi-page menu intently. I pulled into a parking spot that afforded a better view of his location and sat back to wait. With nothing to occupy my mind, I flipped on the radio to help pass the time. NPR was once again asking me for money, so I switched the radio off and settled in to wait and see what would happen next.

What happened next was that Boone had a visitor. I was at a bad angle to see exactly who it was, but while I'd been fiddling with the radio, someone had joined Boone and was now seated across from him in the booth.

Their conversation appeared to be decidedly one-sided, as Boone looked to be doing all the talking, while his visitor merely smiled and dipped a teabag in a cup. And, from the looks of it, made an occasional note on a pad.

I started the car and moved it to a better vantage point to see who the mysterious visitor was. The move was all for naught, though, as reflections on the windows made it impossible to see clearly who was seated across from Boone.

I was so engrossed with trying to identify the mystery person that I barely registered when my phone beeped at me. A second beep finally got my attention and I yanked the phone out of my pocket to find I'd received a text message from Megan.

"U around?" it read.

"No," I texted in reply, typing slowly and carefully on the small keypad. *"I'm in the parking lot of the IHOP."*

A moment later, she texted back. *"Y?"*

"Long story."

"Lunch again? MayB 2morrow?"

"Definitely."

"Gr8. C U."

I spent several minutes trying to come up with a clever closing salutation of my own. As I sat there lost in thought, I glanced up just in time to see Boone's van pull out of the parking lot.

I tossed the phone onto the passenger seat and slammed my car into drive, pulling out so quickly that my tires actually kicked up dust, like Joe Mannix when he was on a case. I looked back at the restaurant in time to see someone who looked, and dressed, very much like Clive Albans also exiting the building, headed toward the other side of the parking lot. I decided that it was more important to follow Boone, so I sped across the lot toward the exit he had taken. I needn't have bothered, as Boone's van merely crossed the busy street and pulled into one of the surface lots in front of the Mall of America. He could have walked the distance in just about the same amount of time.

I followed and found a spot two rows down from his. I then slumped down in my seat and peered over the steering wheel as he crossed the parking lot, heading toward the entrance door. I watched him go and then decided that, since I had trailed him this far, I might as well continue with this plan. I got out of the car and headed toward the entrance that he had just stepped through.

The fourth floor of the Mall of America is referred to as their Entertainment Complex, although that's really overstating it, as it isn't all that complex or even vaguely intricate. It consists of a couple of bar/nightclubs and a massive, sixteen-screen movie theater. I stepped off the escalator in time to spot Boone as he bought a ticket from a theater employee ensconced in a glass booth and then walked into the theater lobby.

From where I was standing, I could just barely hear the voice of the ticket seller as she said, "Enjoy your show."

Through the windows into the lobby I watched Boone as he got his ticket torn by a ticket taker, who then directed him to the left side of the lobby. Boone disappeared down the hall toward one of the eight theaters on that side. I stepped up to the glass ticket booth and had a sudden vision of myself stumbling into eight different dark auditoriums, trying to find the one the Boone had picked. I looked up at the list of movie choices and nothing screamed out as something that might have attracted the movie fan in Boone.

Remembering that simplicity was always the simplest solution, I opened my wallet and said to the ticket seller, "I'll take a ticket for whatever movie the last guy asked for." I pulled a ten out of my wallet and looked up to see a blank-faced teenage girl, all red freckles and braces, staring back at me like a confused guppy.

"What?" she asked, her voiced amplified and disembodied, floating out of a small speaker on the counter.

"The last guy," I repeated slowly, "I want a ticket for the same movie he bought a ticket for."

Another stare, blanker than the first. "I have no idea what movie he asked for."

"It was less than 30 seconds ago," I said, trying to keep an edge of exasperation out of my voice.

"It wasn't a compelling choice," she said flatly.

I decided another approach was in order. I gestured toward the side of the theater he had gone into. "Which theaters are on that side?" I asked.

She squinted as she thought about it. "Theaters one through eight."

"Terrific," I said, "I'll take one ticket for theater eight."

"It's already started."

"I've made my peace with that," I said through gritted teeth.

She sighed as only a teenage girl can, took my ten and pushed a ticket at me under the glass. As I headed into the lobby I could hear her final, rote words echoing out of the small speaker. "Enjoy your show."

When I presented my ticket to the ticket taker, I put the same question to him. He was a very tall kid with a thick mop of brown hair and heavy black-rimmed glasses. "The last guy who came in here...which theater did he go to?" I asked, gesturing down the hall to the left.

The kid perked up, clearly eager for any interaction above and beyond the traditional, repetitive ticket transaction. "Oh, let me think." He screwed up his face and actually scratched his head in thought. "Auditorium three," he said proudly. "I sent him to auditorium three."

"Thanks," I said, as I handed him my ticket and headed toward the auditorium Boone had disappeared into.

Several hours later I emerged from auditorium six, following Boone as he exited and moved mercifully toward the main lobby. If he had headed into another auditorium, I might have begun to scream. In the intervening hours, I had watched parts of five different movies with Boone, as he moved sporadically and nomadically from auditorium to auditorium. I had forgotten my phone on the front seat of the car, so I had no idea what time it was when we left the theater.

I was thankful that Franny had forced two wrapped brownies on me, as they provided sustenance during movies two and three. I did sneak to the bathroom briefly during movie four, but that was really the only break I got.

As to the movies we saw, since we went into each one after it had started and left each before it had concluded, they all had congealed in my brain as one long, epic romantic comedy with action and vampires. And there was something about a talking dog. The rest is very hazy.

I stepped out into a sharp, cold night, feeling oddly jetlagged by the afternoon's movie-going experience. I crossed to my car and tried to keep out of Boone's line of vision as we traversed the parking lot in search of our respective vehicles. I found mine before he had located the gray van, which gave me a chance to check the time on my phone and see if I had any messages. I was surprised to see that it was only a little after eight o'clock—my internal clock would have believed anything up until eleven-thirty or twelve. There were no phone messages and no further texts from Megan. I turned on the car, flipped on the lights, and pulled out into traffic, right on Boone's tail.

He pulled out of the lot and hit the nearby freeway entrance at about fifty; it was all I could do to keep up with him. Traffic was light, so it was relatively simple to keep him in my line of sight as he sped down Highway 77, took the entrance to 494 West, and then transferred to 35W North.

Boone surprised me by getting off the freeway before downtown, pulling off at the Lake Street exit. I followed, keeping several car lengths back, so as not to spook him.

I thought he might be headed to one of the bars that line Lake Street near the freeway, to begin setting up for a DJ gig later that night. However, he revealed his true intentions by pulling up in front of a small but well-trafficked liquor store.

By the time I found a place to park, he was already out of the car, into the store and back with a small brown paper bag in hand. He resumed driving and I followed as he continued north toward downtown.

I still wasn't entirely clear on why I was following him. His verbal tic certainly identified him as the man who called Franny that morning, and if Boone was truly concerned that he had killed Grey, then he warranted observation.

By fate or chance I turned up in his apartment parking lot just as he was leaving, but there had been nothing outwardly sinister in his actions or behavior. However, something in my gut told me to keep following him. Some might call it intuition—Franny, I would imagine, might assign a more supernatural explanation.

As we made our way through downtown I was jarred out of this train of thought when Boone made a sudden turn into a parking ramp. The ramp adjoined a high-rise apartment complex on Third Avenue, right near the river. The building, a 30-story tower called The Carlyle, was a relatively new addition to the Minneapolis skyline. I hesitated for a moment, not sure if I should risk following him into the ramp, but a honk from a car behind me made the decision easy and I hit the gas and pulled in.

Boone found a spot right away, so I rolled past him, keeping my head turned away to avoid identification. I found a place several spaces ahead and slipped into the spot. I heard his van door slam just as I shut off the engine. I got out slowly, peeking over the top of the car next to mine to make sure he wasn't headed my way. He wasn't—he was headed toward the main door to the building. I got out and followed, stopping for a moment to peer in the passenger window of his van.

The interior of the vehicle was a complete mess, a trash can on wheels, but one piece of garbage immediately caught my eye—a pint of Southern Comfort sat on the passenger seat, resting on top of the brown paper bag it had come in. The bottle appeared to be completely empty. Clearly Boone was fortifying his courage, for reasons yet unknown.

As I approached the main entrance, I could see Boone standing in the building's entryway, using the phone on the wall to call one of the tenants. I stepped back against the building, feeling a bit silly but recognizing that it would be even sillier to get spotted now, after all I'd been through with him today. I peered around a corner and saw him hang up the phone and then heard the distant sound of a buzzer as the electronic lock buzzed to admit him. He stepped through the door and across the lobby, into a waiting elevator.

As soon as the elevator door shut, I sprang out of hiding and moved quickly into the entryway. The door to the lobby had re-locked, barring my access. However, I could see the elevator from the entryway, and more importantly, I could see the floor indicator above the elevator door. I watched as the numbers climbed, finally stopping at twenty-three. The illuminated numbers held at that point for a few moments, and then began to descend. Since Boone had entered the elevator alone, I felt it was a safe bet to presume that he was now on the twenty-third floor.

Next to the phone on the wall was a large display board, listing the last names of the tenants and their respective phone codes, which visitors could use to call to get buzzed in. Next to the phone was a cork bulletin board, with messages for the tenants from the management and listings of condos currently for sale or lease. I began to scan the long list of names and codes by the phone. I didn't have to go any further than the Ds.

The name 'Dupree' immediately caught my eye. Arianna Dupree, former lover to Boone's current lover, Nova. Assuming, of course, that Boone and Nova were still a couple—given the way they were arguing at the reception, they could easily have since broken up.

And now he'd waited all day to come down here and had even swallowed a pint of whiskey to get up the nerve to do whatever he was about to do.

I yanked on the front door without really believing that it would open, and I wasn't disappointed. I was about to pick up the phone and call Arianna's number when salvation came in the form of two yippy little dogs.

"Princess! Duchess! Princess! Duchess!" The dogs' owner, a blue-haired woman of a certain age, perfectly tailored and coiffed, was doing her best to negotiate the lobby. For their part, the two little pedigree mutts were doing their best to head in completely opposite directions. Although their combined weight may have been pushing four pounds, their antics were overwhelming Mrs. Blue Hair. She pulled and tugged and cajoled and begged her way across the lobby. When she finally made it to the front door and hit the latch to open it, I was standing by at the ready. I swung the door open for her with one arm, and with the other reached across the small foyer and opened the outer door as well.

"Thank you so much," she said, barely registering my existence as she cooed and pleaded with the two little squeaky furballs. "Come on now, girls. Time to go tinkle before we go to bed. Time to go." I could hear her voice as she struggled to maneuver the two dogs to a small patch of green directly in front of the building.

Before the front door had even closed, I was in the elevator and on my way to the twenty-third floor.

It was a quick ride up, so fast that I didn't really have time to come up with a plan of action before the elevator came to a smooth stop and the doors slid open. I stepped out of the elevator and into a quiet hallway.

I stood for a moment, listening for voices, hoping that would give me a clue as to where to head next, but the only sound was the elevator as its doors closed behind me.

I looked to my left and saw four highly-polished wooden doors, two on either side of the hall. A look to my right revealed a mirror image of what I had just seen on the left. The only difference was that one door, at the far end on the right, appeared to be slightly ajar. It might have been a trick of the light, but I moved toward it anyway. The hall was deathly quiet and my shoes made virtually no sound on the thick carpet.

The door was open a crack and a slim sliver of light shone through in the space between the door and the doorframe. I knocked on the door softly, pushing it open as I did.

"Hello?" I said, my voice cracking from lack of use. I consciously lowered it an octave so as to sound less like a teenager. "Hello? Anyone home?"

The apartment was dark, lit only by the ambient light from the skyline, visible through the large picture windows in what I guessed to be the living room. Something stirred to my left and I turned quickly, only to realize that it was merely the sheer white curtains that hung on either side of the sliding door to the terrace. The door was open and an intermittent breeze lazily swirled the curtains.

I took another step forward and my foot hit something hard.

At first I thought it might be an ottoman, but I quickly realized that the dark lump at my feet was Boone, crumbled over in his dark wool coat.

I knelt down to check his condition, resting my hand on the carpet for support. The carpet seemed to slide out from under me, and I realized that the spot was warm, wet and sticky.

I brought my hand in front of my face and in the dim light I could see that it was covered with what looked like blood.

Then something hit me, very hard, in the back of the head. I could hear what sounded like sirens off in the distance. And then everything went black.

Chapter 15

The blackness was like a deep hole—easy to fall into, but much, much harder to pull myself out of. However, that didn't stop me from trying.

Each attempt seemed to bring me closer to something resembling the real world, and then the fingers of my consciousness would lose their grip and I'd slide back down into the warm and comforting blackness. The state I was in was just this side of dreaming, but my battered brain made no attempt to construct a story out of the random images that flickered by.

If this was my life flashing before my eyes, it was doing so in a very disorganized manner—someone seemed to have left out all of the good parts. I resigned myself to this feeling and floated in a field of nothingness for what seemed like a long time.

And then, like a movie projector popping on after a power blackout, I suddenly opened my eyes and found myself staring at ceiling tiles that were whiter than white. I turned to my left and was blinded by the sun coming through an unfamiliar window.

I squinted involuntarily and turned to my right, where I was surprised to see Deirdre, seated in a chair, casually flipping through a magazine. Her blonde hair was nearly blinding in the bright light that flooded the room. She looked up at the sound of me rolling over.

"Hey, you're back," she said cheerfully, setting the magazine aside.

The intensity of my squinting must have registered with her, because she immediately walked to the window and adjusted the blinds. This, mercifully, brought the light level down to a more manageable, cave-like environment. "I was just sitting here, doing my impression of the last line of your favorite book," she said as she returned to her chair.

"*To Kill a Mockingbird*?" I said, puzzled by the reference.

"Good. Your brain is at least working a little bit. And what's the last line?"

I thought about it for a moment. *"He would be there all night, and he would be there when Jem waked up in the morning."*

"Bingo."

"So," I asked, my mouth dry and my voice raspy. "It's the next morning?"

"Yes, it's about..." she paused, glancing at her watch, "about twelve hours since you walked into Arianna Dupree's apartment and got clonked on the head."

"Who hit me?"

"We're still trying to work that out."

I glanced past her around the room, recognizing that I was in some sort of medical setting. I was clearly in a hospital bed, that much was certain. I was wearing a hospital gown that, now that I was on my side, was affording a comforting breeze up my backside. There was an IV in my wrist and a heart rate monitor clipped on my index finger.

And my head hurt like hell.

The door to the room stood open a crack, and I could see the unmistakable blue uniform of a cop seated right outside the door. I looked back at Deirdre.

"The cop guarding the door... Is he here to prevent me from leaving the room or prevent someone else from coming in?"

"A little of both."

We looked at each other for a moment. There was a lot more going on than she was telling me. "Arianna?" I asked tentatively.

Deirdre shook her head. "Dead," she said.

"How?"

"She jumped...or was pushed...off her balcony. Twenty-three stories."

I lay back on my pillow, which felt as hard as my head. I stared at the ceiling for several seconds, then looked back toward Deirdre. "Was there a playing card?" I asked, not really wanting to hear an answer.

"The King of Diamonds," she said. "They found it in her pocket. It was pretty messed up, as you can imagine, but they found it."

"So Arianna, the full-body healer —"

She cut me off, finishing my sentence for me. "Broke every bone in her body. Yeah, we put that one together right after we found the playing card. Someone has a very sick sense of humor."

"And I suppose Homicide Detective Fred Hutton is still convinced that someone is me," I said, my voice cracking from the dryness in my throat.

"Well, let me put it this way... You may have been unconscious, but you've had a busy night," she said, getting up and handing me a cup of water from the tray near the bed. It must have been sitting there a while, for it was the epitome of room temperature. I didn't care. I took a long sip that began the process of lubricating my Sahara-like throat.

"As the night has gone on," she continued, "you've progressed from the possibility of being charged with first-degree murder and assault, down to accessory to a first-degree murder, down to attempted murder, down to perhaps just assault. If you're lucky. They're still mixing and matching your options even as we speak."

"No wonder I'm exhausted," I said, as I handed the empty cup back to her. She refilled it from the Styrofoam pitcher, and I was glad to hear the sound of ice cubes dropping into the cup along with the water. She gave the cup back to me, and I held it against my forehead for several seconds, enjoying the cold, numbing feeling it produced.

"So why do the charges keep changing?" I asked before taking another long sip.

"As more facts come in, they adjust the charges to fit the facts," she said. "For example, originally they thought that you and this fellow Boone were in on it together and that after you both pitched Ms. Dupree off the balcony, you got into a fight and knocked each other out."

"Interesting," I said. "What particular fly soiled that ointment?"

"They looked at the security tapes. Turns out you got in the elevator at just about the very moment that Ms. Dupree went off the balcony. The tapes are time stamped. If you'd been outside a few seconds earlier, you might have actually seen the fall."

"I'm glad I missed that. So what theory popped up after they looked at the security tapes?"

"They considered accessory to first-degree murder, but Boone is insisting he's only met you once before. He seems adamant about it, although he refuses to tell us why he was at Ms. Dupree's apartment. The last I heard, they're leaning toward sticking the murder charge on Boone and sticking you with some sort of attempted murder charge or accessory after the fact, or at the very least assault on the person of Mr. Boone."

"How do you feel about that plan of action?"

She sat back in her chair and gave me her most serious look. "I'm withholding judgment until you tell me what you were doing in that building and that apartment in particular last night."

"I was following Boone."

"Why?"

"I'm not entirely certain. Where's Boone now?"

"They gave him ten stitches, bandaged his head and took him in for questioning. He spent the night in jail. Apparently his head is much harder than yours." She leaned forward toward me. "So, why were you following Boone?"

"It's a long story."

"I've got all day and you're not going anywhere until the doctor signs you out. And in order to sign you out, he has to get by the cop at the door. So, let me ask you again...Why were you following Boone?"

My head was pounding and this conversation wasn't helping. However, it was clear that I had few options before me, perhaps even none.

I gave her an abbreviated version of my conversation with Arianna at Akashic Records. Then I told her about my meeting with Franny, leaving out only those key details that might—if misconstrued—tie me even closer to the current roster of murders. Details like Franny seeing my image connected to the killings.

"So you followed him around town all day and into the night on the advice of a psychic?"

"It sounds less reasonable when you say it. All I can say is that it felt right at the time."

She leaned back and stared at a point on the wall for what felt like a long time. Then she turned back to me. "Eli, tell me, honestly, do you have any idea why you're mixed up in all this?"

"Deirdre, I honestly don't know. I can't figure it out."

She looked at me for a moment, then reached for her purse and pulled out her ubiquitous tube of lipstick. "Well, let's see what we can do about getting you out of here," she said as she began to apply a new coat to her lips.

Before I could go, I had to wait to be officially discharged. While I waited, a nurse insisted that I eat my breakfast, which had been sitting on the tray by my bed for what tasted like a long time. It was just about as delectable as you might imagine. Finally I received a visit from the attending physician, a good-natured transplanted New Yorker, with thinning red hair and a bushy red beard.

"Back from the dead, are we?" he said with a laugh as he entered the room and started to page through my chart.

"So far," I said.

"Stick around here long enough and we can take care of that." He finished with the chart in record time even for a speed reader, set it back in its holder and turned his attention toward me. "I'm Dr. Levine, I was on call last night when they brought you in. You had quite the smack on the head," he said as he ran a hand over my skull, stopping when I winced. "You'll have a bump for a few days. But, not to worry. We did an x-ray of your head last night and found nothing."

"Rim shot," I said, tapping out a quick drum roll with my fingers on the bedside tray.

"Thank you, thank you, I'm here all week."

"Try the veal."

"To be on the safe side, I'd recommend staying away from the veal in our cafeteria, unless you truly want to be here all week." He peered into my left eye, shining a small penlight at my pupil. "Seriously, it's uncommon for someone to be unconscious for as long as you were after a hit on the head. That's why you spent the night in the hospital while your friend got stitched up and went home."

"Actually, went to jail."

"Well, yes, there is that." He peered into my right eye. "However, what they do to you once you leave here is outside of my sphere of influence. And, my friend, by the looks of things, you're ready to leave my sphere right about now." He put the penlight into one pocket of his lab jacket and pulled a prescription pad out of the other. He scribbled quickly on the pad and tore the top sheet off, handing it to me. "Here's your discharge notes," he said. "Follow these instructions and you should be fine. Take care of yourself."

He gave me a friendly pat on the shoulder and with that he was gone. I could hear him as he entered the room across the hall. "What," I heard him say in mock surprise, "don't tell me you made it through the night. Well, I just lost five bucks." His voice receded as the door swung shut. Deirdre got up and opened the closet, pulling my pants and shirt off the built-in hangers.

I looked at the prescription in my hand. Although he had the typically poor penmanship universally attributed to all physicians, I was able to make out what he wrote with no trouble.

It read simply, "Don't get hit on the head anymore."

It would have been nice to go home and crawl into my own bed, but that was not to be.

Instead, I was transported, in handcuffs no less, from the hospital to the downtown police station, the same squad room Homicide Detective Fred Hutton and his partner had brought me into after Grey's death. The transporting officers didn't take my personal effects this time, just sat me on a bench and told me to stay put.

There was a general bustle in the room, a buzz of activity, and I was surprised that no one paid the least bit of attention to me.

From where I sat, I could see the enclosed interrogation room they had put me in during my last visit. The door to the room was open and through it I could see Boone, looking even worse than he had the day before, slumped in a chair.

Homicide Detective Fred Hutton was pacing behind Boone. I couldn't hear what he was saying, but whatever it was, it wasn't getting any response from Boone, who had a sullen, glassy look plastered on his face.

Deirdre, who had driven herself from the hospital, arrived at that moment. She sized up the mood in the room quickly, immediately establishing my position and its relation to her current husband, like a dog owner who's always on edge trying to prevent two disagreeable mutts from biting each other's balls off. Assured that we were a safe distance apart, she crossed the large squad room.

Homicide Detective Fred Hutton saw her coming and made a beeline toward her. He grabbed her elbow and steered her away from the interrogation room, in the process putting them within eavesdropping distance from me. I looked away and did my best to give the impression that I couldn't hear them.

"Get anything out of Boone?" Deirdre asked.

Homicide Detective Fred Hutton shook his head. "He still insists he walked in the apartment and got clonked on the head. Refuses to say why he was there."

She glanced in my direction. I was looking at my shoes. "How about the security tapes?"

"They've got cameras on all the entrance doors, in all the elevators, in all the stairwells. Our guys sat with the building's security guards and went through the tapes. No one who came in that doesn't belong, with the exception of Boone and your ex. We've got men watching the monitors now."

"What about motive? For Boone? And, for that matter, Eli?" she added as an afterthought.

"Looks like Boone just broke up with that girl, Nova something. She was previously involved with Grey and with Ms. Dupree. Apparently she swings both ways." Deirdre merely grunted and he continued. "Might be some sort of revenge, crime of passion thing. I sent a car to pick her up."

"Where's Eli fit in all this?"

I snuck a look at them. Homicide Detective Fred Hutton was chewing on his lower lip. Deirdre stared up at him and after several seconds he looked away. Poor bastard. "I'll admit that, besides proximity...we don't have much to go on."

"Let's face it, Fred, you don't have anything to go on with him. He's met the other suspect once, has virtually no connection to the three victims. All you've got is a playing card that keeps turning up at the crime scenes. And that's not going to hold up in court."

"So you just want to let him go? Again?"

"I think that would be the wisest course of action at this point."

"Okay. And then what happens if someone else dies and we prove Eli did it and the press finds out we brought him in twice and let him go twice, on the advice of the District Attorney's office?"

"Then I'm going to be updating my résumé and will probably end up going back to the Ice Capades. But until that time, the District Attorney's office doesn't feel that there is sufficient evidence for a conviction in this case."

"That's your final answer?"

"That's my final answer."

I tried to contain a laugh but I couldn't and it burst out, an explosive snort that was louder than the laugh would have been if I hadn't tried to suppress it. They both turned in unison and stared at me.

"Sorry," I said. "For a moment it sounded like I was flipping channels and had stumbled on 'Who Wants to be a Millionaire?'"

Homicide Detective Fred Hutton ignored my observation. "Marks, you're free to go. Again. I'll get someone to uncuff you."

Deirdre walked me out of the office and down the long corridor to the elevator without saying a word. I pressed the button and we waited in silence for the elevator to arrive.

"I hope I'm not getting you into any trouble with all of this," I said. "I mean, I appreciate what you're doing on my behalf."

"Damn straight," she said, giving the button a couple of violent but wholly unnecessary jabs with her index finger. "Now do me a favor and put as much distance as you can between yourself and the other people currently involved in this investigation."

"I will absolutely do that, no problem," I said as the bell signaling the elevator dinged and the doors began to part. Before they were completely opened, I was greeted with a sound that fell somewhere between a yelp of joy and a screech of surprise.

"Eli!" the voice yelled and I looked over in time to see Nova bounding out of the elevator and throwing her arms around me. She was dressed in tight blue jeans and a colorful shirt that seemed to be an artful blend of peasant blouse and halter-top, which left a healthy serving of her tanned midsection uncovered.

"Thank God you're here. Arianna's dead and they've brought Boone in and everything is just colossally fucked up."

Behind Nova were two uniformed cops and from the puzzled expressions on their faces I guessed that they had been the ones assigned to pick her up and bring her in for questioning. I imagined that it had been a very interesting car ride, one that they would be recounting to their co-workers for years to come.

"Let me guess, you're Nova," Deirdre said, as she stepped forward and took charge. "I'm Deirdre Sutton-Hutton, Assistant District Attorney. Thanks for coming down. We just need a few minutes to ask you some questions about the unfortunate events of the last couple days. These two officers will take you to our conference room and get you settled. I'll be in with a representative of the Homicide department in just a moment to speak with you."

I'm not sure if Nova understood, or even heard, much of what Deirdre said. But, as I'd discovered many times in the past, Deirdre's tone and manner were so self-assured, that people generally slipped into a docile mode and instinctively did what she said.

Such was the case with Nova, who unhooked her arms from my neck, smiled meekly, and followed the two cops down the hall. Before she had gotten too far, she turned back to me. "And Eli, thanks again for staying with me the other night. It was great." Nova then averted her eyes from Deirdre and continued down the hall with the cops.

Deirdre turned slowly and gave me a look that was hard to read.

"It's not what you think," I began, trying to come up with something plausible on the fly.

"What I think is that she probably came on to you in a big way and, chaste magic man that you are, you spent the night sleeping two feet from her bed, sitting in a chair, fully clothed."

"Oh," I said, taken aback by her prescience. "Then I guess it is what you think."

"Go home, Eli."

I stepped into the elevator and turned to give her a friendly wave, but she was already headed back down the hall.

Chapter 16

I had gotten home from the police station, walking the several blocks to the Carlyle parking ramp to retrieve my car.

I drove home via side streets, my head still feeling a bit woozy, either from the crack on the head the night before or from the hospital breakfast I'd been forced to eat that morning.

After giving Harry an abbreviated report on the events of the previous day and night and that morning, we both agreed that he could manage the shop while I went up to my apartment to lie down. Which I did with a vengeance, sleeping for what I guessed to be several hours.

At some point, while I was sleeping, I heard a persistent knocking.

The sound of someone knocking on my apartment door is a very rare occurrence. In the months since I moved back in, I don't think it had happened even once.

When I was younger, in my teen years, Aunt Alice and Uncle Harry got in the habit of simply calling me on the phone when my presence was required. Neither one wanted to scale the steep stairs to the third floor, stairs even steeper and more treacherous than those they used to go up and down into the shop from their rooms on the second floor.

At first I thought the knocking was part of a dream. In my dream I was still following Boone, driving slowly behind him as he navigated the twisty streets of Prospect Park. I heard knocking and assumed that there was a problem with the car, but even after I pulled the car over and opened the hood, the knocking persisted. Then something pulled me out of the dream and back to the surface of reality and I woke up.

The knocking continued and it took another long moment for me to realize that someone was at my apartment door.

I stumbled to the door, not fully cognizant of the fact that I was only wearing boxer shorts and a t-shirt. I swung the door open, fully expecting to see Harry and instead came face-to-face with a large gift basket. Wrapped around the basket was a wide, red ribbon.

"I come bearing gifts," a muffled female voice said from behind the basket. "Are you in any condition to have visitors?" Megan's face peeked out from behind the bountiful basket and her eyes widened playfully when she glimpsed my attire. "Perhaps I should come back later," she suggested.

I woke up, fully and completely, in an instant.

"No, no," I said, as I turned toward my bedroom. "Just give me a second." I scampered—yes, that's right, scampered—into the bedroom, reappearing a few moments later in jeans and a cleaner t-shirt. "To what do I owe this surprise visit?"

Megan was already in the apartment and had placed the large basket on the kitchen table.

I stepped around her and shut the door, wondering for a moment if it was more circumspect to leave it slightly ajar. I decided that dorm rules didn't apply after age thirty and closed the door.

"I heard about Arianna this morning and got very upset," Megan said as she straightened the ribbon that surrounded the basket. "So I walked over to your shop to talk to you. Harry explained that you were in the hospital, and so I got this basket together, but by the time I was ready to deliver it to the hospital, he said you were already home. He told me I could come up," she added.

There was an awkward silence as we stared at each other, and then Megan redirected our attention toward the basket. "Anyway, these are just a few things to help you recuperate, although you seem to be doing just fine. How's your head?"

I gingerly touched the bump on the back of my head. "Still sore. But getting better." I looked at the basket, which was filled to overflowing with various and sundry items. "This looks amazing."

"Well, it's a mix of useful items along with some other, I don't know, more playful things." She began to unload the basket. "First, we have some Chicken Matzo Ball soup from Cecil's Deli. Powerful stuff. Good for what ails you." She handed me a quart-size plastic container, which was still warm. I held it between my hands for a few moments, enjoying the warmth and letting the aroma waft around me, and then set it on the counter.

"Just as powerful," she said as she dug into the basket further, "is chocolate. Never underestimate the power of chocolate." She handed me two small wrapped boxes. "I didn't know if you were a dark chocolate guy or a milk chocolate guy, so I got you both," she added. "Personally, I don't have any preference, so I'll be happy to eat any you don't like."

I set the chocolate on the table and watched with interest as she continued to empty the basket. She was having fun and that made it even more fun to watch.

"In case you get bored while recuperating, I got you a book. But not just any book. My favorite book." She held up a hardcover book. "Funniest book you'll ever read. Ian Frazier's *Coyote vs. Acme*. Funny, funny stuff." I held up my hand in a just-a-minute gesture and she stopped talking, holding the book in midair.

One of the benefits of living in a small apartment is that you don't have to go far to find something. I took two steps, which moved me out of the kitchen and into the living room. I reached up to a shelf on one of the two bookcases that line one wall of the living room and pulled out a book, identical to the one she was holding except that the cover was more frayed and worn. Megan gave a small yelp of joy. "You've already got it?"

"Yes."

"Well, now you have two." She handed me the book. "But this one's inscribed." I started to open the front cover, but she put her hand on top of mine to stop me. "Not now. Wait 'til I'm gone. Otherwise I'll get embarrassed." She returned to the basket and I gently set the book on the table, my curiosity now completely piqued.

"Back to foodstuffs. Chicken soup is vitally important while you're sick, but for me the real cure can be found in sugared cereals." The next items out of the basket were six small boxes of sugared cereals, all held together under one cellophane wrapper. "Each box says that it's one serving size, but I think we both know that all six boxes equals one serving." She handed me the cereals and I turned the package over in my hands, seeing several favorites and feeling the pull of their sugary siren song.

She stopped digging for a second and turned to give me a serious look. "Eli, you may not agree with this, but I thought you needed a stuffed animal of some kind," she said, "as the stuffed animal offers a unique level of comfort that may be missing in the life of someone who lives alone. I'm speaking from my current, personal experience. However, you are a very manly man, and so the choice of stuffed animal was particularly important. With that in mind, I believe I have made the correct selection."

From the basket she pulled a small, stuffed version of the cartoon Tasmanian Devil. "He looks quite fierce," she said as she ceremoniously handed it to me, "but in reality he is quite soft. I tested him out for you."

I stood there, holding my stuffed Tasmanian Devil in one hand and the boxes of sugared cereal in the other, feeling better than I had in days, perhaps even years.

My headache was gone and the sore spot on my head was, at that moment, hardly noticeable.

Megan continued to pull items out of the basket. "I also raided my store for a few select items."

She placed the objects on the table as she described them. "A Get Well card, handmade and hand-printed by a local artist with way too much time on her hands. She makes her own ink, for example, and I think the paper is homemade as well. I wouldn't be surprised if she grew the trees and mashed her own pulp." I picked up the envelope, which had the rough, primitive feel of homemade paper. Megan had written 'Eli' in big, broad letters across the front. I set it down on top of the book.

"I also brought some candles and essential oils. The idea is, you put the oils around the wick and they burn as the candle burns. Each one has a different property and is designed for a different intended effect, like harmony, balance, serenity, and so on. I color-coded everything to make it easier for you. Oils with the red dots go on the candles with the red dots, blue goes on blue, yellow goes on yellow. You should be able to figure it out with no problem." She set the small box filled with vials on the table, and then placed several different sized and colored candles next to the box.

"It's like Garanimals for the New Age sect," I suggested as I set down the cereal and the Tasmanian Devil and picked up two of the candles. I gave them each a quick sniff. Unlike the odor that permeated Arianna's shop, these actually smelled quite pleasant.

Megan again stopped unloading the basket and looked up at me with a wicked grin. "Hey, you might be onto something there. Could be a million-dollar idea."

She winked at me and then reached into the basket and reverently withdrew a small, purple velvet bag. A braided gold cord was used to secure the bag around the top. She undid the cord and released the contents into her hand, then held them up for my inspection.

"I've saved the best for last," she said.

Her hand held four stones, crystals I guessed. Megan gazed at them with wonder, but to be honest all I saw were four small rocks. However, I did my best to look sufficiently awestruck. "What do we have here?" I asked.

"I brought you some exquisite crystals," Megan answered, practically cooing at the stones as if she were holding a handful of tiny, adorable kittens. "They all emit a different kind of energy, working on singular vibrational levels. Each one will vibrate with your aura in a different manner. For example, this blue one," she said, picking it up and holding it gingerly with two fingers, "is specifically attuned for healing." She gently handed it to me.

"So, what do I need to do?" I asked as I rolled it around on my fingertips like I would a coin during my magic act.

"Nothing, really," she said. "Crystals are natural forms of energy. You just need proximity. You can carry them in your pocket, put them by your bedside—"

"Wear them as jewelry?" I offered.

She shook her head. "Maybe, but sometimes surrounding them with metal can have a negative impact on their intensity."

"Kind of like how when you put Kryptonite in a lead container, it no longer has any power over Superman?"

She laughed. "Exactly the same principle." She picked another stone and placed it in my hand. The gesture was surprisingly intimate and, well, erotic. "This is a black crystal," she said, looking up to meet my eyes. "It provides protection."

"Great. Where was it last night when I was getting clonked on the head?"

She laughed, quieter this time, and picked up the third stone. "This is a gold crystal, which increases wisdom."

"Yet another item that would have come in handy yesterday," I said as I took the crystal from her. Our fingers touched for much longer than was necessary for the exchange. She picked up the final stone from her palm and held it up.

"And this is my favorite. The red crystal. It provides power, with a particular emphasis on one type of energy."

"What type would that be?" I asked, noticing that she was moving closer toward me.

"Sexual energy," she said and before the last syllable had left her lips she was pressing those very same lips against mine. Our positioning was a little awkward, with the kitchen table between us, but we managed to get around it without disengaging, and before I knew it we were as one, standing there in my tiny kitchen, arms wrapped around each other, trying to find just the right placement of our various limbs.

"Hold me closer," she whispered during a brief break for breathing.

I couldn't help myself and quoted Groucho Marx. "If I were any closer," I said, "I'd be behind you."

As funny as that may have been, the only reaction it produced was a longer and even more passionate kiss. And then, just as quickly as it had started, she stepped back, pushing herself away from me. She ran a quick hand through her hair and straightened her blouse.

"I'm sorry," she said, not quite looking me in the eye. "I probably shouldn't have done that."

"Well," I said, taking a step toward her, "If you hadn't, I would have."

She held up her hand. "No, no, it's too soon. This is too fast. I'm confused."

I took a half step toward her, and she countered with a full step backward. She was almost to the door. "I'm sorry, Eli," she said again. "I think you're great, really I do. It's me. I'm a mess. I'm—"

She didn't even finish the sentence, just yanked open the door and raced through the doorway.

By the time I got to the doorframe, she had made surprising progress down the stairs. She rounded the corner two flights below and vanished into the magic shop, which struck me as ironic for about half a second.

I stood there for a long moment before I slowly shut my door.

The apartment, which had always seemed small, now felt even more undersized. The sudden mix of emotions that had raced through my system in the last three minutes, from instant elation to instant rejection, gave me a sick feeling in the pit of my stomach. I realized that I hadn't eaten anything since that morning, and I wasn't even entirely clear how long ago that was.

I saw the container of chicken soup on the counter and then shifted my gaze over to the two boxes of chocolate on the table, vacillating between the options—healthy food versus a quick shot of pleasure-inducing sugar.

And then I saw the book she had left for me.

Masochist that I am, I immediately picked it up and flipped to her inscription. In a flowery hand, in blue ink, she had written, "Eli, hope this book makes you smile as much as you make me smile. Megan." Under her signature were a line of small, blue Xs and Os, which if my junior high vocabulary was working properly, indicated kisses and hugs.

Figuring if I was going to feel bad, I might as well push it to the limit, I opened the Get Well card, tearing open the handmade envelope with ferocity. The card had a watercolor image of some kind on the front—a splash of yellow that might have been a sunflower or a sunset or just a splash of yellow. I opened the card and read what she had written: "Hoping that the enclosed gifts help heal what ails you. Megan." This was also followed by a row of Xs and Os.

I was in the midst of setting the card back on the table when I heard a feeble knock at the door. I figured it was Harry, making a rare trek up the stairs to learn what I had done to inspire my guest to depart the premises with such speed.

I opened the door without enthusiasm, prepared to block his questions with whatever evasions I could muster on the spot.

Before I could get the door even a third of the way open, Megan pushed her way back in, slamming the door behind her. She grabbed the back of my neck and pulled me toward her, and we started up exactly where we had left off moments ago. It was as if she had never left except now we were standing by the door.

She broke away for one moment, leaning back against the door and surveying me as she took her hand and ran it through my hair.

"Sorry about that. I had to plug my meter," she said, a little out of breath.

"There are no meters on this street," I countered as we returned to kissing with the intensity of teenagers.

As I mentioned earlier, it's only a few steps from the kitchen to the living room. And from there, only a few additional steps to the bedroom. We made the trip in a record number of steps. Not that I was counting.

A short while later—wait, strike that. A reasonable amount of time later, by which I mean a respectable amount of time, nothing too brief and embarrassing, and yet nothing that drifted into the Tantric, we found ourselves wrapped around each other, fitting quite nicely, thank you, within the confines of a twin bed that I'd called my own since about age twelve.

A warm, yellow light dusted the room, courtesy of the streetlamp below my window and the marquee on the front of the movie theater next door. Megan played absently with the few sad hairs that called my chest their home. I looked from her to the red crystal that she had grabbed on our way into the bedroom. I picked it up off the nightstand and rolled it around my fingertips, enjoying the hard, smooth surface and watching as it picked up the dim light in the room.

"Well," I said, holding the crystal up for her benefit, "I think it's safe to say that this one works. I'll put a little Inspected by #24 sticker on it and we can try the next one."

"Sorry to say, I only brought the one," she said. "But I have a feeling that this one will continue to work as the night progresses." She took the stone from me and ran it, slowly and seductively, across my chest. "So, am I your first?" she asked as she peered up at me.

I wasn't sure how to respond and the look on her face was giving me no help at all. And then she burst out laughing.

"My first what?" I asked as I laughed with her. "My first psychic? My first landlady? My first divorcee?"

"Actually," she said, as her voice turned a bit serious, "I'm not yet a divorcee. I'm still technically a married woman."

"Well, then, you are my first married woman," I said. "With the exception of my first wife, but I don't think that counts."

She laid her head back on my chest. "It's so sad," she said quietly.

"What's sad?"

"Divorce. Any divorce. Mostly my divorce." She sighed. "I saw Pete the other day, brought him the divorce papers to sign. He was all set to sign them. And then he just started crying. I felt so bad for him." I ran my hand across her back in what I hope would be perceived as a sympathetic move.

"So I said we could wait a bit," she continued, more softly. She turned back and looked at me again. "But, as I think my actions tonight have indicated, I for one have moved on. At some point he's going to have to do the same."

"It's hard," I said. "I've been in his position, sort of. I'm sure it's difficult to be the one who leaves. But, believe me, it's no picnic being the one who's left."

She sighed again and we lay there in silence. "Pete and I started out so well. I just hope we can come out of this as friends. Do you get along with your ex-wife?"

"We've reached something of a friendly impasse. Basically, I try not to make fun of her husband, and she tries to keep me out of jail." I took the crystal from Megan and set it on the nightstand. "Currently we're each experiencing difficulty in our assigned tasks." I leaned in to kiss her, but she was still looking at the nightstand. Her gaze moved from there to scan the entire room.

"This is almost exactly as I pictured it," she said.

"You've fantasized about my bedroom?"

"No, well, yes. I mean, I just sort of wondered what it would look like."

"Well, as the landlord, I believe you have the right to enter at any time for an impromptu inspection."

"I may have to exercise that right on a more consistent basis," she said. She reached over to the nightstand and I thought she was bringing the crystal back, so was surprised to see that she had grabbed the deck of cards that was lying there. "You play a lot of cards in here?" she asked. "Like solitaire?" she added with a wicked smile.

"Magicians always have a deck of cards within reach," I said. "It comes with the territory. I mean, I'm willing to bet you have quite a few crystals scattered about willy-nilly at your place."

"Willy-nilly," she repeated, raising an eyebrow. "Well, yes, but those are for mystical, not practical, reasons."

"Whoa, full stop. Let's not underestimate the mystical qualities of a standard deck of cards," I said, taking the deck from her and doing a quick fan of all the cards.

"The mystical qualities of a deck of cards?" she said with a note of doubt in her voice. "Such as?"

I squared the deck and then did a series of one-handed cuts while I spoke. "Well, you might be surprised just how interesting an average deck of cards actually is. There's a lot going on in here," I said.

"Such as?" she asked.

"Such as," I said, mentally scrambling to remember all the arcane facts I knew about playing cards. "There are two colors...red and black...representing day and night."

"Okay," Megan said, sounding completely unconvinced.

"There are four suits, each representing one of the four seasons. There are fifty-two cards in the deck—"

"Just as there are fifty-two weeks in the year?" she suggested.

"Exactly."

I pulled the top card off the deck, extended my arm and made the card first disappear from my hand, and then made it re-appear a moment later. "Each suit consists of thirteen cards, which corresponds to the thirteen lunar cycles in a year. And finally," I said, returning the card to the deck and squaring it again, "If you add up the values of all the cards, you'll get 364. Add one more for the Joker, and you end up with 365, or the number of days in one year."

As I finished my recitation, I made one single card—the Joker—rise up out of the deck as a final flourish. Megan laughed and applauded.

"That's all well and good," she said, taking the deck from me and returning it to the nightstand, "but what sort of vibrational energies do the cards emit?

"Nothing like the red crystal," I admitted. "So it's a good thing you brought it along." We started kissing again and I'd venture to say that we both forgot entirely about the cards and the crystals for the next few minutes.

Chapter 17

I awoke to music emanating from my cell phone, which by the sound of it was in my pocket in my pants somewhere on my bedroom floor. I recognized the ring tone as the latest one I had assigned to Deirdre, which I'd come to think of as a sort of musical early warning system.

If anyone ever wanted to chart it, the trajectory of the Eli-Deirdre relationship could be mapped entirely from the ring tones I had chosen for her calls.

I started with a Rolling Stones tune and have stuck with them ever since, each song acting as a mini-signpost of the state of our current emotional battlefield.

The first ring tone I used was *Honky Tonk Woman*—we met in a bar, although to set the record straight, she was not gin-soaked and we were not in Memphis. We graduated to *Let's Spend the Night Together* and then settled in with *Loving Cup* for most of our marriage. You could tell things were headed downhill when I switched to *19th Nervous Breakdown*. That evolved into *(I Can't Get No) Satisfaction*, followed by *As Tears Go By*, *Sympathy For the Devil*, and finally my latest selection, *It's All Over Now*. That one seems to be the one I'll stick with.

I glanced at the alarm clock, which read 7:12 a.m. If she was calling at that hour, it could only be more bad news. I literally rolled out of bed onto the floor, doing a quick sweep with my hands until I found my pants.

"What now?" I said as I leaned back against the bed frame and rubbed something out of my left eye with the palm of my hand. I glanced over at Megan, who appeared to still be sleeping. Even with her hair a mess and with pillow wrinkles covering her face, she still looked amazing.

"Where are you?" Deirdre said. Her tone sounded edgy and a little ticked off. Business as usual.

"You know, when I was a kid, no one ever asked that question on the phone. You always knew where someone was when you called them."

"Let's explore the myriad changes to the daily fabric of our lives wrought by the electronic age at a later time," she said as she cut me off. "There's been another attack."

I sat up straight. "Who? Where?"

"Your friend, Franny Higgins, in her house about three hours ago."

"Franny," I said, louder than I had intended to. Megan stirred and opened her eyes. "Is she...?" I asked, not quite able to say the words out loud.

"She's in the hospital, alive but in a coma. I'd like you to come down here to talk to us."

"And if I don't, Homicide Detective Fred Hutton is going to come get me, right?"

"More than likely. We're at Hennepin County Medical, in Intensive Care."

"Give me thirty minutes." I hung up and looked over at Megan, who was wide-awake now, her head propped up on one elbow, a concerned look on her face. "I've got to go to the hospital. It's Franny. She was attacked. She's in a coma."

"I'm going with you," Megan said. Before I could assemble anything resembling a decent protest, we were both dressed and in my car on our way downtown.

I left a note for Harry on our way out, and Megan called one of her store clerks about opening up without her.

Traffic was light and our conversation was sparse, due perhaps to the early morning hour, or the news about Franny, or the slight awkwardness that settles in after a first-time intimate encounter.

But she took my hand as we walked through the parking ramp and if I had any worries about the likelihood of a second encounter, those doubts vanished in an instant.

So, less than twenty-four hours after I had been discharged, I was back at the hospital, this time with Megan in tow. We made our way through the stark hospital lobby, into the elevator bank and up to the fifth floor.

When the elevator doors opened, I found myself face-to-face with Homicide Detective Fred Hutton.

Behind him was his tiny partner, Miles Wright, and across the small lobby was Deirdre, deep in conversation with a nurse. Two uniformed cops stood near the automatic door that led to the ICU. The doors swung open and an orderly came through—I could see two more cops on duty further down the hall.

Homicide Detective Fred Hutton glared down at me. He was holding his cell phone in his hand. "Marks," he said flatly. "I was just going to call and send someone to pick you up."

"Happy to save you the cab fare," I said, moving past him and toward Deirdre. The nurse said a few hushed words to her as we approached, and then she slapped the silver panel to open the doors and disappeared into the ward.

"She's still in a coma," Deirdre said, anticipating my question. "She's unconscious but stable," she added, looking from me to Megan and then back to me.

"This is Megan, my landlord, er, neighbor. She's a friend of Franny's. And me," I was finally able to sputter out. "What happened?"

Homicide Detective Fred Hutton and his partner joined our small group, standing like silent sentries behind me.

"Someone broke into her house around four this morning," Deirdre said. "The intruder attacked and left her for dead, not realizing that she had managed to trigger the medic alert alarm that she wore around her neck."

"It might have been triggered inadvertently in the struggle." Homicide Detective Fred Hutton corrected.

"However it happened," Deirdre continued, "when she didn't answer her phone, an ambulance was dispatched. They found her alive, but unconscious."

"And what makes you think this is connected to the other murders?" I asked.

Deirdre looked over at Detective Wright, who opened the manila folder he was holding and took out what had become a very familiar sight—a clear plastic evidence pouch containing The King of Diamonds.

"It was found on the nightstand. And once again, our killer is exercising his wit. I understand Ms. Higgins was a phone psychic?" Deirdre asked, delivering her question as much to Megan as to me.

"Almost exclusively," Megan answered.

"Well, she was strangled. With a phone cord."

It made sense, in a perverse way.

"And what's even more interesting," Deirdre continued, "is that Ms. Higgins had two phones in the house. Both of which were cordless."

"The killer brought his own phone cord?"

"Apparently."

"And where's Boone during all this?" I asked.

"Still in custody," Homicide Detective Fred Hutton said.

I turned and looked up at him. "But if he was in custody when this happened, obviously he's not the killer."

"We're still not convinced that this is a one-man operation. Speaking of which, where were you at around four this morning?" He had just the slightest trace of a smile on his lips, like a cat that's convinced that he's cornered a mouse.

"He was with me," Megan said suddenly. All eyes turned to her, surprised at this admission.

"At four a.m.?" Homicide Detective Fred Hutton repeated.

"All night," Megan answered, a bit defiantly.

"And you can attest that he didn't go out and come back?" Deirdre asked.

"He would have had to climb over me to do it." Megan said. "And I'm a very light sleeper," she added, looking up at Homicide Detective Fred Hutton. There was a long silence as the detectives and the Assistant District Attorney exchanged looks.

"Can we see her?" I asked, feeling that a change of topic was in order.

"For a minute," Deirdre said. "The doctors are going to take her down for a scan in a few minutes, to see if there's any brain damage." She hit the plate on the wall and the doors swung open.

Deirdre led the way and we followed. I looked back to see Homicide Detective Fred Hutton glaring after me, and then the doors shut and he was gone.

Both of the times I had met Franny, I had been struck with how tiny she was. Now, seeing her in the hospital bed—with all the tubes and wires and the machines whirring and beeping—she seemed even smaller.

And certainly more frail.

We stood outside her room, the three of us looking through the window at the tiny woman who looked to be on the verge of being swallowed up by the large, white hospital bed.

Megan put her hand to her mouth the moment she saw her.

"I've never seen her be so still," Megan finally said in a whisper. "Every time I've been with her, she's always been moving. And moving and moving."

"She's a tough old bird," a voice from behind us said. I turned to see Dr. Levine, the red-haired and red-bearded doctor from the day before. He recognized my face but I could tell he was having trouble placing me. I mimed being hit on the head and his face immediately brightened.

"Ah, yes, my unconscious friend from yesterday," he said in a jovial, but appropriately quiet voice. "Have you avoided being hit on the head since departing the loving embrace of our care?"

"So far," I said.

"That's what I like to hear," he said, as he looked from me to Megan and Deirdre and then through the glass at Franny.

"Under the circumstances," he said, using an only slightly more serious tone, "she's doing quite well. Breathing on her own, which is a good sign. No bones broken in the struggle. Pulse and blood pressure are both good. Brain activity is strong, but we still need to check for internal bleeding. The problem is, oxygen was cut off from her brain for, well, we don't know for how long. And so we're in wait and see mode right now." He looked at the three of us and then patted Megan's shoulder. "Don't fret. I think she may still have a few surprises in her."

"I hope so," Megan said, her voice cracking just a bit.

He nodded at me and moved back to the large, circular desk that filled the center of the unit. Two cops leaned casually on the desk, conversing quietly. They took turns looking in our direction and keeping tabs on our location.

"What's most distressing about this," Deirdre said to no one in particular, "is that she probably saw who attacked her. She just can't tell us who it is. At least not yet."

We all watched the small figure in the bed for several more minutes, the only sound the hum of voices at the desk and the steady beep-beep coming from Franny's room.

I anticipated another run-in with Homicide Detective Fred Hutton when we left the ICU, so I was pleased to find him in the midst of his own run-in as we exited the ward.

When we came through the automatic doors I could hear him arguing in a low voice with someone in front of the elevators and was surprised to see that his confrontation was with Megan's soon-to-be ex, Pete.

Pete looked a little disheveled and certainly not up to going one-on-one with the iron giant. As soon as he spotted Megan, his face lit up. "That's my wife, right there," Pete said to Homicide Detective Fred Hutton, pointing in our direction. "She'll vouch for me."

Megan and I both stopped dead in our tracks, not certain why Pete was there or what Homicide Detective Fred Hutton may have said to him in our absence. In the momentary confusion of our arrival, Pete was able to sidestep both homicide detectives and make his way over to us.

"Megan, I called the shop this morning and Trina told me about Franny and said you were down here. Is she okay?"

"She's still in a coma," Megan said, taking a subtle step away from me. Pete looked over and seemed to see me for the first time.

"Oh, Eli, hi," he said, clearly a little confused about what I was doing there.

"I gave Megan a ride down here," I said by way of explanation.

"Oh, great, thanks," he said, and then turned back to Megan. "Can I see her?"

Megan shook her head. "Like I said, she's in a coma. They're taking her down for a scan, but otherwise they don't know much. I mean, they're not sure when or if...she's going to come out of it."

Pete moved toward her and they hugged awkwardly. I turned to see Deidre looking at me from one side, and Homicide Detective Fred Hutton looking at me from the other. Their expressions were inscrutable.

"Well," Pete said as they came out of the hug, "as soon as I heard, I thought I should be here. For you. And for her."

"That's great, Pete," Megan said. "I know she'd appreciate that." Megan looked at me but managed to make it look like she was looking at everyone in the group. "Well," she said, "I guess we should be going. Call me if you hear anything," she said to me as an afterthought.

"I will."

Pete took her by the arm and they walked the short distance to the elevator. After a small eternity, the elevator arrived and they stepped into it. Pete threw me a small wave and Megan smiled weakly as the doors closed.

Deirdre and Homicide Detective Fred Hutton were still looking at me with deadpan expressions.

"What?" I asked, my voice coming out a tad higher than I would have liked.

"Her husband?" Deirdre said dryly.

"They're separated. Practically divorced."

"Uh huh," she said, unconvinced.

"Am I needed here any longer?" I asked.

"What's the hurry? Got a date?" she responded, smiling up at Homicide Detective Fred Hutton, who returned the smile in spades.

"I have things to do," I said.

"Fine," she said. She turned to Homicide Detective Fred Hutton. "Do you have any further need for Mr. Marks?"

"I do not," he said, doing a lousy job of suppressing a grin.

Deirdre turned back to me. "Then you're free to go."

As I walked to the elevator I could feel them staring at me, but I refused to give them the satisfaction of turning around. My elevator arrived and I stepped in, turning to press the button for the lobby. I looked up to see Deidre and Homicide Detective Fred Hutton smiling at me from across the lobby.

"You know what I think, sweetie?" Deirdre said to Homicide Detective Fred Hutton without taking her eyes off me.

"What's that, dearest?" he replied.

"I think that someone might want to consider removing *moral superiority* from his list of annoying personal attributes," she said.

"I think you're right," he replied.

The elevator was closing quickly, but I'm pretty sure they both had time to see me flip them off before the doors shut.

"Eli! Hello there, Eli."

I was hustling through the hospital lobby, toward the freedom promised by the front revolving doors, when I heard the voice calling after me.

The nasally British accent could only belong to one person.

I turned to see Clive Albans striding confidently toward me. Once again he was dressed like a modern day Oscar Wilde.

"I thought that was you," he said in a voice way too loud for the setting. "I guess I shouldn't be surprised to find you here," he added as he shifted into a conspiratorial tone that was almost louder than his regular voice. "Being that you're still a person of interest, as the police are so fond of saying."

"Hello, Clive," I said, hoping that he would adopt my quiet, conversational tone. "You caught the scent on this one pretty early, I see."

"Yes, well, the police scanner is my new best friend," he said, his voice echoing. "A phone cord, can you believe it? Isn't that delicious? I mean, I recognize that there's a human life involved here, but you have to admire the chutzpah, don't you? A phone cord," he repeated, shaking his head admiringly. "Wonderful turn of events, wouldn't you say? I believe I've got myself a real page-turner here, not to mention the movie rights, knock on wood."

He saw the look on my face and instantly switched to a more funereal tone. "But, as I say," he said somberly, "there is a human life involved here, can't let that get trampled in the furor. A wonderful woman. Had a chance to speak with her myself just the other day. Tremendous energy, lust for life and all that. Such a shame."

He bowed his head for a brief second, and then a moment later turned and bounded toward the elevators. "Well, good to see you, Eli. Glad to see you're not in jail. Yet."

"Thank you. Thank you very much," I sighed, and then a thought occurred to me. "Say, Clive," I called after him, "was that you I saw talking with Boone the other day at The International House of Pancakes?"

This stopped him dead in his tracks. He spun around and I saw about seven different emotions move across his face in an instant. "International my ass," he said finally, breaking into a wide grin. "They ought to be brought up on charges for that name. They are, to be kind, barely domestic, at best."

"So that was you?"

"Indeed it was. You should have come over and joined us. It might have made for a more enlightening conversation. Our friend Mr. Boone is a lover of the monologue, the more lengthy the better. And he can certainly make quick work of a stack of pancakes, let me tell you. Impressive, in a nauseating sort of way."

"You were interviewing him for the article?"

"The book, my friend, the book. However," Clive said as he slumped back against the wall dramatically, "Mr. Boone, although talkative, says far more than he actually reveals. He mostly spoke in circles, very few of them concentric. The conversation was, in a word, fruitless. Know what I mean?" he added, doing a fair impression of Boone's verbal tic.

"Too bad. You were probably one of the last people to talk to him before Arianna's death."

"And don't think I won't be playing up that angle to the hilt if our friend Mr. Boone turns out to be our killer, knock wood. Well, must get back to the mines, as they say. No rest for the wicked and all that." He tossed a wave in my direction and headed again toward the elevator bank.

"Clive, security is pretty tight up there. I doubt they'll let you in on the fifth floor."

"Oh, my dear fellow, I'm not going to the fifth floor," he said, pressing the down button and turning back toward me. "Perish the thought. I'm off to the cafeteria and then to the employee smoking lounge. When you want the dish in a hospital or any other large, bureaucratic institution, go to where the lowest-paid workers congregate. That's where you get the top drawer information."

Even though he was across the lobby from me, he chose this moment to lower his voice. "In spite of what you may have been taught, my boy," he said, taking on the tone of a wise schoolmaster, "a straight line is not always the shortest distance between two points. At least, that's always been my experience."

He punched the down button twice more. "Here we go," he said as the elevator door opened. "Let the gossiping begin."

Stopping at Akashic Records was not the shortest distance between the two points represented by the hospital and my home, but I ended up veering off course and stopping there anyway.

I wasn't entirely certain why—another bout of intuition, I assumed, which so far hadn't done me any real good. In fact, as I thought about it, I realized that my intuition to follow Boone had put me in the hospital and hadn't helped Arianna one bit. So much for the power of intuition, I concluded as I pulled into the store's parking lot.

As with the first time I entered Akashic Records, I was immediately assaulted by the wall of odor that greeted customers at the door. The smell had not abated since my first visit—if anything, it may have grown even more pervasive. However, the thick cloud of sickly candle smells didn't seem to be hindering business. The store was abuzz with customers.

Several clerks were interacting with shoppers, but there was one clerk in particular I wanted to speak with. I finally spotted Michael, chatting up a customer in the record area. I crossed the store and stood nearby, casually flipping through one of the used-record bins, waiting for an opening.

"Actually," Michael said to the customer, a harried-looking woman in her forties, "our credit policies have recently undergone a change. I know that Arianna used to allow seemingly endless credit, but after some study we've determined that policy was fiscally unsound. Consequently, all outstanding balances will need to be settled before we can begin further treatments."

I couldn't hear the woman's response, due to the ambient noise in the shop and the low tone she was using, but Michael nodded as she spoke, looking like someone who was trying to look sympathetic.

He couldn't quite pull it off.

Michael shifted his weight from one leg to the other and crossed his arms, flexing his biceps and giving his back a stretch while he listened. He obviously spent a lot of time working out, and the tight pants and even tighter shirt that he wore highlighted all his time-consuming efforts. His hair was tousled in a very strategic manner and when he smiled it was clear that the whiteness of his teeth owed more to nurture than nature. His gaze darted around the store while he listened to the woman.

I put my head down and continued to flip through the records, which consisted of easy-listening vocalists from the seventies and eighties. The woman must have finished her plea, for Michael began speaking again.

"Well, I'm sorry you feel that way, but our policies are our policies and we simply can't, in good conscience, make the kinds of exceptions that Arianna was so fond of making." He nodded again while the woman spoke. "Yes, well, we're sorry to see you go, but I would remind you that your outstanding balance is still your responsibility and we will turn it over to a collection agency if the need arises. Thank you. Goodbye." These last words were said to the woman's back as she huffed toward the door, shaking her head.

Michael flexed his biceps once more for good measure and then surveyed the store again. He stepped over to the nearest counter and began tapping away on a computer keyboard. I pulled the first record out of the bin I was in front of and walked over to the counter. He heard my approach but did not look up.

"And did you find everything you were looking for today?" he asked, still tapping away at the keyboard. He glanced at the album in my hand and did a double take, which caused me to look at the album for the first time. It was Olivia Newton John's *Have You Never Been Mellow.*

"Yes, I did," I said. "I've been looking for this one for quite a while," I added.

He glanced up at me for the first time and it took a moment for a look of recognition to settle in on his face. "Mr. Marks, isn't it?" he said, taking the album from me and ringing it up on the cash register. "You were in here the other day, right?"

"Yes, I was talking to Arianna. So sorry to hear what happened to her."

"Yes, a tragedy," he agreed. "We were all devastated. But we must pick up and move on. That's the way she would have wanted it."

I was about to say something, but we were interrupted by another employee, a too-thin girl with stringy bleached-blonde hair and a designer tie-dyed t-shirt. "The ten o'clock reading is here, and the ten-fifteen aura photo is early," she said, glancing at the album in Michael's hand and then over at me.

Apparently I wasn't enough to hold her interest, because she immediately looked back to Michael for instructions. He looked at his watch.

"Serena's late, so you should do the reading. And if Andre isn't here by ten after, I'll do the photo." She nodded and walked away, guiding a customer through the beaded curtain and into the back room.

"Sorry about that," Michael said to me as he continued to ring up my purchase. "We're having some minor staffing issues that still need to be resolved."

"Arianna left some mighty big shoes to fill, I'd imagine," I said.

Michael gave a short laugh that ended up as a nearly silent snort.

"Literally," he said, suppressing a smile. Then his businesslike tone returned. "Arianna always insisted on doing everything, the aura photos, the readings, all that, herself. She never let anyone else help. Since her passing, I've instituted a new schedule, which allows us to fully utilize our treatment space, which in the past was woefully underused. Now we do full-body healings in the treatment room at the same time we're doing aura photos in the studio. I've even got someone back there cleaning and repairing jewelry full-time, which in the past only got done when Arianna had a few spare minutes. Much more efficient use of people, resources, and space."

"And more profitable, as well, I would imagine."

"The album was three ninety-nine, so with sales tax your total is four thirty," he said.

I handed him a five and he opened the drawer for my change.

"Yes, to answer your question, it is more profitable. Arianna had her way of doing business; I have mine. To each his own," he said, handing me two quarters and two dimes.

"So, are you officially the new owner of Akashic Records?" I asked, pocketing the coins.

He put the album into a slim brown paper bag and handed it to me. "Nothing's official, yet," he said. "But I know that was Arianna's wish. We just need her will to go through probate before we can finalize everything. Can I help you with anything else today?"

A thesis occurred to me and I decided to test a few of its elements. I stepped back and looked him over. "Michael, you're in terrific shape. Do you work out?"

He smiled and unconsciously puffed his chest and flexed his biceps. "Every day. You should try it sometime," he added with a fake laugh, giving me a critical once-over as he pulled a cell phone from his pocket.

"I don't know. Ever since Jim Fixx dropped dead while jogging, I've been very skeptical of exercise," I said.

"That was a long time ago. You must have been an impressionable youth."

I shrugged.

"Well, I know this much," Michael continued as he started tapping out a text on the phone. "He would have dropped dead a lot sooner without exercise."

"Yeah, but either way he ended up dead, so what's the point?" This twisted logic brought him up short for a second and he stopped texting, if only for a moment. "So," I continued as he mentally scratched his head, "how much can you bench press?"

"Three fifty, three seventy-five on a good day," he said, resuming his miniscule typing.

"That's a lot of weight to pick up. How much do you suppose Arianna weighed?"

He narrowed his eyes, looking up from the phone's keypad. "I don't exactly know. Is there anything else I can help you with?"

"Yes, you mentioned that you do jewelry cleaning and repair?"

He sighed and dropped his phone arm to his side to dramatically demonstrate the degree to which I was boring him. "Yes we do. Is there a particular piece we can help you with?"

I shook my head. "Nothing right now. I was just wondering, they still use cyanide for cleaning jewelry these days, don't they?"

This got less of a reaction from him than I would have liked. "We use a number of different chemicals. Cyanide may be one of them. Would you like me to check?" he asked.

"No, that's fine. One last question."

"Yes?" he hissed, making no effort to cover his exasperation as he returned to his texting.

"Do you agree that the shortest distance between two points is a straight line?"

He stared at me for a long moment. "I have no idea of what you're talking about."

"Yeah, it's a little fuzzy for me as well, but I'm working on it. Thanks for your help."

I'm a little ashamed to admit it, but I was humming *Have You Never Been Mellow* as I walked out of the store.

Chapter 18

As intriguing as my conversation with Michael had been, I soon discovered that I had more daunting issues at hand. I had a kid's magic show to get ready for, and although it was my intention to simply glance through the material that afternoon—in advance of the show the following day—as soon as I looked at what Nathan had left me, everything changed. And not for the better.

Nathan had brought over all of his props in a grocery sack, which had been stashed, unopened, in a corner of my apartment since his most recent visit to the shop.

It was only upon opening the prop bag and seeing the mysterious paraphernalia within and then reading his instructions for the first time that it dawned on me that I was in trouble.

Serious trouble.

To say that his notes were less than copious would be an understatement. On a small slip of paper, in his neat, legible scrawl, he had written the following:

> *Intro—set character, parrot bit—four minutes*
> *Dinosaur story—confetti or rubber bands as needed—*
> *three minutes*
> *SpongeBob take-off—three minutes (remote controls,*
> *etc. Add extra streamers.)*
> *Balloon animals/song parody—three minutes (adapt*
> *verses for birthday kid)*

*Monkey camp story, with bananas—three minutes (11
plastic, one real)
Balloon finale—four minutes
Encore—rest of balloons*

The only thing on the list that I completely understood was that it added up to twenty minutes plus an encore. Somehow, in my naiveté, I had assumed that he was giving me, you know, his act, including a script and specific instructions for each effect. Instead I got a random list of words, some of which I recognized, but most of which made no sense as a structured magic act for kids.

Granted, he was my friend and I had certainly seen him perform, but not recently and certainly not with the idea of duplicating what I was seeing.

I made several semi-frantic, unanswered calls to his cell phone and then settled into some serious fretting. Then I realized that panicking would get me nowhere, so I sat in the middle of my living room floor and went through all the items in the bag.

There were two bags of balloons. One was the bag I gave him for the special helium balloon gag, so the others, I assumed, were suitable for balloon animals. I hadn't made balloon animals since I was a teenage magician, and as I quickly discovered, it is nothing like riding a bike.

Despite my best efforts, every one that I attempted resembled a sickly boa constrictor in the midst of devouring an anvil.

The bag also included several electronic devices that I didn't recognize, a bag of confetti, some plastic bananas—one which opened to reveal three smaller bananas within, a stuffed monkey that had some sort of remote-control mouth that I couldn't quite figure out, an inflatable version of the cartoon character Sponge-Bob, and several unopened packages of batteries. Stuffed at the bottom were a pirate coat, a pirate hat, and an eye patch.

I looked at the truly random collection of materials in front of me and swore, at first quietly and then at a greater volume. I was screwed. I realized that I would have to look elsewhere for inspiration, as I wasn't finding it in Nathan's accursed shopping bag.

I then spent a fruitless hour digging through my own act, pulling out those pieces that might be suitable for an audience of youngsters.

My act is not particularly *adult*, but it does ask the audience to be hip to certain cultural references. It also requires the people who volunteer to be able to do grown-up things, like follow instructions and care about the outcome.

From my hour-long act I was able to find about three minutes of material that I felt would be suitable for a young audience.

The next hour was spent downstairs in the shop, examining each and every item for its likely kid's show potential. After rummaging through all the stock in the store, as well as numerous discontinued items that had long-since been relegated to the far corner of the basement, I found several possible candidates and carried them up the stairs to my apartment.

Harry, who must have heard me banging around, swung open his door in time to see me passing by, my arms overflowing with a bizarre and sundry collection of objects. He was naturally curious and asked why I had taken to shoplifting at such a late age. I explained my predicament and he nodded sympathetically throughout my recitation of what Nathan had done to me and what I planned to do to him upon his return.

"Not to worry," Harry said, opening his apartment door wider and gesturing that I should come in. "Help has arrived."

"Of course, Buster, you wouldn't know this," Harry said to me once he had persuaded me to put down the armload of junk I had lifted from the store, and take a seat on his worn and lumpy couch, "but I spent the first six or seven years of my career as a children's magician. Loved it, absolutely loved it. But a fellow couldn't make a living at it, at least not back then. So I switched gears and went into stage work, with your aunt. Not that there was all that much more money in stage work, but it was better than the small change I had been making before."

I nodded patiently, waiting for the point of his story, which in typical Harry fashion could be just around the corner or several torturous miles down the road. My face must have betrayed my thoughts, because he winked at me and headed toward the closet.

"Anyway," he said as he opened the door and began to dig through the heavy winter clothes hanging there, all wool and corduroy, "I was a pretty darned good kid's magician, if I do say so myself. And, being the pack rat that Alice always accused me of being, I hung onto all the pieces for that act. At least, I think I did."

He banged around in the closet for a few more moments before I heard a muffled "Aha!" and then he emerged, dragging a worn black suitcase behind him. He set the case on its side and then went to his record collection, flipping through the albums for several seconds before finding the desired selection. He placed the vinyl disc on his beloved stereo, set the stylus on the disc and returned once more to the black suitcase on the floor.

What followed then was nothing short of astonishing.

To the strains of Gershwin's *Rhapsody in Blue,* Harry opened and unfolded the suitcase, which magically transformed into a waist-high table on a stand.

He then proceeded to perform a magic routine of such minimalism and beauty that I was literally awed, sitting on the edge of the sofa, my mouth slack.

Using the simplest of materials—a spool of thread, two coins, three thimbles, a ball of yarn, a balloon, a hatpin, three jumbo playing cards, some flash paper, a single white plastic rose, and a fez— he created a story that could only be called epic.

He performed the routine—which flowed in sync with the music as if Gershwin had written it specifically for Harry—in complete silence, and yet you'd swear that there were sound effects sprinkled throughout the act.

It was thrilling and captivating and when he reached the finale, during which he turned the white rose into a shower of white snowflakes that floated around him like the real thing, I actually found myself fighting back tears. It was, quite simply, magical.

The music ended and Harry took a dramatic bow. "Well," he said, brushing off his hands and smoothing down his hair, even though not one was out of place, "that's the gist of it. Pretty rusty on some of the bits...I've done the thimble routine better back in the day, I can tell you...but that gives you the general idea of the piece. All the props appear to be in working order, with the exception of the flash paper, which has seen better days. You'll want to grab a fresh packet and you'll need more snow, that's for sure. But on the whole, you're all set to go."

I stared up at him in amazement. "I can't do that routine," I finally said. "I mean, maybe if I had a couple months to practice, and even then I'd suck at it. There's no way on earth I can learn that by tomorrow afternoon."

"Nonsense," he said, giving my head a playful swat. "There's nothing to learn. There's not one effect in there you don't already know how to do. And the story flows in a logical order. I could have you up and running on this in forty minutes."

"You're out of your mind," I said, and he gave me another swat on the head. "Hey, careful there, you're whacking someone who was just in the hospital with a serious head injury."

"I'll give you a serious head injury," he mumbled. "Buster, stop complaining and get on your feet," he continued as he turned back to the suitcase and began to reset the props.

I knew that arguing would be a waste of time, and so I moved to where he was standing. And then, just as he's been doing since I was ten years old, Harry began to teach me his magic.

His forty-minute estimate was off by about two hours, but he was right.

By the end of the night, under his often scolding direction ("No, no, what are you, all thumbs? That's the clumsiest execution

I've seen in my entire life. Do it this way.") I had learned the flow of the routine and was able to stumble through a performance that was just this side of adequate.

I spent all of the next morning working on it in my apartment, adding some refinements of my own, and by noon I was reasonably certain that I could, if only for twenty minutes, create the illusion of being a kid's magician.

"Are you off to amaze and delight?" Harry asked as he looked up from his regular table at the bar next door. He was surrounded by a couple of the Minneapolis Mystics—Max Monarch and Abe Acker-man—and the three of them were eating Juicy-Lucy burgers, swapping stories, and topping each other with complaints about their various aches and pains.

"I'm all set," I said. "I practiced all morning, got the stuff in the car, and I locked up the shop." I looked at my watch. "With plenty of time to spare."

"Then sit down and eat the rest of this burger," Harry said as he pulled out the chair next to him. "There's enough here to feed an army and you can't do a show on an empty stomach."

I sat next to him and he pushed the plate in my direction. I hadn't eaten breakfast and suddenly lunch seemed like a good idea.

"I make it a rule never to eat before a show," Max said as he wiped a glob of hamburger grease off his chin. "Makes me logy."

"How can you tell?" Abe said, taking a bite of potato chip and shooting a playful glance at Harry, who smiled in return.

"Well, during your show *you* may be wide awake, but believe me, the audience is sound asleep," Max shot back.

"At least I have an audience. What was the size of that last crowd you played for? Two homeless guys and a stray cat?"

"It was a small crowd," Max admitted. "But I had them in the palm of my hand."

"They'd just about fit."

"Ah, you with the jokes all the time. I don't care how big the crowd is. I've had audiences of just one person that I have amazed," he said, starting to build up steam.

"Here it comes," Abe said quietly to Harry.

"For example, you may not be aware of this fact, but I performed one-on-one for the late, great Dai Vernon."

Harry and Abe both mouthed *Dai Vernon* in sync with Max. This was Max's big story.

"I fooled him, The Professor himself. Flummoxed him and baffled him," he continued.

"Blinded him with artistry," Abe said.

"Pulled the rug out from under him," Harry added.

"Make jokes all you want," Max said, turning to the two cronies. "Dai Vernon was the only magician to ever fool Harry Houdini, and I fooled Dai Vernon. So do the math. That's all I'm saying." He turned back to me, studiously ignoring the other two men.

"That's cool, Max," I said, feigning ignorance on the topic. "How'd you fool him?"

"Here's how I did it," Max said, leaning in closer. "Dai Vernon knew all the tricks, believe me. He was a sharp one. So, to fool him, all I did was, I added a flourish to an old standard. And Dai, God rest his soul, got caught up in the flourish. The flourish made him think I was doing one trick, but I was actually doing another trick altogether."

Max continued with the story, relating the post-trick conversation he'd had with Dai Vernon and the lavish praise he had received from the master, but I wasn't listening anymore.

I was thinking about what had fooled Dai Vernon.

He thought it was one trick, but it was actually another. He got fooled by the flourish.

"What's a flourish?" Deirdre said once I got her on the phone. "What are you talking about?"

"The Ambitious Card," I said as I held my iPhone in one hand and steered with the other. "The killer wants us to think he's doing The Ambitious Card, but that's not the trick he's doing. He's trying to fool us with the flourish."

"Eli, he's not doing a trick. He's killing people."

"Yes, I understand that, but he wants us to think he's doing The Ambitious Card. That's a trick where the same card keeps turning up, again and again and again. But that's not the trick he's really doing...that's just the flourish. I think he's doing a version of One Ahead."

Deirdre sighed into the phone. "And what is One Ahead?"

I checked my rearview mirror as I merged onto the freeway, headed toward St. Paul. "It's a technique more than a trick, but the idea is that the magician has information that his audience doesn't know he has...he's one ahead. He knows this piece of information and he spends the whole trick covering that up."

"And how does this apply here?"

"The killer knew all along who his primary victim was going to be...Arianna Dupree. The other psychics were murdered to make it look like she was just part of a series, just one of a bunch of psychics who were being killed. She was the main trick, the others were just a flourish. Just like the playing card. We think he's doing one trick, when he's actually doing another."

"And who is this *he* you're talking about?" Her tone told me she was graduating from placating me to being just a little bit interested in what I was saying.

"Michael, Arianna's assistant. Her boyfriend, boy toy, whatever he was. I don't know his last name, but he runs her store, he ran her life, and according to him he's set to inherit everything she's got. Which I think is probably a lot."

"Is that all you have?"

"He had access to cyanide, because they use it at the store for cleaning jewelry. He certainly had access to Arianna's apartment, and he's strong enough to have thrown her over the balcony."

There was a long silence on the phone. I could tell she was considering all the angles. "So if his goal was to kill Arianna, why make the attempt on Franny?"

"To make it look like Arianna's death was just one in a series. To make it less special," I said, emphasizing that last word.

"Okay," she said slowly. "That's all interesting, but if this Michael guy killed Arianna, what was Boone doing in her apartment, and how did Michael get in and out of her building without showing up on the security tapes?"

Now it was my turn for the long, thoughtful pause. "I'm not sure," I said finally. "Boone and Nova were on the rocks. Arianna was Nova's former lover. Michael was Arianna's current lover. There's something there, I just can't connect the dots yet."

"I don't know, Eli. This all sounds a little far-fetched."

"Do you have anything that's any nearer-fetched? What's the harm of sending Homicide Detective Fred Hutton to talk to him?" I could hear her sigh on the other end of the line. "I tell you, Deirdre, there's something in this. Trust me. I'm not far off."

"I'll see what I can do."

"That means it's as good as done." But she didn't hear this last bit. She had already hung up.

Spiderman was crying.

At least, it looked like he was crying. With a mask pulled over his head, it was tough to know for sure. But he had his head down and his shoulders were quaking a bit. He was sitting on the curb in front of a large, expansive house in North Oaks and to be honest, he looked sort of pitiful.

North Oaks is just northeast of St. Paul, a private community filled with large homes, wooded areas and lakes.

Expensive cars were parked haphazardly up and down the street near the house. I found a space further away than I would have liked and lugged the boom box and Harry's old black suitcase toward the house. It must have been a magical case, because the nearer I got to the house, the heavier it seemed to get.

I stopped to catch my breath a few feet away from Spiderman. He didn't look up.

"Are you okay?" I asked tentatively.

I could hear a sniffle from within the mask and he turned to look at me. His eyes were the only part of his face that was visible. There was a redness around the eyeholes that was, I think, unrelated to the mask. He looked me over, top to bottom, and then noticed the suitcase and the boom box.

"You here for the birthday party?" he asked, his voice sounding hoarse.

"Yes."

"Well, all I can say is, good luck."

"A rough crowd?"

"The worst. Seven-year-olds with money. They're like a disease." He lowered his head again and I heard another sniffle muffled by the mask. "I'm done with this. This is just brutal. I'm going back into phone sales."

I could sense that he wanted to be left alone, so I picked up the suitcase and boom box and headed up the driveway toward the house.

I was met at the front door by one of the official party planners, a blonde woman in her late twenties. She wore a freshly starched red polo shirt with an emblem on it that read "P2: Perfect Parties." Her nametag read "Candy."

Candy radioed my arrival to some sort of party planning war room, where an authoritative voice noted with pleasure that I was early and okayed my admission into the house.

I was led through the immense house by the too-perky Candy, who chatted nonstop about how well the party was going, interrupted by two brief and tense radio conversations with the crew on the back lawn who, apparently, were running into some difficulties while setting up the fireworks.

She ended both dialogs by harshly hissing, "I don't care, just do it," into the radio.

"A problem with the fireworks?" I asked.

"No," she said confidently. "They're just worried that it's going to rain, which apparently is a problem in their world, but not in mine. The forecast said snow, not rain, and I'm more inclined to believe the National Weather Service than this pack of idiots. Believe me, one way or another, there will be fireworks."

"I can imagine," I said.

Candy steered me down a wide staircase that emptied into a mammoth lower level room. One wall was filled with windows and sliding glass doors that overlooked the lawn and a lake beyond. The other walls were covered in what looked to be real wood. The carpet was wall-to-wall, and that's saying something, because there was a lot of distance between the four walls.

The room was brimming with children running, playing, screaming, and in some cases, all three. Food was at the far end of the room, where linen-covered tables had been set up and the red-shirted staff was serving custom cake and homemade ice cream to kids who had clearly already had too much cake and ice cream.

A few of the parents stood around in small clusters, doing a terrific job of ignoring their children and the bedlam they were creating. Most of the children were gathered around a new Wii game, which played on the largest plasma screen I had ever seen outside of a major league ballpark.

"This is your performance space," Candy said, pointing to one corner of the room. "You can set up here."

"Great," I said, realizing that she had placed me in the only dark space in an otherwise well-lit room. I called her toothy smile and raised her a grin. "It should just be a couple of minutes."

As I began to set up the props and plug in the boom box, one of the parents—a balding guy in his forties with a drink in one hand—stopped by to watch. "You're the next entertainer?" he asked.

"Yes, I'm a magician."

"You're a braver man than I," he said. "This group has chewed up and spit out a lot of performers in the two hours I've been here."

"Oh, I'm sure it will be fine," I said. "Where's the birthday boy?"

"Take a guess," he said, using his drink to point toward the kids gathered around the Wii. One kid pushed another kid over and grabbed the game's remote.

"That's mine," whined the kid, who was literally snot-nosed. "I'm going to play until I win." He pushed another kid out of the way and hit the reset button on the game box.

"Wow, someone's a little wired. What's his name?"

The guy shrugged. "I forgot his given name. Around here, we just call him Satan." He looked into the suitcase as I pulled my few props out of it. "You got any tricks in there that will make him disappear?" he asked hopefully.

"Oh, probably," I said, "but currently I'm a person of interest in three homicides and one attempted homicide, so I'm trying to keep a low profile."

He chuckled awkwardly at this and then pretended that someone across the room wanted to see him.

"Anyway, have a great show," he said as he scurried away.

As it turned out, I did have a great show. One of the best of my career, I think.

Over the years, I've had a lot of experience performing for bad audiences. I've performed for drunk audiences and angry audiences and bored audiences and exhausted audiences.

For one Fortune 500 company, I performed right after they finished a memorial ceremony for a well-loved and recently-deceased employee. That was a cheery show. For another company,

I was the entertainment for the employees who didn't reach their sales goals that year. People who did reach their sales goals got a private performance by Bruce Springsteen. Even I didn't want to be at my show that night.

So I know bad audiences. And, believe me, this started out as a bad audience.

Once I was all set up, Candy announced that the magician was starting. The announcement fell on deaf ears—all the kids who weren't stuffing their faces with cake and ice cream were gathered around the TV and didn't look like they were leaving any time soon.

Nevertheless, Candy gestured that I should begin, and so I did.

I pressed play on the boom box, cranked the volume and George Gershwin did his best to compete with the music and sound effects emanating from the television's theater-style sound system.

I had made only minor alterations to Harry's act, not so much to personalize it but to make it possible for me to perform with any authority after seeing it for the first time less than twenty-four hours earlier.

The biggest change I made was the addition of two inanimate audience members, which turned out to have been prophetic, because when I began the show I had exactly zero actual audience members.

I created this fake audience by taking a couple of balloons and blowing them up with the tube that snaked down my sleeve from the helium-oxygen tank I had strapped to my back. Once inflated, I quickly sketched a face on each one with a black marker. Then I began the show proper, while these two balloon heads floated at eye-level nearby, seemingly watching me perform.

With the balloon audience in place, I began to execute the simple moves that Harry had so artfully strung together. It really was a beautiful and elegant routine and I was having a great time with the material. I got so involved in going through the act and playing to the balloon heads, that I was surprised to look up at one point and see that two kids had wandered over from the video game to check me out. Moments later they were joined by another kid and then another.

I made no effort to acknowledge them and kept playing to the balloon heads, which somehow must have made the act all the more magnetic, for every time I glanced up a few more kids had joined my crowd.

I persisted in steadfastly ignoring them, instead directing the act toward the floating balloons, occasionally reaching out and turning the balloon heads so that they were facing me and not the wall. This got a huge laugh every time I did it, and so I found several more opportunities to work it into the act.

By the time I reached the climax of my show, I had all the kids seated in rapt attention in front of me, with the exception of the birthday boy. Satan sat glumly alone in front of the large television screen, doing his best to pretend that he was exactly where he wanted to be.

For a few seconds I considered trying to do something to draw him in, and then thought *to hell with him* and continued to perform for my audience.

If he wanted to be a seven-year-old North Oaks spoiled brat, that was fine by me.

I reached the finale of the act—turning the white rose into a snowstorm—and was greeted by a tremendous round of applause. Well, as tremendous as you can get from thirty tiny pairs of sticky hands clapping together.

Then the parents set down their drinks and joined in, giving the ovation a bit more volume. I feigned surprise at the crowd that had appeared before me, then grabbed two longs strands from the ball of yarn on the table in front of me. I tied one to each of the floating balloon heads and presented them, with a bow, to the first two kids who had come over for the show. This produced yet another round of applause.

*   *   *

"That was terrific," Candy said as she escorted me back to the front door. Good thing she did, as I could have easily gotten lost in the maze of halls and doorways.

"Glad you liked it. The kids seemed to like it, too," I said, hefting the suitcase and the boom box through the wide front door. "Sorry I couldn't entice the birthday boy into the fun."

Candy looked around and then whispered, "Oh, screw him, the privileged little fucker. I hope he chokes on a Lego." Then she handed me my check, smiled sweetly and closed the door.

After I made the short hike back to my car and got everything loaded into the trunk, I checked my phone to see if I'd received any messages from Deirdre. She hadn't called back, but I did find an enticing text message that had come from Megan about ten minutes before.

"Hey, where are you? Are you interested in having some fun? Megan."

I sat in the front seat and quickly typed a response. *"Just finished a gig in North Oaks. Fun – yes, please."*

I waited, impatiently, and a few moments later I got a response. *"Perfect. I'm at the Wabasha Caves. Can you join me? Megan."*

That was intriguing, I thought, but it didn't stop me from quickly typing a response. *"I can be there in 20 minutes,"* I wrote. I hit send and started the car.

A smarter man—one less smitten by a beautiful woman and pumped up on the adrenaline rush that comes after a great show— might have recognized the warning signs in those text messages, the clear signs that something was amiss.

Clearly, I was not that man.

Chapter 19

The sky had turned silver-gray and it looked like the snow that had been threatening for days was finally going to arrive. I pulled my car into The Wabasha Caves' virtually empty parking lot and parked next to the only other car in sight—Megan's small, green Mini Cooper, which was parked slightly askew near the front entry.

The main door to The Caves looked closed as I approached it, and then I noticed that it was propped open with a worn, red brick, which matched the cobblestone-style walkway that led from the parking lot.

It took a few moments for my eyes to adjust to the dark foyer, which was lit only by a small, bare bulb over the box office window, which was shuttered. The main room straight ahead of the lobby was completely dark, but I could see some light to my right, down the corridor to the bathrooms.

I turned and headed in that direction.

"Megan?" I said, momentarily surprised at the echo that bounced off the walls as I moved toward the light, which appeared to be coming from up ahead and around the corner.

I remembered that chamber as the one where I'd had makeup applied before the fateful television broadcast with Grey. I moved more confidently toward the light, and turned into the large cavern. The room was lit by a single light, an old-fashioned beer sign showing a smiling bear touting the benefits to be found in the land of sky blue water. The flowing stream in the two-dimensional sign actually produced the illusion of motion, casting a shimmering light throughout the room. This provided a festive look to the cavern, but did little to cut the murk that emanated from the dark corners.

Even though she was heavily silhouetted in the dim light from the beer sign, I recognized Megan standing behind the far end of the bar. I moved toward her.

"Thanks for the intriguing invitation," I said as I ran my hand across the smooth, cold surface of the bar. "I mean, I like the mood lighting and all."

"Eli," she said.

If I'd been really listening, I would have heard the stress in her voice, but I was already onto the next subject.

"Well, you'll be happy to know that not only did I just have a great show, but I may have also cracked the murders," I said as I arrived at her end of the bar. I pulled up a stool and sat down.

The shimmering water in the beer sign was doing interesting things to her face, making it look as if she were crying.

"Turns out, Arianna's assistant, Michael, was killing all the psychics to direct attention away from his desire to get Arianna out of the way. The Ambitious Card was just a flourish to hide the real trick he was doing."

Megan shook her head sadly. "No," she said quietly. "That's not it."

"Well, I might be off on some of the details," I admitted, "but I think I have the general concept figured out."

"Yes, you do," said a voice from behind the bar. I looked around, surprised to hear another voice, but didn't see anyone.

And then Pete, who had been crouching behind Megan, slowly stood up. He was holding a gun and it was pointed at Megan. "You've got the concept right, Eli, you're just a little off on your identification of the players."

I looked from Pete to Megan and for the first time I saw the fear in her eyes. And, finally, moron that I am, I recognized that it wasn't just a trick of the light from the beer sign.

She actually *was* crying.

"Hey, buddy," I said to Pete, trying to sound as affable as possible, "Take it easy. If you handle that gun the way you handle a deck of cards, someone's gonna get hurt."

"Thanks for the advice, but I'm actually *counting* on someone getting hurt," he said as he took Megan's arm and pushed her out from behind the bar. He clutched her tightly as they rounded the corner and stood in front of me. "And thanks for responding to Megan's text messages, although you've probably figured out by now that I sent them."

I nodded as the other shoe dropped and I realized where I had screwed up. "Abbreviations," I said, shaking my head. "That's what was wrong."

"Pardon me?"

"I should have realized that the texts weren't really from Megan. There were no abbreviations."

Pete looked from me to Megan. He actually looked hurt.

"My wife and I don't text each other," he said, "because she told me once she didn't like it. But apparently she really likes texting with you," he said, making it sound almost kinky.

He gestured toward a small, silver flashlight resting on the bar. "Pick that up and turn it on," he said.

I did as instructed. "You know, Pete, if this is about Megan and me, I think you're blowing it all out of proportion."

"Don't worry about that, Eli," Pete said. "Your relationship with my wife is just icing on the cake. Now head over that way." He gestured with the gun toward the darkest corner of the room. I turned and pointed the flashlight beam ahead of me.

The ceiling sloped down as we got closer to the far wall, and, in the dim light of the flashlight I finally saw a door set back within the murk. It was nearly the same color as the cavern walls, making it practically invisible until you were right on top of it. I heard the rattle of keys and turned to see Pete tossing me a key ring. I grabbed the ring out of the air.

"Unlock the door," he said flatly.

There were two keys on the ring. I focused the flashlight on the door with one hand while trying one of the keys with the other. The first key didn't fit at all. The second key slid into the lock roughly and on my initial attempt it refused to turn. I gave it a hard twist and could feel the vibration of the old tumblers in the lock as they slipped into place. I gave the handle a hard tug and the heavy, solid door swung open slowly.

The space on the other side looked even darker and danker than the room we were in.

"Go in," Pete said.

I stepped into the pitch-black space and turned to see Pete pushing Megan in ahead of him. She stumbled up alongside me, trembling. I wanted to put a comforting arm around her, but under the circumstances I felt it was best to wait and see how this played out.

I held up the key ring. Pete shook his head.

"You can hang on to that," he said. "You'll notice that there's not a lock, or even a doorknob, on this side of the door. So the keys will do you little good, but they will at least explain how you were able to get in here."

I pointed the flashlight toward the door and saw that he was correct. An old, rusted metal plate was welded to the door where a lock and door handle should have been.

"I'll take that flashlight now," Pete said, holding out a hand to me, while he kept the gun in his other hand pointed in my general direction. I handed it to him and he stood back, partially closing the door, holding just a small opening with his left foot. "Don't want to let too much air in here," he said. "Sorry about the gloomy setting, but it was the best I could do, under the circumstances. The pattern must be maintained."

"The pattern?"

"Sure, you know...the psychic with second sight stabbed through the eyes. The hypnotherapist who is murdered in his sleep.

And on and on. And now, the psychic who works with crystals is found dead in a cave full of them. And, as an added bonus, the murderer dies along with her."

"So, you're going to lock us in this room?" I asked.

"Well, yes, but to the police it's going to look like you accidentally locked yourselves in this room," he said, putting an odd emphasis on the last word. "But what's interesting is that this isn't a room, is it Megan?"

She shook her head slowly. "No, it's not."

"What is it?"

"It's the entrance to the rest of the caves. The part that's not open to the public."

"That's right, honey. It's the rest of the caves...a few miles of tunnels and nooks and crannies and maybe even a couple places where one could fall from a great height and do considerable damage. And you know what's interesting about these caves?" he asked. Neither of us answered him.

I couldn't see his face—he was silhouetted by the dim light coming from the cavern behind him.

"What's interesting," he continued unabated, "is that over the years the St. Paul Parks Department has systematically sealed off all the outside entrances to these caves. You know, to keep bums and homeless people out. However, every few years someone finds another way in and they wander about for a while and then you know what happens?"

Again, we stared back at him, unwilling or unable to answer. He didn't seem to mind.

"They die," he said. "They die because all the entrances are closed up and there's no air and before they know it they're only breathing carbon monoxide...only they don't realize that...and a little while later they get tired and fall asleep and die. Which, essentially, is what's going to happen to the two of you in the next hour."

My mind was doing its best to figure out what was going on, but I couldn't make all the pieces fit. "This can't be just about me and Megan," I said finally. "Because there was no me and Megan until well after Grey and Bitterman were killed. So, if it's not about us, what is it about?"

"Real estate," Megan said in almost a whisper. "It's all about money and real estate."

"Bingo," Pete said.

"Real estate," I repeated as I looked around the dark space. "Really?"

"Not this real estate," Megan said softly. "Not the Caves. My corner. The stores."

"Here's something interesting," Pete said as he leaned casually against the doorframe, still holding the door open a bit with the toe of his shoe. "When Megan and I were in couple's therapy, I learned that finances are the one thing that couples are most likely to argue about." He looked over at Megan. "And that certainly is true in our marriage, wouldn't you agree?"

Megan didn't say anything in reply, but I could sense her fury just below the surface.

"When Megan inherited all that property from her grandmother," Pete continued, "I was all for unloading it. In fact, I even found a consortium that was looking for a corner just like ours, and they were willing to pay well above market price to get it. Unfortunately, my dear wife, and I should point out, you are still my dear wife, as no divorce papers have yet been signed, wanted to hang onto it for what she called sentimental reasons. She said I could sell the caves, if I wanted, but not her precious corner."

"So this is all about money?" I asked.

"Not just money, Eli. *A lot* of money. The consortium's plan was linked to federal money for a new light rail line and some state money for new housing and some city money for park improvements. We're talking millions here, for the right developer. They were looking at several locations, but ours was favored. But I couldn't get Megan to sell."

"So you had to get rid of Megan," I said.

"Yes, as it turned out. But in reality nothing would have happened if I hadn't bumped into Grey in the parking lot after his show that night here in The Caves. We'd crossed paths before, and so we started chatting. He knew about the consortium and said he was putting together his own plan to bring to them, including ideas for another location. I needed time to convince Megan and didn't need that old faker screwing up my plans, so I followed him home."

"You stabbed him and used my playing card as the flourish."

Pete shrugged. "It was right there in his pocket, so I figured why not? Then, at the reception after Grey's memorial, Bitterman started talking about a meeting he was supposed to have had with Grey. I couldn't take the chance that he was putting together his own deal, so I got some rat poison from the car, emptied out a couple of Ibuprofen capsules, refilled them with the poison and put them in his sleep apnea machine."

"You carry rat poison in your car?"

Pete chuckled. "I'm a real estate guy, trying to unload a bunch of friggin' caves. You bet your ass I carry rat poison in my car. And because I've religiously followed the rules that you taught me," Pete continued, "I also always carry a deck of cards. So I left a King of Diamonds under the machine. At that point, as far as the police are concerned, there's a pattern...someone's knocking off psychics."

"And you're one ahead," I said, "because now if you do need to kill Megan, it will just look like one in a series."

"Exactly. And on the other hand, if I can finally convince her to sell the property, I don't have to kill her and at the same time I've successfully eliminated the competition."

"I guess that's what they call a win-win," I said dryly.

"That's exactly the way I looked at it," Pete agreed. "The problem was, Megan was insisting on the divorce, and as soon as those papers were signed, there was no way I was getting my hands on the property. Then I remembered that Megan had consulted two different psychics, and both of them had, bless their hearts, recommended that we get divorced."

"Arianna and Franny," I said.

Pete's silhouette nodded. "Those would be the two."

"So you decided to continue the series?"

"I needed a couple more to make sure that no one made the connection to the real estate angle. And I also needed more suspects besides you."

"That's where Boone came in."

"Yes, Mr. Boone. That boy was born to be a suspect."

"So how did you get Boone to go to Arianna's apartment?"

"Didn't have to. He had a standing appointment at her place, same time every week."

This gave me pause. "Really? A weekly appointment? What was that all about?"

"I have no idea, but saw no reason not to use it to my advantage. And I thought it wouldn't hurt to have you there as well."

"So it was you who called Franny, pretending to be Boone?"

"That was me...know what I mean?" he said, doing a dead-on impression of Boone's verbal tic. "Now, I hope you both understand that the longer we talk, the more precious oxygen you're using up in here. I helped things along by coming in earlier and starting a couple fires further along in those passages," he added, gesturing toward the darkness behind us.

"I'd like to have it all make sense in my head before I pass out and die."

"Have it your way."

"So how did you get in and out of Arianna's building without showing up on the security tapes?"

"Real estate, Eli. Don't forget what Megan said. This is all about real estate. There's a furnished unit for sale on Arianna's floor. I made an appointment to show it to a couple earlier that day. I came into the building with them, but let them leave on their own. Then I just stayed in the condo until it was time for the Boone and Arianna show. Then I took care of the two of them. After you arrived, I whacked you on the head and returned to the unit down the hall. The next day, I had another showing set up. I buzzed this new couple in, showed them around, and then left with them. Nothing out of the ordinary about that...the place is always crawling with realtors."

Another pause. I wanted to keep him in with us as long as I could, but I was running out of conversational gambits. "So, the idea is that the police will find us in here and assume that we got locked in when I was attempting to kill her?"

Pete nodded. "Something like that. They may find another way to spin it. But the most incriminating piece of evidence against you will be that after you die, the murders will stop. Of course, that will be because I've stopped committing them, but that's not how the police will read it."

He shone the flashlight on my face, and then on Megan's. He was quiet for a long moment. "What a cute couple," he said. "It's kismet that you found each other. Now, if you'll excuse me, I have one more loose end to tie up in Minneapolis. I'll be back in a couple of hours," he added as he stepped through the door, "but I think I'll say my good-byes now."

He closed the door and we could hear the lock snick shut. And then we were alone in the inky blackness.

Chapter 20

We stood together in silence for what felt like a long time. The noise the door had made while closing had the sound of real finality to it, like it was sealed tight. I listened closely, but couldn't hear any noise from the room on the other side of the door. There was no air movement where we were standing. The only sound was our breathing.

"Perhaps this is the wrong time to bring this up," I finally said, "but I think your divorce may not be as amicable as you thought."

Megan sighed, long and hard. "The little bastard. Have I ever mentioned that he has a small penis? Well, he does. Tiny little thing. Almost laughable."

There was another long silence in the dark. "Thanks for sharing. Feel better?"

"Not a lot," she said, and then she sighed. "I spent a lot of time here with my cousins when I was little. I hate to think that this will spoil all my great memories of these caves."

"Hey, if we walk out of here with memories of any kind, we can consider ourselves lucky." I squeezed her hand gently and she returned the gesture. A thought occurred to me. "When you say 'a lot of time,' do you mean in here or in the public spaces on the other side of that locked door?"

"Both really. Back in those days, it wasn't locked up like this. My cousins and I used to play hide and seek in all the caves. Of course, that was before the outside entrances were all sealed up.

But yeah, we'd run through here for hours on Saturday afternoons with flashlights."

"Doesn't seem like a very safe activity for kids," I considered.

"Well, there were a lot of us, so I guess the grown-ups figured that if we lost one or two, it didn't really matter."

"Having just come from performing at a kid's birthday party, I can fully endorse that point of view."

Another pause and then I felt Megan lean into me. I hugged her and held her close. "I don't want to die in here," she said quietly.

"Ditto," I said, kissing the top of her head. "So let's see what we can do to ruin Pete's day."

I stepped back and gave the locked door a useless thump with my fist, and then turned back toward Megan.

"You know your way around here. They couldn't have boarded up all the entrances. The job was performed by city workers after all...they're not known for their work ethic. There must be at least one way out of here."

I could hear her sniffle. "Maybe," she said. "But how do we find it in the dark before the carbon monoxide gets us?"

A thought occurred to me. "You know, we might not be completely screwed," I said as I quickly searched through my pockets. "My iPhone has a flashlight app on it. It doesn't throw off a lot of light, but it would be better than nothing." I came up empty-handed and then remembered when I had last used my phone. "Of course, the phone would be more helpful to us right now if it weren't sitting on the front seat of my car. So I guess we *are* completely screwed," I added.

"Well, it was a good idea while it lasted," Megan said.

I patted my pockets one last time just to make sure, and then reached again into the inside pocket on my sport coat. "However," I said, realizing what I had stashed away there, "I do have the ability to make it light, if only for a couple of seconds at a time." I stepped toward what I thought must be the center of the pitch-black room.

"Turn away from me and open your eyes. There's going to be a short flash of light, so you need to look around and gather as much information as you can in just a second or so."

I took one of the pieces of flash paper from my pocket, attached the small igniter to my finger and set it off. There was a bright burst and for just an instant the cave was illuminated. And then, just as quickly, we were thrown back into the thick darkness.

"Okay, I remember this room," Megan said. "There are two corridors straight ahead of us. The one on the right is a dead end. My older cousin used to go in there and make-out with her boyfriend. He was gross. Big guy, football player. Cute but really dumb, which was the type she always went for. She's married three just like him."

"That's great, Megan," I said softly, "but I think we need to focus."

"Right," she said. "Focus. We don't want the one on the right. It's the one on the left that branches off into other corridors."

"Then let's make our way down the left corridor." With one hand behind me holding Megan's hand, and one ahead of me—to prevent us from walking into a stalactite or stalagmite or whichever it is that hangs from the ceiling—we slowly made our way toward the left corridor.

Once we were safely through the small archway, I gave Megan a warning and then ignited another piece of flash paper. This new small room lit up briefly and I could see Megan's face for an instant as her eyes scanned the space.

"Okay, I know where we are. There's a crawlspace over to our right. It's kind of tight, but once through it, we'll have a lot more options." We moved toward it together, getting down on our knees and feeling the dimensions of the opening in the rough wall. It didn't feel very big.

"Do you want me to go first?" I asked.

"It's not so much that I want you to go first, as it is that I would prefer that I go second."

"Oddly enough, I completely understand," I said.

I took a deep breath and bent down, preparing to crawl through the passage. Then I sat up again, unable to force myself to wiggle into the small opening. "I don't know why this is so hard," I said. "I'm only going from one really dark place into another really dark place. Sort of the story of my life, really." I could hear Megan chuckling behind me. "That's what we in business would call a polite laugh," I said.

"No, it was funny," Megan said. "I'm just worried that we're using up too much oxygen talking. Do you know the symptoms of carbon monoxide poisoning? I feel like I'm starting to get a little light-headed."

"How can you tell?" I made a quick rim shot sound effect.

"Again, funny, but do we really want to waste the oxygen?"

"You're probably right. I'll do my best to keep the graveyard humor to a minimum," I said. "Must be the way that I cope with stress, although to be honest I've never reacted this way in the past."

"Eli, you're still talking," she said patiently.

"Yes, I agree," I said. "But as to your earlier question about the symptoms, in a situation with a really heavy concentration of carbon monoxide, I don't think there really are any symptoms. I think you just pass out."

"Then shut up and start crawling."

I heeded her advice and bent down, pulling myself into the small space. Megan had described the passageway as kind of tight, and if that was her recollection of it as a child, I looked forward to hearing how she described it as an adult. At its narrowest point, it felt like it was about a half-inch wider than my shoulders, and just exactly the size of the height of my horizontal body. And, since I couldn't see anything ahead of me, I had no sense of how long I would be stuck in this confined space. I was truly unnerved and I could feel myself begin to sweat, the moisture rolling off my neck and down my shoulders, making me shiver.

I dragged myself along, silently cursing the small helium tank strapped to my lower back, which dug deeply into me at a couple of really tight points in the journey. I began to wish that I had taken it off back at the car.

And then, after what felt like a long trek but was probably only about eight feet, the passageway opened into a larger black space.

I pulled myself out, not wanting to go too far into the darkness but still wanting to put some distance between myself and the claustrophobic passageway.

"It's all clear," I called into the hole. Megan didn't respond, but I could hear her struggling to pull herself through.

"Here's my hand," I said, groping in the dark. Our hands found each other and by counter balancing my weight against hers, I was able to provide some traction to get her out of the tight channel and into this new, unknown space. We sat for a moment, catching our collective breath, leaning against each other and the rough wall behind us.

"There used to be a hole leading to the outside in this chamber," Megan said finally as she caught her breath. "It should be over to the right, but since we can't see outside right now, I suspect that they sealed it up."

"Let's see what we can see," I said. "Here comes the flash." I ignited another sheet of flash paper and for just an instant we got a quick snapshot of where we had landed.

The headroom was a lot lower than the last chamber, maybe four feet at the highest point. There were two passages out, both to the left of where we were sitting, and a large gray spot on the wall on the right.

"How many of those flash paper things have you got left?" Megan asked.

"I didn't count them, but whatever the number is, I'd be willing to bet you that it will be one or two short of what we actually need."

"Those were the numbers I was thinking of, too," she agreed.

"So the exit you mentioned..."

"It's that gray spot on the wall. I was right. Looks like they filled it in."

"Let me check." I crawled across the bumpy ground to the wall on the right and felt along the uneven surface. The texture of the wall changed to something much smoother for a couple of feet, and then back to the rough texture.

"Hard to say for sure," I said, "but I'm guessing they cemented this one shut. We're not getting out here. Ready to press on?"

She didn't answer and after a moment I heard a whimper that indicated she was crying. I crawled through the dark until I found her. We hugged awkwardly. She buried her face into my chest.

"I really, really hate him," she said. "I'm just kicking myself for being so nice to him about the divorce."

"Well, with any luck, in an hour or so, you can stop kicking yourself and start kicking him. And when you're done, I've got a couple places I'd like to kick him as well."

"But they sealed up the exits," she said, trying to control her crying and coming up short. "All of them."

"Maybe. But maybe not. So we've got to keep moving. We have two options ahead of us. Do you remember which one is which?"

She sighed and it sounded like she was wiping her nose on her sleeve. "Hey, what are you doing, that's my sleeve," I said in mock horror, which made her laugh. She sniffled again and I could sense that she was done crying, at least for the time being.

"Okay, we saw two corridors in here, correct?" she said. "And then the filled-in hole as well."

"That's right. The corridors are to our left, the filled-in spot is to our right."

She took a deep breath. "Both corridors are good, but I think the one on the far left has more exit options."

"Then I vote that we take the one on the far left. Follow me." I started to crawl in the direction of the opening. I heard Megan start to move behind me, and then she stopped.

"Eli," she said quietly. "I'm really starting to feel light-headed."

Now that she mentioned it, so was I, although I was unwilling to admit it just yet. "Really?" I asked. "How bad?"

"It's hard to tell," she said. "Being in the dark makes everything disorienting. But something's going on, that's for sure."

I had made it across the small cavern and found the space that I believed was the corridor on the far left. I leaned back against the rough wall and felt an immediate sharp pain in my back, which made me call out.

"What is it?" Megan said, a hint of panic in her voice.

"It's this stupid thing," I said. "For the kid's show. I keep jabbing myself in the back with it." I took off my jacket and began to unstrap the tank when an idea occurred to me.

"You know," I continued as I removed the tank and then reconnected the long tube and the nozzle, "We could actually use this thing."

"What thing?" Megan asked from across the small space. "Can we use it to punch through the concrete they used to seal up the exit?"

"No," I said as I crawled back to her. "I think we can use it to buy ourselves some time. It's a mixture of helium and oxygen that I use in the act. As luck would have it, though, I didn't use much of it today. Normally, after a show, it would be completely empty."

"And we can breathe it?"

"I don't see why not. There's really only one side effect."

"It's carcinogenic?"

"No," I explained. "It's cartoonogenic."

"What's that mean?"

"It will make us sound like cartoon characters. You know that high-pitched voice you get when you suck the helium out of a balloon?"

"No, I've never done that."

This stunned me into momentary silence. "Never? Even as a kid?"

"Not that I recall."

"Well, you're in for a treat," I said, handing her the nozzle. "Place this in your mouth and press down on this switch. That will start the flow of air. Then just breathe it in." She took the device from my hand and a moment later I heard the tell-tale hiss of gas as it flowed out of the tube. I could hear her breathing deeply for a few seconds and then the hissing stopped. "How did it work?" I asked.

"I'm not sure," she said in a high, squeaky voice. It was as if I had suddenly been joined in the cave by Minnie Mouse. "Let me try it again." She took another hit off the nozzle. "That feels better," she said, her voice a notch higher now, almost up to Betty Boop range. "You should have some, too," she added in her new, squeaky voice as she placed the nozzle in my hand.

I put the nozzle in my mouth and hit the release button, which immediately filled my mouth with the gas. I tried to breathe it in, but the first pass went down wrong and I started coughing. "This is like the first time I tried a cigarette," I said.

I tried it again and this time was able to pull the air into my lungs. I breathed out and took another hit, and then one more. I'm not sure if it was a placebo effect, but my head did feel a bit clearer.

"I think it's working," I said, sounding very much like Alvin or one of the other lesser-known Chipmunks. "I feel a little better."

The sound of my voice produced a huge laugh from Megan. "You sound ridiculous," she said in her new falsetto, in between bursts of laughter.

"Well, you've lost your Kathleen Turner quality as well," I said. "Now it's like being stuck in a cave with Cyndi Lauper."

"Or the munchkins," she added.

This last example sparked a thought. "You know," I said, "Franny told me that she saw something in my future that involved the dark and munchkins. And here we are. Isn't that weird?"

"Did she say how you got out of it?"

"That didn't come up." I handed her the nozzle and waited while she took another hit. She handed it back and I filled my lungs to capacity. We sat for a moment in silence, knowing that the next person to speak would re-start the wave of laughter. Finally I spoke.

"We should keep moving," I said, trying to deepen my voice and coming up short.

Megan stifled a laugh. "Yes, you're right," she finally said. "Let's see if we can find the yellow brick road out of here."

After several minutes of slowly making our way through the various sized caverns, we fell into a sort of routine. We'd crawl into a new cavern, take a couple hits off the tank, use one of the diminishing sheets of flash paper to determine our next step, and then move on.

Then rinse and repeat, as the saying goes.

I had to hand it to the men and women of the St. Paul Parks department. So far they had done a very thorough job of blocking each of the potential exits we had come across. Any image I'd had in my mind of lazy, indolent public works employees had been completely shattered. Those guys were good and even though it might end up killing me, in a way I grudgingly admired their determination to find and plug every damned hole in the bluffs from Wabasha Avenue all the way down to the Sibley Memorial highway. It was evident that at some point in the past someone had taken his job very seriously.

It was hard to keep track of time in the dark, but after traversing several small and medium-sized caverns, I guessed that nearly an hour had gone by.

As we moved forward, Megan's memory of the layout of the caves had started to become less precise. I didn't blame her—it had been over twenty years since she'd played hide-and-seek in this space and we had gone deeper and farther than the areas she had previously played in. However, she wasn't looking at it that way and her level of frustration grew with each new, unfamiliar cavern.

Unfortunately, I was unable to take her self-recriminations seriously, because the madder she got at herself, the more she sounded like Donald Duck in the midst of a bout of cartoon road rage. And of course, my laughing only made things worse.

"Shut up," she snarled at me after one particularly hilarious outburst. "It's not funny. We're going to die in here."

"That may well be," I said, my voice just a tad lower than hers. "But we'll die laughing."

"And it's all my fault," she continued. "If I'd only let Pete sell the corner when he first suggested it, nobody would have died. Nothing bad would have happened. We wouldn't be stuck this cave right now."

"Megan, I don't think your ex-husband's murderous tendencies really fall under the heading of your fault," I suggested. "You're the victim here and Pete is the bad guy and you didn't do anything wrong. Here's what you should do," I said, moving into therapist mode. "Instead of beating yourself up, you should push that energy outward and use it to get out of here and bring that little bastard to justice." I paused for a moment, waiting for a response.

Megan burst out laughing. "Maybe what you're saying makes sense, but there's no way I can take advice from anyone who sounds like that," she spit out between peals of laughter. "You sound absurd."

"So do you." This led to more laughter, followed by another couple hits off the nozzle. The tank was feeling considerably lighter, but I didn't think this was the ideal time to mention it. "Are you ready to move on?" I asked.

"I think so."

I ignited another sheet of flash paper, revealing that we were in a pretty large cavern. In the brief burst of light, I could see at least three corridors leading out of it. "Which one looks good to you?" I asked.

Megan responded with a yelp of surprise. "What was that?" she cried and even though her voice was ridiculously high and squeaky, I could hear real terror in it.

"What happened?"

"Something just touched my head," she said, still panicked. I heard the sound of her tousling her hair frantically. "What was it?"

"It wasn't me. Let's take another look." I ignited another sheet of flash paper. The room was too large to really see everything in that quick flash, but the burst of light triggered a response from somewhere above us, deep in the murk. I could hear the distinctive, unsettling rustle of wings. "I think we've got bats," I whispered.

"Oh crap," she replied, not even trying to keep her voice down.

"No," I assured her. "Bats are good."

"I hate bats. And I don't want to hear that shit about how they eat mosquitoes. Right now, I don't care. I hate them."

"I'm not talking about mosquitoes. If we've got bats, that means there must be a way out somewhere around here."

"How do we know?" she said, calming a bit. "I mean, maybe they just live in here all the time."

"Well, I'm no bat expert," I said. "But I think bats have to go out every once in a while to get things like food. That's the good news."

"What's the bad news?"

"The bad news is that we won't be able to see what direction they're going when they go. And, now that I think of it, I believe bats can get out of a place through a hole about the size of a quarter, which wouldn't be much help for us."

"So tell me again...how is this a good thing?"

"Well," I said as a new thought occurred to me, "if it's safe for them to breathe in here, it's probably safe for us." A doubly important point, I realized, as the helium tank was feeling dangerously close to empty. "We just need to see where they go when they leave and find a way to follow them."

"When do they typically go out?"

I paused, wondering at what point I had suddenly become the de facto bat expert. "They head out at night, if you can believe all the old horror films. Or maybe dusk."

"And when is that?"

I had gotten so used to her high-pitched voice that it no longer struck me as odd. "I'm not sure. It should be soon, though," I said. "It gets dark pretty early now."

As if they heard and understood me, there was more rustling above us. It was quiet for a moment, and then it started again. The sound was moving away from us. I pulled out my dwindling stack of flash paper. I ran the pieces through my fingertips. It felt like I had maybe three left. The noise continued above us.

"I think the bats are moving. I'm going to set off another flash. Watch and see if you can tell where they're headed." I ignited the sheet as I tossed it in the air in front of us. In the brief light, I thought I detected shadows moving.

"I saw movement toward the opening on the far left," I said. "How about you?"

"I'm sorry, when I see bats, I shut my eyes," she said. "It's a primal kind of thing."

"Actually, I don't blame you," I said. "But I think the left corridor is the one we should head down."

"With the bats?"

"After the bats. Or as the French might say, *après le* bat."

"So you're promising me that there will be no bats in the corridor when we go through it?"

"Absolutely," I lied. "We're following them. At a distance."

"Okay then."

We groped our way through the blackness across the cavern until we located the far wall, which I discovered first with my forehead and then, less painfully, with my hand.

I felt around the wall until I found the opening to the passageway. "We're going to have to duck down to get through here," I said, "but at least we won't have to crawl."

I went through first and could hear Megan moving into the space behind me. The cramped corridor got even skinnier for a few feet, requiring us to turn sideways in order to keep moving. I began to fear that it would get narrower and narrower, forcing us to retrace our steps, and then it suddenly became wider and I stopped worrying about that.

That's when they came.

First I heard the hum of wings, which resembled the noise of static on a radio, but the acoustics in the passage were such that I couldn't really place where the sound was coming from. And then suddenly the bats arrived and it didn't really matter anymore.

They hit us from behind like a cold breeze, hundreds of them, bouncing off our bodies like pinballs.

Apparently we were standing between the furry little winged bastards and their night on the town and they were determined to get around us by any means available.

They fluttered between our legs, under our arms, past our ears and eyes, slapping us in our faces with their cold webby wings. I've never walked through a car wash, but I think that's the closest thing to what we experienced, except that we weren't being sprayed with water. Water would have been great, a welcome treat, but that's not what the bats were carrying. They were flying and flapping and peeing and Megan and I were getting the works, the Deluxe Super Wash. Only a couple dollars more, but absolutely worth it.

Did I mention that Megan screamed continuously through all of this? I don't know how that slipped my mind. Yes, she freaked out completely and I really didn't blame her, except that the majority of her screaming was done directly into my right ear. She clung to my arm like a deer tick and dug her nails so far into my skin that I think her fingers actually met halfway through my limb.

And then, as quickly as they had descended on us, they were gone. It was quiet again, with only the echo of Megan's screams reverberating in the cavern. She still clung tightly to me but I could feel her muscles relax, just a bit, and her breathing slowed.

"What's that smell?" she asked, her voice still carrying a trace of Betty Boop in it.

"You don't want to know," I said, using my free sleeve to wipe my eyes.

"Oh, yuck," she said after it finally dawned on her, and I could feel her body shudder. "That's just gross."

"Well, what do you expect? You scared them."

"I scared them? How do you figure?"

"I'm sure they come through this passage all the time and didn't expect to run into anyone."

"Don't tell me you're taking the bats' side?" she said, her voice still high, but more from incredulity than helium.

"I'm neutral on the subject," I finally said. "I'm the Switzerland of bats and bat guano."

Chapter 21

The previous hour or so had felt like a ping pong match between good and bad news, and when we entered the next chamber, bad news continued its winning streak.

The good news, which was meager at best, was that the moment we made it out of what I had come to think of as the Bat Corridor, we were hit with actual fresh air and could see the night sky ahead of us.

We breathed in the crisp cold breeze and, for a moment, I didn't mind being covered in bat pee. Or I minded a little bit less.

The first wave of bad news was the realization that the only thing that separated us from our well-earned freedom was a two-foot by two-foot metal grate, a thick, barred grid with square holes large enough for a bat to crawl through. We headed immediately toward this barrier and I grasped its bars tightly, giving them a hard shake. The grate was very solid and didn't budge.

If that wasn't bad enough, the next piece of bad news became vividly apparent as we looked through the grate. The clouds had lifted and it was a crisp clear night. It appeared to be just after sunset and we could see the tops of the trees and, in the distance, the river and the lights of downtown St. Paul.

"Uh-oh." I said quietly.

"What?" Megan asked, turning to me. "What is it? We found the way out. What's the problem?" Her voice had almost entirely returned to its normal pitch.

"We're near the peak of one of the bluffs. I can see the tops of trees. We're pretty high up."

"Is that bad?"

"Yes, but that's our second problem. Our first problem is this grate. It's really solid." I stood back, my eyes still adjusting to the dim light, and examined how the grate was attached to the wall.

"It must be fastened on the outside," I said, as I stepped closer and tried to see what was holding the grate in place. Megan stepped next to me to see.

Just at that moment a tardy bat flew between the two of us, brushing the side of my face as it maneuvered through one of the larger holes in the grate. Megan jumped back and yelped.

"Son of a bitch," she said, immediately checking her hair for unwelcome visitors.

"Boy, there's something about bats that really brings out the sailor in you," I commented, and then returned to the fruitless task of shaking the sturdy, heavy grate. I was ready to give up but just for the hell of it I gave it one more obligatory yank. And then I felt it give. Just a little.

I rattled the grate again. "What did that TV guy say before Grey's performance in the cave? Something about not touching the walls, because of how soft they were?"

Megan shook her head. "I wasn't there," she said. "But my grandfather used to lecture us about that, about how the cave walls were made of sandstone and how easy it was to dig into them. Didn't matter how much he said it, though, we still did it."

"So even though this is a really solid piece of metal," I said as I examined the grate more closely, "it's attached to what is essentially soft rock."

"Soft rock? Like Fleetwood Mac?" Megan asked, trying to hide the traces of a smirk.

"I see someone's sense of humor is creeping back in," I said. "So if the rock that's holding this is soft, it really doesn't matter how sturdy the actual grate is."

I stepped back and then rushed at the grate, hitting it with the full force of my shoulder and all the weight behind it. I was unable to gauge the impact I made on the grate, as the impact on my shoulder was so intense, pain-wise, that for a second I felt like I was going to pass out.

This made me so mad that I stood back from the grate and lifted my right leg as high as I could and kicked with the full force of my body. I did that twice more, with less force each time, before falling backward onto the dirt. I tried to keep my whimpering to a minimum. The grate hung exactly where it had for years and glared back at me with a silent superiority that I found annoying.

"I'll give it a try," Megan said, taking a position in front of the metal grid.

"Don't bother," I said from my place on the ground. "They found the one spot in all the caves where the rock isn't soft."

She ignored me and prepared to make her own Bruce Lee-style karate kick, balancing on her right leg and arcing her left leg directly at the grate. She gave her best karate yell and kicked firmly at the grid. Her foot bounced off the metal like a tennis ball off the side of a garage and she tumbled backwards to the ground, landing neatly on top of me.

"Son of a bitch," she grumbled as she rolled off of me, placing her elbow squarely into my kidneys in the process. She saw a fist-sized rock on the dusty ground where she had landed and grabbed it, throwing it with fury at the barred metal.

The rock hit cleanly at the center of the grate, making a resonant clang before falling back to the ground.

We turned away, but the sound of metal grinding on rock drew our attention back to the opening. A second later the grate slipped effortlessly away from the wall and tumbled out of sight, down into the woods below.

The only unsettling part of the temporary victory was how long it took for us to hear the sound of it hitting the ground. It took a lot longer than I might have liked. I pulled myself painfully to my feet and stepped forward to examine the obstacle-free opening. Behind me I could hear Megan as she gave a small cheer of joy.

"Now what?" Megan asked as she joined me. She was grinning ear to ear.

"Now we transform ourselves into mountain goats and climb down," I said as I began to pull myself through the hole.

The bluffs that line the riverfront across from downtown St. Paul are, admittedly, not exactly Mount Everest.

Even if there had been snow on the ground, there was no chance of an avalanche. And we were within sight of civilization, so there wouldn't be any Andes-style snacking to worry about.

Be that as it may, it looked to be a long way down. Given the distance between us and the footpath below, I seriously wondered how a lone Parks Department worker had made it up here to install the grate, poorly or otherwise.

I crawled through the hole and stood precariously on a small ledge beneath it. I looked up the bluff and gauged that climbing higher wasn't a practical option. It looked like quite a hike, a steep one at that, and I had no idea where it would ultimately leave us. Going down made more sense, because I could see the road below and knew that it would take us to my car and, more importantly, to my phone.

"Let me go first," I said to Megan as I helped her through the hole. "I think I can see the safest way down."

I stepped back to make room for her on the small ledge and felt the ground give way as my feet came out from beneath me. Then I felt a bush, followed by the branches of a small tree, some shrubs, followed by some stones – both large and small – another tree and then a series of shrubs – this time of the prickly variety – as I slid down the face of the hill.

It was not unlike riding down one of those huge slides at a state fair or carnival, except that the sliding surface was far from smooth and there was nothing between me and the hill but my pants.

Somewhere between seven and ten seconds later I was lying in a heap at the bottom of the bluff, with bits of my pants (and some of my skin) spread out on the hill above me. It was clear that I had discovered the fastest, albeit not the least painful, way down.

I heard Megan, above me, swearing as she struggled to make her way down the hill without following the express route I had just taken. As I listened to her slow and profane progress, I did a quick systems check, wiggling first my fingers and then my toes. After that proved moderately successful, I tried moving my upper limbs and then the lower ones. I felt pain throughout every inch of my body, but nothing sharp or specific, leading me to believe that while much of me was badly bruised, none of me was actually broken.

By the time Megan reached my side, I was able to sit up, although the flashbulbs going off in my head made me wish I hadn't. I touched a sore spot on my forehead and my hand came back red, so apparently I was bleeding in at least one area.

"What took you so long?" I asked, and then spit some dirt out of my mouth.

"Are you okay? That looked really painful."

"Not a problem. Luckily, my body broke the fall. Help me up." I began the deliberate process of putting my feet under me and, with Megan's assistance, I was able to stand shakily.

I looked back up at the dark opening into the cave and shook my head at how far away it appeared. Then I turned my gaze toward the road. "This path should lead us to Water Street," I said. "From there, we can walk or hitch back to the parking lot." I leaned on Megan and we started toward the road. The pain, which was equally dispersed throughout my body, started to fade the more I moved and by the time we reached the road I was able to walk on my own, with only the trace of a limp.

"You know what we're learning?" Megan asked several minutes later as we made our way along the side of Water Street.

"Don't marry a psycho? Don't let him lock you in a cave? Don't scare a flock of bats in a small space?"

She cut me off, sensing, correctly, that I was just getting warmed up. "No, we're learning that no one wants to pick up hitch-hikers who are dirty, battered, bloodied, and smelling of bat pee."

"Well, to be fair, they probably wouldn't know that we smell of bat pee until after we got into their car."

"I'm not so sure," she said. "Some people have a sixth sense about bat pee and many of them seem to be driving down Water Street tonight."

On some level she was correct. Consequently, what would have been a five-minute trip with the help of a friendly, open-minded driver turned into a twenty-minute walk back to The Wabasha Caves' main entrance. My car was the only one in the lot—Pete must have taken Megan's, with the idea of placing it back in its traditional spot behind her store.

I had to admit, his plan looked good on paper.

To outsiders, it would appear that I had driven Megan to The Caves, and then gotten trapped inside with her. The case would be closed, he'd get all of her assets and could sell them as he wished. And no one would be any the wiser.

"We should get out of here," Megan said, a trace of fear in her voice. "In case Pete comes back."

"I don't think Pete is coming back until he's certain that we've expired due to carbon monoxide poisoning," I said as I opened the passenger door and picked up my phone. I was about to dial Deirdre when I noticed that I had received three calls, all from her. She had left the same number of voicemails. I listened to the first one.

"Eli, where are you?" she said in the message, her voice sounding more than usually stressed. "I'm at your uncle's shop. There's been an accident. Call me. Now."

I didn't bother listening to the other messages, but started the car and then proceeded to violate several traffic laws as I made my best time yet getting back to Minneapolis.

*   *   *

From a block away it was clear that something was going on at Chicago Magic. An ambulance, a fire truck, and several squad cars were parked haphazardly in front of the store, their flashing lights creating psychedelic patterns on the storefronts. A crowd of onlookers were being held at bay by several uniformed officers. As we approached, a voice yelled out to me.

"Eli! Eli, old boy. What's going on?" It was Clive, standing on the edge of the crowd, holding his portable police scanner in one hand while he held a small video camera above the crowd and pointed it in the general direction of the front door of our shop. "There was one call on the scanner and since then they've been completely mum on the topic. Occasionally one of the medics or the fireman will come out coughing, then they turn around and go back in. What the devil is going on?"

"Clive, I haven't a clue," I said as I pushed through the crowd with Megan right behind me. I got to the front and was ducking under the police tape they'd strung around the front sidewalk when a uniformed officer yelled at me from the curb.

"Hey, you, stay behind the tape."

"It's okay," a familiar, but not friendly, voice bellowed. "We've been waiting for him."

I looked up to see Homicide Detective Fred Hutton standing over me. He lifted the yellow tape up high enough for Megan and me to scamper through, then waved us into the store. The flashing lights were creating weird patterns on his face. I couldn't really read his expression, but I didn't like the fact that he had been borderline polite to me. That couldn't be good.

Deirdre was waiting for us on the other side of the door.

"Deirdre, what happened? What's going on?" I asked, scanning around the shop. It was a small space and didn't really seem large enough to hold the number of cops, EMTs, and firemen that were currently encamped there. They were all standing at the front of the shop, making it impossible for me to see what was going on in the back.

"Eli," she said, putting out a hand to stop me from moving forward, "there's been an accident. That's why I was calling you. Your uncle—"

I didn't wait for her to finish but pushed past her and through the wall of civil servants until I got to the back of the shop. The back counter was blocking my view, but I could see a pair of legs sprawled on the floor at the base of the steep steps that led up to our apartments.

"Harry," I called out. I moved toward the body, but a hand reached out and stopped me.

"I wouldn't go back there if I were you," a voice said. I turned and was completely surprised and thrilled to see Harry, seated on a stool by the counter. One of the EMTs was bandaging Harry's hand, but otherwise he looked unharmed.

"Harry? You're okay?"

"I'm fine. What happened to you?"

"I'll tell you about it later. Who's that back there on the floor?"

"It's that terrible magic student of yours," he said, and then gestured next to me. "That young lady's husband."

"Ex-husband," Megan said. She had made her way through the crowd and was standing by my side. "Or at least, he will be as soon as I get the papers signed."

"I'm afraid he won't be signing papers any time soon," Harry said with a sad shake of his head.

"Why? Is he—" I wasn't sure the best way to ask the question with Megan standing next to me.

"Is the little prick dead?" Megan said, cutting me off.

"No," Harry replied quickly. "Quite the contrary. The little prick is very much alive. But he's taken a bit of a spill and I suspect that he'll be in the hospital for the foreseeable future."

"So, if he's alive and needs to go to the hospital, why is he still lying back there?"

Harry shrugged. "They got a neck brace on him, and put him on one of those back boards, to prevent any further spinal injury. But I think they're taking a short break." He glanced over at the EMTs, who were in the front of the shop, taking turns with an oxygen mask. "There's the problem of the smell." He looked us over, head to toe. "You probably didn't notice it yourselves, given your current olfactory situation." He sniffed the air around us. "Bat guano, am I right?"

"On the nose," I said. "So what happened?"

"Well, he came in here about an hour ago, pretending to want to buy a cups and balls set. Of course, I refused to sell it to him, as he hasn't begun to master the cut-and-restored rope trick we sold him two weeks ago. So then he pulled a gun on me," Harry recounted indignantly. "I told him flat out that wasn't going to change my mind, but he started yammering about how he needed to tie up the loose ends. Turns out he's the fellow that's been killing all the psychics. He said he had it all worked out that the police would think you did it, but that he knew I was the only one who would ever put all the pieces together, so I had to be, in his words, 'taken care of.'"

"You always did scare the hell out of him," I said.

"Well, be that as it may, he kept pointing the gun at me and told me to head upstairs. So I did as I was told and went upstairs. When we got up to the top, in my kitchen, I started coughing and doubled over."

"Were you okay?" Megan asked.

"I was fine, my dear," Harry said. "I just needed him to step a bit closer to me. And when he did, I fired at him, right in the face."

"With a gun?" Megan asked, her eyes wide.

"No, no, nothing like that," Harry said reassuringly. "On my way upstairs, I palmed one of those horrible cans of fart spray that Eli has had sitting around on the back counter for the last two weeks."

"Good thing I never got around to restocking those shelves," I said.

Harry clucked his tongue. "Perhaps, perhaps." He turned his attention back to Megan. "I blasted him right in the face with the putrid stuff. Then I pulled the rug out from under him."

"What did you do?" I asked

"I just told you, I pulled the rug out from under him. You know that little braided rug that your Aunt Alice had at the top of the stairs? After I blasted him in the face, I reached down and pulled it out from under him. Backwards he went, ass over tea kettle, landing with a thud at the bottom of the stairs."

Megan and I exchanged looks, marveling at Harry's resourcefulness. "Aunt Alice always said someone was going to break their neck on those stairs someday."

"And she was right," Harry agreed. "As always, the old girl was right."

In spite of the smell, it was ultimately decided that Pete should be moved to a hospital, given that he probably had a broken back and certainly had broken one leg, one arm, and several ribs. The EMTs lifted him, on the backboard, to a stretcher and the cops and firemen cleared a path so they could roll him out of the store.

Pete was conscious, although clearly in pain, and the double take that he gave when they wheeled him past Megan and me must have been painful indeed. At least I hope it was.

"How the hell did you get out of the cave?" he croaked in a thin, raspy voice.

I shook my head at him and wagged a finger in the air. "A professional magician never reveals his methods," I said with a smile.

It felt really, *really* good to have the last word.

They continued to roll him out. He tried to look back at us, but between the neck brace and the intense pain, it wasn't going to happen. After he was gone, the smell lingered on.

"How are you doing?" I asked Megan as I put a hand on her shoulder.

"I'm okay," she said. "I just wish Harry hadn't pushed him down the stairs."

"I know, it looks like it was very painful."

She shook her head. "No," she said. "I wish I had been the one to push him. And, just between you and me, Eli," she added more confidentially, "if all those cops hadn't been swarming around here, I would have dragged the little bastard to the top of those damned stairs and shoved him down again."

I nodded in agreement. "I think I understand," I said. "And I'll make a mental note never to get on your bad side."

I looked up to see Deirdre waving me over from across the room. She and Homicide Detective Fred Hutton had been conferring in a whispered conversation.

"You smell almost as bad as our perp," Deirdre said as I approached the pair. "What did you get into?"

"It's really more what I got out of," I said. "Pete's final victim was going to be his wife, Megan. She's a psychic who works in crystals, so he locked us in a cave with no oxygen, with the idea that it would look like I was the killer and I had somehow screwed up."

"I would have bought that premise," Homicide Detective Fred Hutton said dryly.

"He was counting on that. And I guess he figured that somehow Harry would have been able to put all the pieces together, so he had to remove him from the equation."

I looked back toward the stairs that Pete had intended to push Harry down before inadvertently making the trip himself.

"It would either look like an accident, or maybe you guys might have figured I did it and that I just tried to make it look like an accident. Either way, Pete would be free and clear and could go on his merry, murderous way."

Deirdre nodded. "That fits with the conversation we had with Harry and the brief conversation we had with your girlfriend's husband before the EMTs took him out. We would have questioned him further, but the smell precluded that."

"You actually sell that product?" Homicide Detective Fred Hutton asked.

"More of them than I'd like to admit," I said.

"After experiencing the results, I would argue that a permit should be required for purchase," he said.

"Anyway," Deirdre said, pointedly turning the conversation away from the impending fart spray legislation, "Fred and I have discussed it, Eli, and we're both confident that you're no longer a suspect in this case. We have a few loose threads to tie up, but the DA will indict your hospital-bound friend on three charges of murder in the first degree, along with four counts of attempted murder. Plus assault charges for his attack on you and Mr. Boone, if you wish to pursue those charges."

"I would love to pursue those charges," I said. "I'd like Pete to be locked up for a good long time."

"I can pretty much assure that," Deirdre replied.

And knowing her as I did, it was as good as done.

I watched as she turned and continued to confer closely with her husband and I determined at that moment to no longer call him Mediocre Fred—at least for the time being.

Homicide Detective Fred Hutton and Assistant DA Deirdre Sutton-Hutton left a short while later and soon after their departure the rest of our visitors made their own exits. In a matter of a few minutes, the shop went from being completely packed to just the three of us—me, Megan, and Harry.

I walked Megan to the door while Harry pretended to be busy re-stocking the fart spray. When we got to the door, Megan turned and looked up at me.

"So, what did you think of our second date?" she asked.

"In a word, memorable. So what's next for the two of us?"

"I'm headed home to take a long, long bubble bath," she said.

"That sounds very inviting," I said.

"That's why I'm inviting you," she said, flashing a wicked little smile. "Unless you have other plans."

"No, that sounds wonderful. Just wonderful. The thing is," I said, and then cut myself off, picking my words carefully. "This may sound weird, but before I come over to take a bath, I'd like to take a long hot shower. And maybe burn my clothes. No, wait. Not maybe. Definitely. Definitely burn my clothes."

"I hear you," she said. "Meet me at my place in an hour." She stood on her tiptoes and gave me a quick kiss on the lips, which turned out to be not so quick after all. And then she left.

I locked the door and turned to see Harry, who was still pretending to be occupied with restocking the gag shelf.

"If you want something done right, you have to do it yourself," he grumbled as he put the last product in place. "You got a date?"

"Looks like it," I said as we headed toward the back stairs. "Did you eat yet?"

"No," he said. "Haven't gotten around to it. Been a busy night."

"That it has." We stopped at the base of the stairs. "Why don't you throw some leftovers in the oven and I'll sit with you after I take a shower?"

"Buster, that would be nice. Oh, will you look at that." He bent down and picked up three dimes that were lying at the base of the steps. He held them up for me proudly. "Three more dimes from your aunt," he said, smiling widely.

"They probably came out of Pete's pocket," I offered.

"That's plausible," he said as he started up the stairs.

I considered for a moment, and then spoke again. "Harry, you know those dimes aren't really from Aunt Alice, don't you?"

He turned and looked down on me, his face beaming. "Buster, every time I find a dime, I'm reminded of how much Alice loved me. When you look at it that way, why in the world would I care where they came from?"

He turned and continued his slow climb up the stairs. A moment later, I followed him.

Chapter 22

"Okay, I asked you once and you didn't give me a straight answer so I'm going to ask you again."

"Ask away," I said, "although I can't guarantee an improved result."

It was a cloudy, crisp day in late November and Megan and I had decided to take a walk along the Minnehaha Parkway. After some charming, aimless strolling, we found ourselves seated on a wooden bench.

She pointed at the object in front of us.

"What's the deal with that bunny?" Megan asked. The bench was just a stone's throw from the giant rabbit statue.

"I have no idea," I said finally. "Harry's intrigued with that rabbit, as well," I added. "Although I don't exactly remember why."

"How's he doing?"

"Harry? Harry's good, I think," I said, taking off my gloves and setting them on the bench next to me. I pulled off my wool cap as well, since it was starting to feel a little warmer. A little warmer for November, that is. "He's started talking about Aunt Alice more, which I think is a good sign. He's not exactly moving on, but he's moving ahead, if that makes any sense."

"I think it does," Megan said as she took off her gloves. We had both bundled up for cold that, apparently, wasn't happening.

"Which reminds me," I said. "What are you doing for Thanksgiving?"

She wrinkled her nose. "Well, normally we go see Pete's family for Thanksgiving, but I don't think that's happening this year—"

"Well, if you want, you could join us," I interjected as off-handedly as I could. "It's not a big deal. It's just Harry and me. And my friend Nathan. And that British writer, Clive. And whichever of the Minneapolis Mystics don't have a gig that day. Which generally means all of them. Basically it's everyone we know who doesn't have anywhere else to go."

"That sounds like fun. I did tell Franny that she and I might get together"

"Bring her along. The more the merrier."

"I think she'd like that," Megan said. "She's almost back to normal, health-wise. And, who knows, there might be some sparks with Harry."

"Two psychics at his dining room table? I can pretty much guarantee that there will be sparks with Harry," I said.

We both laughed and then I felt a need to amend that thought. "Although, actually, I'm not so sure that's the case now. It might have been true a month ago. But now, I'm not so sure. He's mellowed in that area. And I think that's due, in no small part, to you."

I picked up Megan's hand and held it. She leaned her head on my shoulder.

"But if Franny's looking to hook up with a guy her age, I can promise you that we'll have plenty of options for her to choose from," I added.

"Speaking of hooking up," Megan said, sitting up straight and turning toward me, "I meant to tell you. I ran into Nova. She and Boone got back together. And, you'll never believe this, she's running Akashic Records!"

"What happened to pretty boy Michael?"

"Out on his ass. Turns out Arianna didn't leave him squat."

"Nothing?"

"Not a thing."

"So he wasn't even mentioned in the will?"

"Oh, from what I heard, he was mentioned. He was mentioned at great length. Remember the language I used in the cave with the bats? Multiply that by ten."

"Wow."

"Arianna left it all to Nova. So she's running the store and Boone is in charge of the record department." Megan sat back and we continued to look at the rabbit.

"You didn't happen to find out," I asked finally, "why Boone was at Arianna's that night, did you?"

Megan looked around to make sure that no one was within listening distance. "As it turns out," she said quietly, "Nova confided in me that Arianna was one of the reasons she and Boone got back together again. Turns out, he'd been taking private lessons from Arianna, in order to learn how to please Nova the same way Arianna had. I mean, you know, sexually."

"Shut up," I said, my mouth dropping open in an almost comic reaction to this news.

"No, not like that," she said as she slapped my knee. "They weren't doing it. She was giving him actual lessons, with reading assignments and written tests and everything. Nova told me all about it. And, get this...it was Boone's idea. He talked to Arianna, told her he really wanted things to work with Nova, and she took him on as a student, to teach him her secrets. The night she died was supposed to be their fourth lesson."

"Well good for Boone," I marveled. "But now I can see why he didn't want to tell the cops the reason he was at her apartment."

"You men," Megan said, shaking her head. "You'd rather rot in jail than admit that you're bad in bed."

"Hey, speaking of things we meant to tell each other," I said, not so subtly changing the subject, "I didn't tell you that I found the script for Nathan's act."

She look puzzled. "I didn't know it was lost."

"It was," I said. "I couldn't find it among all the stuff he left for me when he went out of town. All I could find was a sheet that said how long each bit was supposed to be. But no script. So I ended up doing Harry's act instead. And then when I went to pack up Nathan's gear, I found the script. It had been sitting in the bag the whole time. Although I'd swear it wasn't there before. Weird, huh?"

"Spooky," Megan said, and then she added, "But these things often have a deeper meaning. So you have to ask yourself, what would have been different if you'd found the script and done Nathan's act?"

I thought about it for a moment. "Nothing, I guess," I said. "Except that I would have been a lot less stressed out. And I would have blown up a lot more balloons."

"Really," she said thoughtfully. "So, if you'd blown up more balloons, then you and I would have had less oxygen in the tank when we were in the cave?"

"Oh, yeah," I said. "A lot less. Nathan's act calls for a ton of balloons. I probably would have drained the tank."

"So," she said slowly, "if you had found Nathan's script, you would have done Nathan's act, and then you and I would have died in the caves from lack of oxygen."

"Well," I said just as slowly, "you're making a bit of a leap there."

"Not much of a leap," she said. "These things always happen for a reason."

I thought about this for a long moment. I could feel her looking at me while I thought. It felt like she was smiling at me.

"So let me see if I understand this," I said, turning to face her. "You think some supernatural force hid Nathan's script from me so I wouldn't use up all the air in the tank. And this supernatural force did that so we'd have enough air to survive on when we were trapped in the cave? Is that what you're saying?"

Megan shrugged. "Franny says that the supernatural is much more powerful than the natural. That's why they call it super."

"Franny says that, does she?" I asked, looking up at the gray sky and trying to sort out all the thoughts in my head. Megan was staring at me, her eyes sparkling with laughter that the rest of her face wasn't willing to express yet.

"She does," Megan said. "She also had a few choice thoughts about my future with you."

"Did she?" I asked, moving closer.

"She did," Megan said. We were very close now.

"What did she say?" I asked in a whisper.

"I'll tell you later," she whispered back. She kissed me.

And as she did, right on cue, it finally began to snow.

Reader's Discussion Guide

1. Eli clearly doesn't trust Grey from the beginning and is able to expose all of his mentalism tricks. Have you ever had a psychic experience that you couldn't explain?

2. Eli has moved back to his childhood home after his divorce. In general, does that seem like a good idea?

3. Megan is just getting started as a psychic and is (clearly) having mixed results. Do you think psychics actually improve with time?

4. Harry refuses to sell Pete a new trick until he masters the one he recently bought. Is that a reasonable expectation for a shop owner and have you ever been treated like that when trying to buy something?

5. As the story went along, Eli suspected different people as being the killer. Did you agree with his assessments and did you ever get ahead of him?

6. Eli ultimately succeeds at the birthday party by focusing on the audience members who seem interested and ignoring the birthday boy. What's the perfect kind of entertainment for a child's birthday party?

7. Eli turns down Nova's offer to sleep with her because of his feelings for Megan, even though they weren't involved at the time. Was that a reasonable thing for him to do?

8. Harry's mourning of his late wife is softened every time he finds a dime on the ground. Does it matter that he doesn't assign a mystical reason for the discoveries?

9. Eli embarrasses Homicide Detective Fred Hutton by singing the song "Mediocre Fred" in the interrogation room, knowing that the recording will be passed around later. Given his relationship with Fred, was he justified in doing that?

10. Megan is convinced that some supernatural force prevented Eli from doing the kid's show as written, which helped them survive while in the cave (because otherwise he would have used up all the oxygen/helium mixture in his air tank). Do you think she's right?

11. Both Eli and Megan are at different stages of getting over a divorce. What do you think their chances are of surviving as a couple?

John Gaspard

In real life, John's not a magician, but he has directed six low-budget features that cost very little and made even less—that's no small trick. He's also written multiple books on the subject of low-budget filmmaking. Ironically, they've made more than the films.

His blog, "Fast, Cheap Movie Thoughts," has been named "One of the 50 Best Blogs for Moviemakers" and "One of The 100 Best Blogs For Film and Theater Students." He's also written for TV and the stage.

John lives in Minnesota and shares his home with his lovely wife, several dogs, a few cats, and a handful of pet allergies.

IF YOU LIKED THIS HENERY PRESS MYSTERY,
YOU MIGHT ALSO LIKE THESE...

ARTIFACT

BY GIGI PANDIAN

Historian Jaya Jones discovers the secrets of a lost Indian treasure may be hidden in a Scottish legend from the days of the British Raj. But she's not the only one on the trail...

From San Francisco to London to the Highlands of Scotland, Jaya must evade a shadowy stalker as she follows hints from the hastily scrawled note of her dead lover to a remote archaeological dig. Helping her decipher the cryptic clues are her magician best friend, a devastatingly handsome art historian with something to hide, and a charming archaeologist running for his life.

Available Now
For more details, visit www.henerypress.com

Lowcountry BOIL
by Susan M. Boyer

Private Investigator Liz Talbot is a modern Southern belle: she blesses hearts and takes names. She carries her Sig 9 in her Kate Spade handbag, and her golden retriever, Rhett, rides shotgun in her hybrid Escape. When her grandmother is murdered, Liz hightails it back to her South Carolina island home to find the killer.

She's fit to be tied when her police-chief brother shuts her out of the investigation, so she opens her own. Then her long-dead best friend pops in and things really get complicated. When more folks start turning up dead in this small seaside town, Liz must use more than just her wits and charm to keep her family safe, chase down clues from the hereafter, and catch a psychopath before he catches her.

Available Now
For more details, visit www.henerypress.com

DINERS, dives & DEAD ENDS
by Terri L. Austin

As a struggling waitress and part-time college student, Rose Strick-land's life is stalled in the slow lane. But when her close friend, Ax-ton, disappears, Rose suddenly finds herself serving up more than hot coffee and flapjacks. Now she's hashing it out with sexy bad guys and scrambling to find clues in a race to save Axton before his time runs out.

With her anime-loving bestie, her septuagenarian boss, and a pair of IT wise men along for the ride, Rose discovers political corruption, illegal gambling, and shady corporations. She's gone from zero to sixty and quickly learns when you're speeding down the fast lane, it's easy to crash and burn.

Available Now
For more details, visit www.henerypress.com

BOARD STIFF

by Kendel Lynn

As director of the Ballantyne Foundation on Sea Pine Island, SC, Elliott Lisbon scratches her detective itch by performing discreet inquiries for Foundation donors. Usually nothing more serious than retrieving a pilfered Pomeranian. Until Jane Hatting, Ballantyne board chair, is accused of murder. The Ballantyne's reputation tanks, Jane's headed to a jail cell, and Elliott's sexy ex is the new lieutenant in town.

Armed with moxie and her Mini Coop, Elliott uncovers a trail of blackmail schemes, gambling debts, illicit affairs, and investment scams. But the deeper she digs to clear Jane's name, the guiltier Jane looks. The closer she gets to the truth, the more treacherous her investigation becomes. With victims piling up faster than shells at a clambake, Elliott realizes she's next on the killer's list.

Available Now

For more details, visit www.henerypress.com

DOUBLEWHAMMY

by Gretchen Archer

Davis Way thinks she's hit the jackpot when she lands a job as the fifth wheel on an elite security team at the fabulous Bellissimo Resort and Casino in Biloxi, Mississippi. But once there, she runs straight into her ex-ex husband, a rigged slot machine, her evil twin, and a trail of dead bodies. Davis learns the truth and it does not set her free—in fact, it lands her in the pokey.

Buried under a mistaken identity, unable to seek help from her family, her hot streak runs cold until her landlord Bradley Cole steps in. Make that her landlord, lawyer, and love interest. With his help, Davis must win this high stakes game before her luck runs out.

Available Now

For more details, visit www.henerypress.com

malicious masquerade
by ALAN CUPP

Chicago PI Carter Mays is thrust into a perilous masquerade when
local rich girl Cindy Bedford hires him. Turns out her fiancé failed
to show up on their wedding day, the same day millions of dollars
are stolen from her father's company. While Carter takes the case,
Cindy's father tries to find him his own way. With nasty secrets,
hidden finances, and a trail of revenge, it's soon apparent no one is
who they say they are.

Carter searches for the truth, but the situation grows more volatile
as panic collides with vulnerability. Broken relationships and
blurred loyalties turn deadly, fueled by past offenses and present
vendettas in a quest to reveal the truth behind the masks before no
one, including Carter, gets out alive.

Available Now
For more details, visit www.henerypress.com

FRONT PAGE FATALITY
by LynDee Walker

Crime reporter Nichelle Clarke's days can flip from macabre to comical with a beep of her police scanner. Then an ordinary accident story turns extraordinary when evidence goes missing, a prosecutor vanishes, and a sexy Mafia boss shows up with the headline tip of a lifetime.

As Nichelle gets closer to the truth, her story gets more dangerous. Armed with a notebook, a hunch, and her favorite stilettos, Nichelle races to splash these shady dealings across the front page before this deadline becomes her last.

Available Now
For more details, visit www.henerypress.com

PORTRAIT of a DEAD GUY
by LARISSA REINHART

In Halo, Georgia, folks know Cherry Tucker as big in mouth, small in stature, and able to sketch a portrait faster than buck-shot rips from a ten gauge -- but commissions are scarce. So when the well-heeled Branson family wants to memorialize their murdered son in a coffin portrait, Cherry scrambles to win their patronage from her small town rival.

As the clock ticks toward the deadline, Cherry faces more trouble than just a controversial subject. Between ex-boyfriends, her flaky family, an illegal gambling ring, and outwitting a killer on a spree, Cherry finds herself painted into a corner she'll be lucky to survive.

KILLER IMAGE
BY WENDY TYSON

Philadelphia image consultant Allison Campbell is not your typical detective. She's more familiar with the rules of etiquette than the rules of evidence, prefers three-inch Manolos to comfy flats and relates to Dear Abby, not Judge Judy.

When Allison's latest Main Line client, the fifteen-year-old Goth daughter of a White House hopeful, is accused of the ritualistic murder of a local divorce attorney, Allison fights to prove her client's innocence when no one else will. But in a place where image is everything, the ability to distinguish the truth from the facade may be the only thing that keeps Allison alive.

Available October 2013
For more details, visit www.henerypress.com

CPSIA information can be obtained at www.ICGtesting.com
Printed in the USA
LVOW13s1456220114

370535LV00002B/385/P